dup -

The HOUSE
of DEEP WATER

The HOUSE
of DEEP WATER

Jeni McFarland

G. P. Putnam's Sons
New York

PUTNAM
—EST. 1838—

G. P. PUTNAM'S SONS
Publishers Since 1838
An imprint of Penguin Random House LLC
penguinrandomhouse.com

LIBRARY OF CONGRESS CATALOGING-IN-PUBLICATION DATA

Names: McFarland, Jeni, author.
Title: The house of deep water / Jeni McFarland.
Description: New York: G. P. Putnam's Sons, 2020.
Identifiers: LCCN 2019049488 (print) | LCCN 2019049489 (ebook) |
    ISBN 9780525542353 (hardcover) | ISBN 9780525542377 (ebook)
Subjects: LCSH: Small cities—Fiction. | Domestic fiction.
Classification: LCC PS3613.C43945 H68 2020 (print) |
    LCC PS3613.C43945 (ebook) | DDC 813/.6—dc23
LC record available at https://lccn.loc.gov/2019049488
LC ebook record available at https://lccn.loc.gov/2019049489

Printed in the United States of America
10 9 8 7 6 5 4 3 2 1

Book design by Nancy Resnick

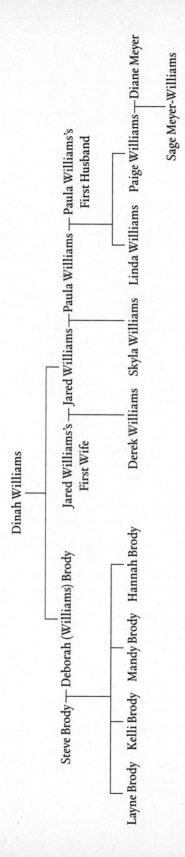
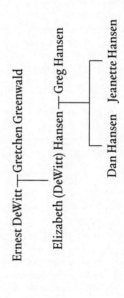

The HOUSE
of DEEP WATER

COMINGS AND GOINGS

In a fertile corner of Michigan, perched just above the state line in the soft crook of the St. Gerard River, lies the village of River Bend. The highway bypasses town to the west, in a curve mirroring the eastern sweep of the river. The town's romantics describe this pattern as a heart, including Mrs. Tabitha Schwartz, who teaches a section on River Bend in her seventh grade history class. When she puts the town map on the screen, some of the boys in her class invariably snicker and exchange knowing looks: It is commonly agreed upon among teenagers that, when viewed together, the town, its river, and the highway resemble a vulva and the labial folds surrounding it.

The bluffs to the north of town shelter that tender spot where teenagers go when they wish to be alone with each other. This pleasure center goes unnamed—River Bend has no "Make Out Point" as such—because nobody talks about the bluffs. Yet many teens know instinctively, like salmon intuit their own spawning ground, and every spring and all summer long the teenagers trickle in, two by two in their cars, assuming this place is theirs alone. They are shocked, always, when they arrive to find another car parked there, another couple. Or when they're already at the bluffs, screened by a steamy windshield, and hear another vehicle approach. The girls might perk up, listen, try to determine its trajectory. They have a knack for buttoning up just before another car arrives.

In many families, multiple generations share a direct link to this location, for without the cover of the bluffs, and the covert fumblings they enable, the lineage would not have endured.

Sitting anywhere in their houses, the women of River Bend can feel a car running in their driveways, so preternaturally attuned are they to the comings and goings of family, friends, solicitors, neighbors. They feel these arrivals as vibrations in their chests, a skill they developed not for gossip's sake—or, at least, not solely. Instead, they are primed by an old evolutionary need. Women, especially those of limited means, must learn to read the signs. A lingering rumble of a familiar engine in the driveway at day's end means her husband is home, that he is held up in his car collecting something, perhaps his temper, before entering the house. An unfamiliar vibration at an unusual hour means a surprise visit— from an ex maybe, or a long-lost relative, a salesperson or the repo man.

In her two-bedroom house, which squats in the V of land between Main Street and Schoolhouse Road, Deborah Brody hears an engine idle in the driveway. It's the first Saturday in June, and her girls—Kelli, Mandy, and Hannah—are with their grandmother. Her husband, Steve, is working. Deborah peeks through a chink in the blinds to see a car she does not know, an old beat-up Buick. She has to squint to identify the driver, Gilmer Thurber, a man who has lived in town his whole life. She isn't sure what he's doing here. She lives next to the pet store, so she suspects he's headed there, though the longer she watches him, the longer he sits, his car facing the grade school across the street. How sad he must be. He never married. He lives with his sister in a house he inherited from his parents. Deborah has seen him before, watching the children playing, and the longing she sees in his face makes her body go cold. She tries to think what her life would be like if she'd never had kids. She used to dream of moving to a city, of having a job where she could wear high heels and blazers. But here she is, almost forty, living in the same cramped house her husband had when they met. Gilmer looks up and sees her, and his expression is a little sheepish as he puts his car in gear and drives away.

On the outskirts of town, a police car races down the dirt road past Dinah Williams's farm. She hears it approach from her barn, and looks out in time to catch a glimpse. She's pretty sure it was Sheriff Hudson she saw behind the wheel, and wonders where he's going with such urgency. She turns back to her task; today, she's teaching her granddaughters how to milk cows. The youngest girl, Hannah, peeks out of the barn, too late to see the police car. The older sisters, Kelli and Mandy, are too busy brushing the horses and petting their velvet noses. The girls aren't much help to Dinah, but she loves having them at the farm. It's good for them to remember their roots. Moreover, Dinah's daughter, Deborah, needs some time at home without them. As she sets a bucket under her prized cow, Dinah hears an engine in her drive, and she knows her son, Jared, is leaving, heading for the bar. It's only three in the afternoon. Ever since his wife, Paula, left fourteen years ago, Jared has spent most of his free time at the bar.

Back in the heart of River Bend, a car pulls into the drive at the Muylder Mansion, a historic home open to the public from twelve o'clock to three o'clock on Saturdays during the summer, unless its curator, Mrs. Tabitha Schwartz, is sick or out of town with her seniors' club. Mrs. Schwartz—who often feels lonely since her husband died, and who thought her seniors' club would do the trick, and who thought curating this mansion would occupy more of her time in the summer, and who was distraught to find the funding of the mansion was practically nonexistent and that the Muylder Foundation wouldn't open the museum more than three hours a week, not when there is a perfectly good replica of the mansion at the Muylder Museum in Kalamazoo, and who was downright dismayed to learn that her seniors' club consisted only of her and a bunch of old biddies eating deviled ham on white bread—rushes to put on a pot of coffee and open a box of butter cookies. It has been ever so long since the mansion had a visitor. Mrs. Schwartz fluffs her hair and waits, but nobody comes in. When she looks through the window, she's disappointed. It's only one of River Bend's boys in blue, stopped in her parking lot in an unmarked car, talking on his radio. When a beat-up brown Buick drives by, the officer pulls his car out after it. What a waste of a pot of coffee.

Derek Williams sits with a low heart at the kitchen table of his under-furnished modular home, waiting for the sound of his uncle Steve's truck. His kitchen sink, clogged again, is beyond his ability to fix—his ability being limited to emptying bottles of drain cleaner into the pipes. When he hears the engine, his heart sinks further. No doubt his uncle will give him shit for calling about such a simple task. Steve will leave his own tools in the truck with the sole purpose of borrowing Derek's just so he can judge his nephew. Why on earth does Derek have an adjustable wrench instead of a good crescent wrench set? Really, his uncle should shut it, given that Derek works so many hours at the hospital, and doesn't have time for tool shopping, or energy to complete his own home repairs. That's another sore spot with Uncle Steve, who staunchly believes a real man takes care of his own home. How Derek wishes he could call a different handyman. But no doubt if he did, if he not only called but *paid* another man, it would get back to his uncle and his father, Jared. No, it's easier to steel himself. Stiff upper lip and all. As Derek answers the door and lets his uncle inside, he hears police sirens in the distance.

As his uncle sets to work on the sink, Derek's phone dings: a text from his half sister, Skyla. She has sent the same message to him and her older half sisters, Linda—who lives in Texas—and Paige, who lives up in Kalamazoo. Skyla is sixteen, bored, and always on her phone. She sends her siblings five or six texts a day, emoji-heavy missives from River Bend. Today, the text is a shaky video of a crummy old Buick pulling into the drive of the house next to the park. The owner of the Buick gets out and goes into his house, and then a white car—an unmarked police car—pulls through the alley and parks behind the house. Skyla can't believe her family is missing this. *Some shit's going down at that creepy house,* she texts, with a Wow emoji: the wide eyes, the mouth an O.

Two houses down, Ernest DeWitt is on the phone with his daughter, Beth. She's going through a rough patch, has been going through one for years. He worries for her, and for her children, Dan and Jeanette.

"Elizabeth," he says, over and over. He only uses her full name when he means business. "You can always come home."

Ernest hasn't even seen his grandkids since they were very small, but Dan's a teenager now, and Jeanette is in the eighth grade. They've been living in Charlotte, North Carolina. But now Beth's lost her job. As Beth tries to explain that she'll be fine, she's sure to find a job soon, his attention is lured away. Ernest watches Sheriff Hudson get out of a car parked next door, where he greets another officer waiting in an unmarked cruiser. What on earth is going on?

Over the phone, Beth simply thinks her father has lost interest in the conversation. If she had known the police car was there, if she had guessed the scene unfolding, she might have had time to ossify her heart before the story breaks. But she doesn't hear.

In the derelict house next to the park, Gilmer Thurber also fails to hear the car in the alley behind his house. But his sister hears. Encoded into her DNA, generations of women help her feel the vibrations, to suss out whether the driver is friend or foe. This is an unfamiliar engine: not a family member. The engine cuts off, and the silence that follows is terrifying. The best she can do is crouch down in her living room, ball herself, still her breath, diminish the space she occupies, and hope she will be overlooked. This tactic seldom works for her, but still she tries.

Her brother, Gilmer, goes about his business in the basement unbothered.

As soon as his officer is stationed near the front, Sheriff Hudson makes his way up the walk to the back door of the Thurber house. He has to knock three times, has to call out that he has a warrant for Gilmer's arrest, before Thurber's sister, as wan and frightened as a half-skinned rabbit, opens the door.

Elizabeth DeWitt
4

My babysitter, Mrs. Thurber, is old and mean. She makes me drink water standing by the kitchen table. She won't let me sit down. After I drink the water, she pushes me back outside to play. She won't let me in until lunch at eleven.

She has toys, but she won't let us play with them. She lives next door to the park, but she never takes us there. I play with the other kids in the yard. There's another girl whose name is also Beth. And there's a boy, Mikey. He has long hair and thick, dark eyebrows like a grown-up. I like him because even though he's white, he's nice to me. We make a game out of jumping over the dog doo in the grass. We run, jump, and don't land on the dog doo. Some of it's soft and some of it's hard if you poke it with a stick.

"You two are gross," the other Beth says. She tells Mikey, "You shouldn't let her *make you gross."*

I don't know what time it is, but I have to pee. I knock on the door and call to be let in. Then I whine. Then I cry. I can't hold it anymore, and when I let go where I stand, Mrs. Thurber yells at me, then sits me in the corner with my wet underwear on my head. She makes me wear a diaper for the rest of the day.

Her kids still live at home. They both look the same age as my mom and dad. The girl child, she's growing a baby in her belly, even though she's not married. You don't ask questions about it. I like to watch her chewing her breakfast. She chews on one side only, her jaw sticking out, popping. I try to chew crooked like her.

The man child lives in the basement. He walks around the house, the yard, wearing just a little swimsuit, and his belly moves like Jell-O.

After lunch, I hide in Mrs. Thurber's coat closet. It's hot in here, crowded with smelly coats. It's also dark, and I focus my eyes on the line of light coming in beneath the door. I stare at it a long time, until my eyes are dry. Cigarette smoke clouds the light. I'm sweating, watching smoke coming in beneath the door. The man child is home. He's smoking, looking for me, but he won't call for me. His mother is taking a nap. He won't risk waking her. All I can do is wait, pressed in between the coats, my feet hidden in adult-sized snow boots.

WRAPPING UP

Linda drives until the Gulf Coastal Plain gives way to soft hills, golden in the evening sun. She drives until the hills go flat again, dipping into the hot brown parts of central Texas, then roll on into the foothills of Arkansas, rising and falling in the dark, promising mountains she never sees. Next comes corn, the stalks smoothed to an ocean under a bright moon, her eyes sailing along the surface of the fields. She has to check herself, remember to watch the road. Around morning, she enters the glacial hills of Illinois. By the time she arrives in Michigan, the sun has crested again.

Knee-high sweet corn grows here, tall for early June, the fields dense and glossy green. The sky is a hazy kind of blue, the air Michigan-muggy, which is hardly muggy at all. Her car strains—its knocking engine has been on the verge of dying for ages—and Linda shuts off the air conditioner, cranks her window down, and breathes in the fresh air, the smell of hay and manure. For a moment, she has a hard time remembering why she couldn't wait to get away from River Bend six years ago. There's the poverty, yes, and the shabby houses, and the fact that the place becomes a food desert when the farm stands close in the winter. Then there's the politics: the everyday goings-on of a small town, and the inability to keep private things private. And, of course, there's the fact that, at twenty-two, when Linda met Nathan, there had been nobody worth dating, worth marrying in River Bend. Nathan was better than the boys she grew up with, which made him seem perfect. He wore polished black dress shoes and collared shirts. He went to the gym. He used product in his hair. Some mornings, he took longer than she did to get ready. He was always so impeccable—that was the word that came to her mind—in his manner, in his speech. Best of all, he had ambitions, plans to move away from East Lansing, the college town where they met. He did, too, going off to law school, while Linda slunk back to River Bend to wait for him.

Making a life with Nathan seemed wildly adventurous. When he proposed, it never even occurred to her to think it over, to consider all the ways they were ill-suited for each other. She thought she knew herself, and what she wanted. She thought she was done growing. She was twenty-five. He proposed the day he graduated from law school, and even though Linda was already impatient from the three years they had dated long-distance, she stayed in River Bend until their wedding; at twenty-five, she didn't have the guts to tell her grandma Dinah she was moving in with her fiancé before the wedding.

She'd gotten out of this town, had married, moved, tried for six years to make a go of it. But she didn't belong to that life. The Houston suburbs, with their busy streets, their noise, their lights, their genteel aggression, had seemed to her a foreign country. The humidity was foreign, as was the smell of a city always damp. The roaches, as long as Linda's index finger, were foreign. The unholy heat, and the wind off the ocean, and the lizards that sunned themselves on the side of her house, and the grackles, and the palm trees. Foreign.

Yesterday, Nathan dragged her to yet another luncheon at the house of his business partner, Guy Wexler. The man lived in a three-story in Upper Kirby, a mansion that smelled like a warehouse, a thin, industrial, empty smell. She and Nathan had already been fighting for months, maybe even years. They'd found themselves in the middle of a divorce, having agreed to walk away before things got ugly.

It was no longer her duty to accompany Nathan to these parties, and she told him so. But the divorce was affecting him more than it was Linda, and she felt bad for him. He seemed to take it as not just a personal failure but also a professional one, as if the end of his marriage would stunt his career growth.

As always, Linda was underdressed and out of place at the party, ill fed and over-drunk. Bottomless glasses of wine need an equal abundance of pasta to soak them up, but lunch meant only a fistful of pasta per guest, a small salad each. Even with the food and wine, the house smelled blank. Guy and his wife, Sophie, resembled a pair of stick bugs in business casual and perfume, beetling around the dining room, clinking wineglasses, laughing their insect-clicking laughs, ignoring their meager portions of food. When Linda's meal was gone, she sneaked food off their plates. And why not? Who was she trying to impress?

After dinner, the group was herded into the drawing room, where Guy and Sophie hoped to awe with their artwork (which made Linda feel nothing but poor), their eclectic tastes in world music (though, when pressed, the Wexlers couldn't tell you the names of the instruments in the recordings), and their immaculate white furniture. Linda hunted out a love seat in the corner, hoping to hide behind a sculpture, but Guy found her, wine bottle at the ready to refill her glass. He seated himself next to her, his thigh touching her own. The wine had pickled Guy, ripening him into a bolder flavor of man. He let his hand wander along her leg. Linda said nothing, so he kept his hand there. And while he knew that no meant no, he hadn't yet realized silence also meant no.

He leaned in to whisper in her ear. "What did Cinderella do when she got to the ball?" He paused just long enough to laugh through his nose, a puff of air on her neck. "She gagged."

"I saw that one on Facebook," Linda said.

"Wait, I got another."

His breath smelled of Chianti and cabbage, even though no cabbage had been served. At some point that afternoon, Guy left the seat, and Nathan took his place. Linda didn't even notice the change.

"You and Guy were awfully cozy," Nathan said. Linda would have liked to blame the anger in his voice on the wine, but knowing Nathan, he had been carrying around the same half glass all afternoon, only pretending to sip it for show.

If she'd had any doubts about the divorce before, they'd dissolved last night. Back at home, Linda quietly packed a few belongings, wrestled her cat, Arthur, into his carrier, loaded her car. Nathan had already refused to move out during the proceedings. It would have been much less awkward if he had. He was still there, in the house, hovering around the edges of the rooms as Linda walked through them, telling herself she wouldn't miss any of it: the china hutch, the leather upholstery, the silver tableware, the brocade drapery, the wood floors, the marble counters, the gilt mirror over the fireplace, the garden tub, round and deep enough to sink up to her neck. Okay, she might miss the garden tub.

"At least sleep here tonight," Nathan said finally. "You can go in the morning." He hoped that if she delayed she'd change her mind. He knew she wasn't happy in Houston, but he couldn't fathom why she would want to move home to that backward little town when she could live in an elegant house, shop at the Galleria, dine at posh restaurants, and drive a sleek black car.

Linda wouldn't stay. She was never one for dragging things out. Instead, she drove nineteen hours straight, stopping only for gas, coffee, and rest areas. She arrived with very little money in her purse and no food in her stomach, her hands shaky on the steering wheel, her eyes crusted in the corners with sleep crud even though she hadn't slept.

River Bend has hardly changed since Linda left six years ago. The only difference is that the townspeople finally voted for the highway bypass, so that the highway now skirts around town. Linda gets lost on the way, foolishly following the highway instead of the business loop; she finds herself at the next town north before she realizes her mistake, and on her way back, she takes another wrong street and ends up turning around in the Thurber driveway, that creepy old house next to the park, its bright paint at odds with the gnarled crabapple tree, its knee-length grass as dry as tinder and full of dog shit. She'd never paid it much attention before, but on the drive here, she kept catching snippets of a national news story, surprisingly out of River Bend. Gilmer Thurber and his sister. The things they were accused of. This must be what was happening in the video her half sister, Skyla, had sent; the cops were waiting to arrest Thurber. Now the yard and house lay empty, quiet.

Linda has a hard time believing this could happen in her hometown. Her knee-jerk reaction was that it couldn't possibly be true; the street is so peaceful, how could anything bad have happened here? Hearing the story from her car in the middle of the country, Linda had felt sick, but also safely isolated from it all. She couldn't connect the news with her memories of the town. The report from River Bend was just another story in a vast sea of bad news. Still, it feels odd to see the house again in person.

As she backs out of the drive, her car shudders and dies, its dashboard lighting up. Linda turns the key, but the car's only response is to release a hot electrical smell. How many times has Nathan tried to get her to junk this car? He even bought her a big black Lexus when her Ion failed its first safety inspection. This car isn't even registered. She'd cringed every time she started it; the muffler had been shot for ages, and the vehicle made an ungodly ruckus, causing neighbors to pause in their driveways or peek out from behind their blinds, but she couldn't bring herself to get rid of it. As much as she'd wanted to get out of River Bend, out of Michigan, she found herself nostalgic in Texas, clinging to anything that reminded her of home.

She gets out and pushes her car to the side of the road, pops the hood. The smell is overwhelming. It makes her turn her head into her shoulder, bury her nose in her sleeve. She doesn't really know what she's looking for—the engine on fire, maybe?—but she sees nothing of obvious concern. In the backseat, Arthur's cat carrier is unusually quiet. In a moment of insight, when Linda packed Arthur in the car, she'd draped a sweater over the carrier, and her cat had been sleeping peacefully. She's surprised he's lasted this long; she figured along about Arkansas, he would start scratching to be let out.

She checks on Arthur now. Still asleep, on his side, one paw draped over his face, his gray fur looking bluish in the sunlight. Despite the noise from the car and the open windows, he doesn't move. He's old and arthritic, and she'd had a terrible time wrangling him into his carrier. Her blouse is still covered in cat hair, has made her itch the entire drive.

Fuck it, she thinks, then puts the car in neutral and pushes it down Main Street, her shoulder wedged into the open driver's-side door, her hand on the wheel. It's only a few miles to her family's farm. Little town like this, there's almost no traffic. She'll push it the whole damn way if she has to. She has spent long Houston summers imagining the feel of freedom as a cool breeze on her face, only now that it's here, it's a metallic heap on the side of the road. And what do you do with that? You get out and push, that's what.

Despite its recent emergence into the national spotlight, River Bend is stubbornly the same. It still has one stoplight, one bar, one church, no grocery store, a single block of two-story buildings marking its downtown—the street there lined with faux gaslights. The village was a shipping hub in the 1830s, and is hugged on three sides by the St. Gerard River, which once carried goods to Lake Michigan. Then the railroads came, nowhere near River Bend, and the village was forgotten. It struggled for a century and a half, unable to grow beyond the river's stranglehold.

Main Street is quiet, the houses lying sleepily along it. As far as Linda can tell, the only soul around is an old man sitting on the front porch of a pale blue house framed by columns, with turrets running up the west face and a round cupola at the top. The DeWitt place, the oldest house in town. Which would make the man Ernest DeWitt. Linda vaguely remembers him; his daughter, Eliza, used to babysit her. He watches Linda as she pushes her car up the road. When she looks closer, she sees that he isn't as old as she thought. His hair is graying, yes, but his eyes are bright. And laughing. At her.

He doesn't mean to laugh. He just can't believe his good fortune, that a car should break down in front of his house, and the driver should be such a doll. Dirty-blond hair, curvy body.

"Need a hand?"

"I think this might be the end," she says.

"Will be if you don't go catch it." He nods at the car, and Linda turns to find it gaining speed down a slight hill. She chases it. Climbs in and puts it in park. Before she gets back out, she takes a second to check him out in the rearview mirror.

Ernest DeWitt had a reputation. The aging bachelor. The ladies' man. Although, come to think of it, Linda remembers talking to him a few times. He seemed nice enough. He seemed very nice, in fact. Linda finds herself wanting to touch him.

"I'm Linda," she says, her hand outstretched.

And even though his eyes are laughing at her again, he takes her hand in both of his. "You haven't been gone so long that I don't know who you are," he says. His skin is warm, and a little calloused. His response throws her. She had hoped she was safe from recognition, that she could return anonymously, but already, here's someone who knew her. Knows her.

Ernest pushes the car into the alley behind his house. Linda steers. In her rearview mirror, she watches his face turning red, a vein protruding in his forehead. What is he, like, sixty? He doesn't look sixty. He looks pretty good, in fact, even when he strains like that. Once he gets the car into his driveway, he pops the hood. Linda stands behind him, peering over his shoulder.

"Mind fetching my toolbox?" He gestures toward his garage.

Linda is loath to leave his side. The effort of pushing the car has left his tee shirt damp with sweat, and his skin and hair release a scent that makes Linda take deep breaths. After she gives him his toolbox, she shakes her head clear. She goes to the backseat and checks on Arthur again. He hasn't so much as moved. God, what Linda wouldn't give to be able to sleep like that. When she was fourteen, after her mother, Paula, left the first time, she'd had problems sleeping. She went through a phase where she slept with the radio blasting, the mindless chatter of DJs and the top forty drowning out her thoughts. Her stepdad, Jared, would come into her room after he thought she was asleep and turn it down. Sometimes she was asleep, and she would wake up in the morning with the radio on quiet. Other times she would lie awake most of the night, straining to hear the low drone. She'd resumed this habit not long after she was married, listening to headphones all night to drown out the sounds of traffic and sirens, the neighbors' dogs barking.

"You can leave it here for now," he says, shutting the hood. "I don't know if I can fix it, but I'll try. You want to call your sister, maybe?" He hopes her sister doesn't answer. He doesn't really want her to go.

It's Saturday. Her sister Paige is likely busy with her son, and while Linda knows that Skyla just got her license, she isn't sure whether Skyla has a car. She could try her grandma Dinah, but she would be out in the barn or the fields. And Jared, Dinah's son, would be anywhere but at home today—maybe at the bar shooting pool, or at his hardware store, even though he's supposed to be semi-retired.

Linda dials Skyla, but her sister doesn't pick up. She leaves a message.

"I can give you a ride," Ernest says. Linda grabs her suitcase and the cat carrier. Sitting in Ernest's car, she pulls back the sweater, puts a finger through the grille, and scritches Arthur's head. He still doesn't move, doesn't purr. Linda has to admit it. Her cat is dead.

Grandma Dinah's house sits on a drumlin, the land falling sharply in the backyard. Linda and Paige sledded down this snowy hill when they were girls, rolled down its grassy shoulder in the summer. At its base, a creek trickles, all but dry now. The sisters had picnicked in this grass. In her teens, Linda escaped to this place when she wanted to be alone. By then, Paige wouldn't come here anymore, said it was too muddy. Skyla was just a baby and wasn't allowed out of the yard. That was the summer before Linda set out for college, the summer their mother left for good, having come back to Jared just long enough to get pregnant and birth, ween, and potty train Skyla. When the creek flooded, the grindstone in their old flour mill still ran, groaning out of its rust, spooking the cows, so that even the animals shied away, preferring to drink from the pond. This was where Linda planned to bury Arthur.

She isn't sure how her family will respond when she gets to their farm; she didn't tell them she was leaving her husband. She didn't tell anyone. In the six years she was away, she visited home only twice. She imagines her family's shock when she shows up—will Grandma Dinah gloat? She never liked Nathan to begin with. For that matter, neither did Jared. But when Linda arrives in the early evening, waving goodbye to Ernest, Dinah asks no questions. Instead, she offers to bury Arthur.

"I suspect you've been through enough already," Dinah says.

These girls, she thinks. *Always uprooting their lives.* Dinah grew up on this farm, as did her mother before her. She'd never felt the need to go traipsing around the country like this generation does. She sets up a small cat funeral, Dinah digging when Linda starts crying too hard to use a shovel. Afterward, Dinah fixes Linda a plate of leftovers, lets her settle in.

While Linda finishes her dinner, Skyla comes in from the fields. She's wearing boots and jeans, has her hair up in a baseball cap. She's been out riding horses, and is in a mood from it. Unlike Linda, Skyla doesn't enjoy riding. Even before Linda moved away, Skyla had been on her grandma to sell the horses, since it had fallen mostly to Skyla to make sure they got enough exercise.

When Skyla sees Linda sitting at the dinner table, though, she squeals.

"You're back!" she says, and hugs her sister fiercely. "Where's the boy toy?"

Skyla usually tries to pass for the kind of angsty teenager who doesn't care, but in reality, she's as tender and fragile as Linda had been at her age.

"I suppose he's still back in Texas," Linda says.

"So you're home for good?" Skyla says, doing a little skip. "Thank God. You can ride the horses now."

"I don't even know if I could anymore," Linda says with a sigh.

Skyla shrugs. "At least it'll be fun now that you're back. It's been so boring here with just me and Grandma."

Linda's other sister, Paige, got married two years ago, and moved with her wife to Kalamazoo. Paige's wedding was the last time Linda had been back in town. Linda's stepbrother, Derek, had bought a house on the outskirts of town soon after Linda left River Bend. Poor Skyla has been experiencing what it is to be an only child. With Jared never at home, it had to be lonely.

19

Skyla grabs a yogurt from the fridge and settles in at the table to gossip with Linda late into the night. And while Linda loves catching up with her sister, part of her feels like she's taken a huge step back. She knows that, being back under Grandma Dinah's roof, she is once more subject to house rules.

Grandma Dinah's idea of raising girls had mostly consisted of criticism: Don't sit with your mouth hanging open; button up that collar; stand up straight; a lady doesn't take any bull, but she doesn't give any, either. It had all seemed impossibly rigid, especially to Paige, who often struck Linda as being more boy than girl. Paige never liked dresses, even to wear to church, and completely rejected makeup and crushes and slumber parties. Linda had always had a boyfriend and a backup, was sure to keep the latter close enough that he could be called up at a moment's notice. She spent more time on the backups than the boyfriends, chatting on the phone, bringing them homemade baked goods. Even as a teenager, Linda had had a profound fear of being alone.

When Paula left the first time, Linda had watched her father's loneliness, watched him split his time between his hardware store and the bar, coming home only to fall into bed for a few hours. When Paula returned a year later and slipped back into his life like nothing, Linda had made no attempt to forgive her.

"We don't need you," she'd told her mother one day out of the blue.

They were in Grandma's kitchen. Linda had snapped beans for dinner; Paula had shucked corn. Without looking up from her task, Paula had said, "You got a mouth on you. Just like your daddy."

"I'll go live with him, then. Better than being around you." An empty threat, since neither Linda nor Paula knew where Linda's biological father was.

Paula stuck around about three years, then. In that time, Jared had insisted on adopting the girls, and giving them his name, ensuring he had a legal tie to them. When Paula left again, nobody was surprised, and nobody went into mourning—Jared having never fully come out of it from the last time.

All of this comes back to Linda now. Now that she's here, she has the support of family, sure, but she also remembers all the ways family tears you down. Sitting at the kitchen table with her sister, Linda wonders whether she made the right choice in coming back.

Early the next morning, Dinah knocks on Linda's door, ostensibly to collect laundry, although really Dinah wants to let Linda know it's inexcusable to sleep past eight, especially when there are chores to be done.

"I saved you some breakfast," Dinah says. "After that, you can help with the wash."

Once they've eaten, Linda and Skyla lug the baskets out to the clotheslines, strung along the drumlin to catch wind from all directions. Weak sun and a sky hazed with thin clouds. The air will leave the laundry smelling like summer by the end of the day. Linda feels a strange excitement in the pit of her stomach. She looks forward to wearing the clothes once they're dry.

Linda and Dinah hang sheets, the breeze billowing the fabric like sails. Skyla has been asked to help, too, but instead ducks in and out of the rows, making a game out of dodging the cloth. Dinah holds the fabric while Linda stretches up to pin it and Skyla limbos underneath, her long hair brushing the ground. When she straightens, she gathers her hair over her shoulder, holding it like a pet as she picks grass from it. Skyla looks so

21

much like their mother, too, Linda realizes, with dishwater-blond hair and light brown eyes—just like Linda. Unlike Linda, though, Skyla has inherited Paula's slenderness.

"I didn't get to hang laundry in Texas," Linda says. Somehow, she can't keep from referencing the life she just abandoned, even though her family's default mode is to ignore uncomfortable situations. She watches Dinah stiffen.

"I don't see why we don't just use the dryer," Skyla says.

"It's cheaper," Dinah says.

"And greener," Linda adds. "The HOA in our subdivision said clotheslines portrayed a 'certain class of people.'"

"What's an HOA?" Skyla asks.

"It stands for Horribly Oppressive Asshats," Linda says.

Dinah sighs. "Homeowners' association. We don't have them in the country, and we seem to do just fine." She didn't like that Linda married Nathan. She disapproved of his perfectly pressed trousers, his gelled hair, his manicured hands, his fancy car. Grandma Dinah considers anything not manufactured in Michigan to be too fancy. But Dinah most disapproved of his branch of real estate: rural development. He *would* have to live somewhere that doesn't allow clotheslines.

Skyla has disappeared again behind the sheets. Only her silhouette is visible to Linda, and from the angle of the sun, which is still low, it seems as if Skyla is well over six feet tall. Come to think of it, Linda notices that Skyla is a lot taller than when Linda last saw her. In Linda's mind, Skyla was still a ten-year-old child. She was never able to replace her memory of family with the reality; even when she last visited two years ago, Linda had been surprised to see a woman in Skyla. And Skyla has gone a little feral in Linda's absence, not wild like a normal teenager, but independent in the way of children who've raised themselves. Skyla seems, in some ways, girlish and vulnerable, and, in other ways, mature beyond her years. She dodges around the fabric not with childish agility, but with a kind of strength Linda hasn't seen in her before.

"You could be helping, you know," Dinah says, in that tone of voice that implies that ever since Skyla turned sixteen, she's gotten too big for her britches.

Skyla peeks her head around the sheet. She plucks a towel from the basket, flops it over the line, and sticks a clothespin on it. When she bends for the next towel, Dinah reaches up and straightens the one Skyla just did.

Linda finds her own blouse in the basket, the one she had been wearing yesterday. It's been mostly de-furred in the wash, although a few of Arthur's gray hairs still cling to the fabric. And as she stretches up to pin the blouse on the line, she finds herself fighting back tears. Her cat is gone, and these hairs clinging to her blouse are among the few reminders she has of him, of Texas, of her marriage. To see this blouse clean somehow makes everything seem final.

"What's PRW?" Skyla pulls a monogrammed towel from a basket of bedding. She glances at Linda out of the corner of her eye in a way that makes it apparent she has seen Linda's distress and is offering a distraction.

Linda and Dinah both look away.

"Period-Ruined White?" Skyla says.

The towels are stained, but from rubbed-off makeup and drying the dogs, washing them with colored clothes and taking them on trips to the beach. The sheets are from Jared's bed. As teens, they were allowed to pass any bouts of illness downstairs in their dad's room, while their dad slept on the couch. Grandma Dinah always said this made it easier on her, saved her from going up and down the steps to take their temperature and bring them juice, but really, she wanted them to feel they weren't alone. There were people who loved them, right nearby. The poor things had been abandoned, first by their biological father, then by their mother. When Paula left, Jared sold his house and moved himself, his son, and his girls—he still referred to them as "his girls," even though they were Paula's—to his mother's farm. Grandma Dinah said she was glad for the company and extra hands, yet as much as she claimed they were no burden, the girls weighed on her. She could often be caught giving Linda or Paige sidelong glances, just staring for a time, as if trying to figure them out, until finally, she'd shake her head; clearly she didn't like what she'd gleaned.

Now Linda understood it must have been hard for her, to have in her house two young women who were no blood relation.

How many times had Linda sweated out a fever on these sheets? How many bowls of chicken soup had she eaten on them? They are yellowed with age, frayed at the edges from wear. Beige sheets would have fared better.

"Purity Really Wrecked?" Skyla says.

"They were a wedding present," Dinah says, as if that ends the conversation.

"Parental Responsibility Waived," Linda says.

"That's enough," Dinah says.

"Paula—what? What was Mom's middle name?" Skyla asks.

"Ruthless," Linda says.

"Ruth," Dinah says.

"Who leaves home without taking her towels?" Skyla says. Her eyes dart to Linda before fixing back on the laundry basket.

"Maybe she was in a hurry," Linda says.

"In a hurry to start her life in Vegas." Skyla is forever building stories based on family gossip: Their mother always wanted to go to Vegas. Skyla talks about the absence with a nonchalance that's possible only because she can't remember their mother enough to miss her.

Linda remembers, though. She's come to hold up her step-father, Jared, as a saint. He stuck around when Paula left, continued to care for his stepdaughters, Linda and Paige; he moved in with his mother to give all of his children more stability. He's a good guy, the only dad they've ever known. And who does that? Who leaves a good guy?

"Your phone was vibrating this morning," Dinah tells Linda.

She left her phone in her room, which means Dinah has been up there. Maybe she saw it when she was gathering laundry. Or maybe she was going through Linda's few possessions.

"I think you should talk to him," Dinah says. "Whatever the problem, it's not worth walking away."

But Linda doesn't want to. The last message he left, he'd told her, "The house feels bereft without you." He didn't say that he missed her, or that he loved her. She was beginning to realize that what he missed were all the ways in which she took care of him. She'd turned the ringer off after that. He didn't need her back. He could afford to hire a housekeeper.

"You never even liked him," Skyla reminds Dinah. And it's true. But Linda knows Dinah fears, above all else, that Linda and Paige—and someday Skyla—will follow in their mother's footsteps, making their own families and then breaking them. Linda's return is proof.

The truth is, Linda walked away from Nathan a long time ago. Maybe even before the wedding. She married him because he was the first man to ask her to, and because it was what you did when you were in your midtwenties. Even in the beginning, she wasn't really invested in him. Something in the way he smelled, she couldn't abide. It wasn't like he had poor hygiene or wore too much aftershave. It was more like he invaded her senses. It was all she could smell when she was in the house. Their bedroom was potent with him, a scent she couldn't name, but it reminded her of lounging in the sun with Paige when they were girls, of lying in the yard on a picnic blanket, giggling and smelling her sister's head next to her own, the perfume of shampoo, yes, but also something else, something more personal. A smell like family. Nathan smelled like her sister.

"How is school going?" Dinah asks.

"Fine. Mandy and I got detention for sitting on the tables at lunch."

Dinah raises an eyebrow, but doesn't scold Skyla. She's always been most lenient with Skyla, and Linda often wonders whether it's because Skyla is blood, or because Dinah has lost the strength to argue. Skyla reaches for another towel and a handful of clothespins.

"I bet Mom's a showgirl or a bartender," Skyla continues, un-fazed. "Or she cleans hotel rooms." Even as her list deteriorates in glamour, she still speaks with a sense of wonder. Linda suspects this is less Skyla envisioning their mother, and more Skyla imag-ining her own future.

"Maybe she deals blackjack," Linda says.

"She probably has at least half a dozen boyfriends," Skyla says.

"And she makes them do her bidding," Linda says. She's always considered her mother to be heartless, but today, she's not quite feeling it. While coming to terms with her own divorce, she has begun to understand her mother, at least a little.

Dinah says, "I hope you two wouldn't talk that way if your father were here."

"Is he working late, or at the bar?" Linda asks. "Or has he up and left for Vegas, too?"

"I bet they bring her flowers," Skyla says. "And chocolates. Lingerie."

"Lordy!" Dinah mutters through a mouthful of clothespins.

A breeze picks up, and the sheets engulf Skyla for a moment. She fights her way back out of them, only to disappear again, running down the rows, angling her body to avoid the fabric. Linda knows it's only a matter of time before her youngest sister takes off, too. The only question is whether she'll manage to stay out once she leaves, or whether she'll come back like Linda, with a broken-down car and a failed marriage, an extra fifteen pounds and a giant gap in her résumé. Acquired experience that doesn't seem to inform her current life in any way. She watches Skyla dodge the blowing sheets, now visible, now hidden, the sunlight casting an elongated shadow on the fabric, showing only the ghost of the girl Linda once knew.

River Bend is so fanatic about football that even off-season skirmishes are well attended. And so, in late July, Linda makes her way to the high school football stadium to see the varsity play against the junior varsity, because what else is there to do in River Bend on a Friday night? She's spent the past few alone in her bedroom.

Linda worries about being spotted, about running into people she should remember. She worries for nothing—Linda Williams no longer looks like the girl she was in high school. As a teenager, she'd been athletic, her body thick with muscle, her hair as long as Skyla's. She'd been busy with 4-H and school clubs. Now her hair is chin-length, and she no longer bleaches it. Her face has grown dark in the Texas sun, with lines around her mouth and eyes. When she was younger, lipstick and perfume and dress shoes were reserved for special occasions. Somewhere over the past few years, though, she developed a love of makeup she never knew before, and now she feels naked leaving the house without at least concealer and mascara. As she seats herself in the metal stands, she spots a few people who look familiar, but only vaguely so.

It's hot by Michigan standards. The spectators are dressed in tee shirts, tank tops, shorts, sandals, tennis shoes with no socks. Linda wears jeans and an old flannel shirt. She feels strange, out in public in such casual clothes; people *dressed* in Houston. Around the third down, a warm drizzle settles in, soaking the players, muddying their jerseys. The ball keeps sliding out of the boys' hands. Even the cheerleaders are halfhearted in their shouts, their voices going rough, their shoes slick with rain. They kick up their legs, giggling as they almost fall, and make a kind of game out of seeing who will be the first to slip. Linda had wanted to be a cheerleader in high school, but didn't have the guts to try out. Not that she thought she wouldn't make it, but Grandma Dinah was always so dismissive of anything too girly. If it wouldn't put food on the table, or at least win ribbons at the county fair, it wasn't worth doing.

The stands begin emptying before halftime. Even though the evening is still warm, Linda is cold in the rain, having not yet acclimated to the Midwest. She's miserable, thinks of leaving. Everyone knows how the game will end. But by halftime, when the band takes the field, neither team has scored.

This is what she really came for, the nostalgia of seeing her half sister in the same heavy wool uniforms Linda had marched in. She easily spots Skyla, her hair wet on her face, the plume on her helmet looking like a soaked rodent. Skyla's gloves have the fingers cut out so she can grip her piccolo. Linda remembers those days, marching in the same uniform whether it was eighty degrees or twenty. Shivering in the stands because the band director wouldn't let you wear a coat. Nearly passing out from heat exhaustion during the Memorial Day parade. It could always be worse.

Linda has a terrible time spotting her cousins, though. She can't even remember what instruments they play. The formation of the band brings Skyla close to the bleachers, and Linda fumbles in her pocket to find her phone. She wishes she were sitting closer; the zoom on her phone's camera isn't great. She knows the photo won't turn out well, but still she tries. The damp makes it impossible for the fingerprint reader to register, and as she tries to input the passcode, the phone slips from her hands and falls below the bleachers. And Ernest DeWitt, who'd been sitting near the top of the stands, climbs down.

"I got it," he says, with a hand on her shoulder. And what a funny thing, to have a man she's known all her life, and yet barely knows at all, climb down to retrieve her phone.

He limps his way back up the bleachers, and Linda wonders whether the change in weather makes his joints hurt. Grandma Dinah can foretell a cold front by the feel of her knees. But Ernest DeWitt isn't as old as Dinah. His hands are warm as he passes Linda the phone. He sits next to her.

"It still work?" he asks, and she sees the screen is cracked.

"Ah, hell," she says without conviction. Part of her hopes the phone is dead, that it will no longer receive calls.

"Game's a wash," Ernest says. "And you look like you're cold."

"I'm fine," she replies, but Ernest offers her his poncho anyway. It's the sort of gesture Linda's husband, Nathan, would never have thought to make. She's been back a month, and Nathan still calls her daily. At first she would talk to him, hoping maybe a little distance had let her gather her thoughts. When Nathan was in law school, they had spent every night on the phone. Something in the way his voice hummed in her ear made her nostalgic. It was like he was inside her head. She liked having him contained there. On the phone, maybe she would remember what it was that had first attracted her to him, and then she could figure out what he'd done to drive her away. Only it wasn't anything he had or hadn't done. They simply didn't want the same life.

The stands are all but empty now. Linda burrows deeper into Ernest's poncho—army surplus, stiff green canvas, a hood that crinkles around her head so that she can't make out the brass instruments anymore, only the rhythmic pounding of the percussion section. Neither can she hear Ernest talking, so she lowers the hood and lets her hair get wet. When she continues to shiver, he slips an arm around her.

She forgets all about her sister on the field.

Back at Ernest's house, he offers her a mug of coffee with whiskey in it. Brash, cheap coffee that punches its way down her throat, cut with too much booze. They sit together on his couch. She's ashamed to find that she's grown accustomed to expensive coffee, to the extent that she no longer finds Grandma Dinah's palatable. Ernest's is even worse.

"This is strong enough to stand a duck in," she says, and immediately wishes she hadn't. She doesn't even know what that means really, but growing up, Grandma Dinah said it so often she can't not repeat it.

"Not a whiskey drinker?" He's sitting very close to her now.

She tries to think of something to say. She did her share of drinking in the suburbs; there wasn't much else to do, and she wants to let him know this, wants to impress him for some reason, although there is nothing particularly impressive about a thirty-two-year-old bragging about drinking. What she wants most is to let him know she's changed. She's no longer the awkward twentysomething she was when she left here six years ago. She wants him to understand the heat that's building in her stomach and spreading through her whole body, but she doesn't even understand it. She's never felt this before, not even with her husband.

She takes another sip and tries to smile. Ernest has lines around his eyes, etchings in wood. When he smiles back at her, his teeth are impossibly bright, uneven, a strange combination. His eyes are pale blue, almost silver. She can't think. She sets her coffee down and leans in to kiss him. He pulls back.

She leans in again, and again he pulls back.

"I'd rather take my time with you," he says. His voice is low, almost a growl, but his eyes are, once again, laughing.

Only that won't do. These moments that are close, but not close enough, are too much. They make Linda feel like her skin is blistering, like her face has ants crawling on it. She never could linger in the in-betweens. She leans back into the cushions of his couch and pulls him against her by his belt. He takes both her hands in one of his to still her.

"Where's the fire?" he says. His lips look serious, but his eyes are still creased at the corners. She supposes he's past the age of urgency. He touches his thumb to her chin, and she kisses his hand. He leans in, almost touching his lips to hers, and then pauses en route, hovering until she jerks her head forward. And then she's moving all at once, pulling his belt off, tugging her jeans down, burrowing her hands under his shirt to push him against the couch, straddling his lap. Too soon, it's over.

It hasn't been so quick since she was a teenager, since she and Nathan were first dating sophomore year in college. It leaves her feeling confused and vaguely dissatisfied. Like she isn't entirely sure it really happened. She feels as though she should apologize, but she doesn't know what she would apologize for, so instead she nestles against him, her head tucked up under his chin. She's so warm; she radiates heat from head to toe. He smells like hot summer grass. He has his arms wrapped around her waist, and he kisses the top of her head.

"Why don't we go upstairs and do that again, but slower," he says. When she looks at him, his eyes are no longer laughing. He looks at her like he might like to bite her. She takes his hand and lets him lead her to his bedroom.

In her purse, which she dropped by the back door, her cellphone buzzes. Nathan again. Her husband has spoken to his lawyer. If she doesn't want to talk, they'll continue to move forward with the divorce. He says this like a threat. She won't hear his messages until Monday, so wrapped up is she in Ernest DeWitt.

Elizabeth DeWitt
5

Gilmer grabs me by my arm, drags me down to his bedroom in the basement. He doesn't turn on the light. There are high windows, dirty, smoky. Clothes thrown on the carpet. The other children are there, too, Mikey and Beth. Both of them look down.

He gives us a choice. We can do what he says, or else we'll get a licking. I don't want to get a licking. Only naughty children get spanked.

His Jell-O belly comes closer. Too close. I don't even know the words for the things he shows me, for the things I do.

I find new places to hide in my babysitter's house. The closets, the bathrooms, even the garage, even in the cold. No matter where I go, he always finds me.

EXPOSURE

It's Saturday afternoon, early July, and I'm sitting in an overly air-conditioned high school auditorium between my ex-wife, Beth, and my current wife, Mara. We've been married three months. This is the first time Beth and Mara have met face-to-face, maybe the only time they will ever meet, since Beth has decided she'll move my kids out of state, back to her hometown of River Bend.

Beth is on her best behavior. For now. She's fidgeting with items from her purse—her nail file, her lip balm. She's anxious, I can tell, but she's hiding it pretty well. She keeps smoothing her hair down, which she does when she's nervous, but also, it's raining outside. Beth is half black, and I see she still presses her hair every morning with a flat iron, a habit she tried to kick when we were married. She was forever fussing about her hair going frizzy in the slightest humidity.

"How was your drive over here?" Mara asks, leaning forward in her seat to talk around me.

"Not bad," Beth says. "Traffic is moving in spite of the rain."

"Greg and I saw an accident on the freeway," Mara says, a hand on my sleeve. "I'm glad you weren't caught up in that."

I'm surprised. Beth doesn't usually have a lot of patience for small talk, but then Mara is easy to get along with. She's smart, well educated. When she's sweet, it's genuine. She doesn't go out of her way to be nice to people she doesn't like. We're here to see the kids' concert for band camp. Last year, Jeanette didn't go to camp, just Dan did, so I could skip the other part of the show. This year I have to sit through both halves of the program.

I shouldn't say that. I paid for this band camp; I should at least enjoy their performance. The high school–aged group, which Dan plays percussion in, is pretty good. And the middle school isn't bad, for middle school. Jeanette is actually a better singer than she is a clarinet player, but she decided to join band because her big brother is in band, and because Beth played clarinet in high school. I try to focus. I should be savoring every moment with my kids. I already don't get to see them as often as I'd like, and it's only going to get worse when they move to Michigan.

"I heard you're getting your house ready to sell," Mara says. "Let us know if we can help."

"You're so sweet," Beth says, reaching across me to put a hand on Mara's arm. "I may take you up on that."

Mara and Beth continue talking around me, Beth sweet, even flirty in that social way some women can be. She's putting on a show for Mara. I wait for the concert to begin so that it can be over. Beneath the stage curtain, I see movement, kids scooching chairs and music stands, getting situated. The middle school is up first, and I wonder whether Jeanette is nervous. I'm always impressed by anyone who can get on stage, under such bright lights and in front of so many people. And, I realize, I actually am going to miss this.

The move makes no sense to me. Beth hated growing up in that cow town. She says that they treated her like she was less than. I don't understand why she's moving back there, back in with her father, rather than letting me cover the mortgage until she finds a new job.

"You mean let Mara pay?" Beth said when I offered. A low blow. She knows that Mara makes more money than I do, but we don't keep our finances separate. We don't squabble about money like Beth and I did.

"It was Mara's idea, if that's what you're implying." This has been a sore spot with Beth, that I haven't seen Dan and Jeanette as much as I used to since meeting Mara. I think Beth blames Mara, assumes she doesn't like the kids. Even though Mara doesn't want kids herself, it's important to us both that Dan and Jeanette are well provided for.

I hate the idea of them moving in with their grandfather Ernest, who they haven't even seen since they were both too young to remember him. And Gretchen, their grandmother who lives a few towns over from him, doesn't ever visit or call. She's not really a grandmother, not like my mom is. I only hope that Ernest helps temper Beth a little, because Beth has always been weirdly strict with the kids, especially Jeanette. She doesn't like them going out much, doesn't encourage them to join clubs or school sports. She didn't even want them in band, which I think is the real reason Jeanette joined. It's like Beth thinks it's the kids' job to stay home and keep her company.

Also, River Bend is sick. I mean, for Christ's sake, just last month they arrested a man preying on children there. When I brought this up with Beth a few days ago, she looked disgusted with *me,* as if I were the guy who'd been hurting kids.

"You think this shit doesn't happen everywhere?" she said. Beth is a master of shutting down a conversation.

"But why River Bend?" I asked. "Why go back there?"

"Enough," Beth said. "It's time to give it a rest." The way she said this, the absolute defeat in her voice, and the way her eyes darted from mine, it was like she'd given up. Like she thought she deserved River Bend. Like she was a failure for having to move the kids there. She was hugging herself. She looked like she was on the verge of tears. I know Beth's tears. Once they start, they don't stop for a long time. I let it drop.

Beth and I were married for four years. Truth be told, we got married too quickly, too young. It was doomed from the start. My mother warned me. Beth's mother, Gretchen, warned her. When that failed, Gretchen warned *me.* Beth never talked much about growing up in River Bend, but Gretchen told me about it, and about Beth's ex, Steve. Getting Beth to talk about Steve—about anything, really—is like pulling teeth, but according to Gretchen, Beth and Steve were inseparable, even though he was also dating the woman he ended up marrying. What was her name? Deb. Gretchen made it sound like Beth was half-crazed; there was no reasoning with her about Steve. Like he had Beth brainwashed. I can't even imagine Beth brainwashed. My ex-wife is nothing if not strong-willed.

"By the way, sorry I missed your wedding," Beth says now to Mara. "Jeanette tells me it was lovely." She keeps reaching across me to paw at my wife, and I want her to knock it off. She's not fooling anyone.

"No worries," Mara says. "Thank you for the gift, though."

I can tell Beth's not sorry. She hates weddings. I don't think she even liked our wedding. Not long after it, it was like a curtain came down over her, and when it rose again, she'd changed into another character. This version of Beth was moody, angry, surly, destructive. She blamed me for everything. And I really mean everything. There were the normal issues couples fight about: miscommunications and money and sex. I got blamed for those, but also for Beth having a rough day at work. She's a chef, or at least she was until very recently, and she always felt like the men she worked with didn't respect her. They hit on her, which, like, that's what men do. I never understand why women get so offended. And she said she got passed up for promotions. They treated her like a prep cook. She said it was because she's a black woman. She was always playing those cards. Really, if she wants people to treat her well, she needs to treat them well first, but I pray for the poor bastard who tries to tell *her* that.

So it's surprising to see Beth being so nice to Mara, who is tall and slender and white, with the kind of hair you see in shampoo commercials. A lot of women get insecure around Mara. Shit, a lot of men do, too. Add to that the fact that Mara is a professor at UNC, and I assumed Beth would be feeling threatened. But if she is, it sure doesn't show.

I tried with Beth. I tried to placate her. When we divorced, I gave her everything she asked for. I didn't argue. I just wanted out. But she stayed just as miserable. Even now, while she talks with Mara, there's an edge to her voice. She's still miserable. And I worry, deep down. I worry that the problem isn't her. It's me. Somehow, I did this to her. If she were talking to me instead of Mara, she would be Angry Beth. Something in me poisoned her— and what if I poison Mara? Part of me wants Beth to turn on Mara, to show just a bit of the woman I divorced, to prove that the problem is her, but she doesn't. The two of them are still chatting like old friends as the house lights dim and the curtain goes up to show all those young faces, Jeanette among them, all squinting out into the darkened audience. Jesus, how will this move affect Jeanette? At least if she stayed here, she'd be around Mara, might learn how to behave in the world. And my son, too, I worry for him. He and Jeanette will probably end up angry and mean, just like their mother, blaming the world for their faults. Dan is already antisocial like Beth. And he's turning into kind of a know-it-all like her, too.

Who am I kidding? Even if they stayed, my kids are doomed to turn into little Beths. It's awful, every time I see them and see how much like her they've become. I could work myself stupid trying to prevent it. Maybe it's time to move on.

Wrapping an arm around Mara's waist, I brace myself for the hour to come. Really, maybe this move will be good. For me, at least.

Elizabeth DeWitt
6

Mrs. Thurber renames me. I used to go by Beth, but she says I'm to be called Liz or Eliza.

"My granddaughter is 'Beth,' and I won't have my own kith and kin sharing a name with a nigger child."

These are all the new names I've learned today: Liz, Eliza, Nigger.

"Choose. Now. And hurry up, before I get angry."

EXPERIENCE

Ernest wishes Linda could stay. Every time she's over, when the evening quickly wears away, he asks her if she'd like to stay the night, and every time she declines. He's been through this before, but women usually give in eventually. With Linda, he supposes she's not ready to tell people, and this throws him. Is he getting so old that women are embarrassed by him?

To get her to stay, he tries tempting her with food, with wine (which he's never really liked, but from watching movies and TV, he's gathered that's what women prefer), and with foot massages. He's never worked this hard for a woman in his life. He kind of enjoys it.

And every night before she leaves, she'll kiss him long and soft, her arms going around his neck. He's sure she doesn't want to leave him. This isn't a casual thing for her. The town, with the way they talk about him, might be surprised to find that it isn't casual for him, either, but then it seldom is. In his life, he has loved and been loved by many women. The problem is, he falls in love with women before he really knows them, and once he's in love, he's completely in, body and mind, until he's completely out again. But that's still a long ways off. Right now it's the middle of August, and the sky is a hot, deep blue. He has been seeing Linda about a month, and he's absolutely smitten. And if he's not mistaken, she's smitten with him, too.

Paige knocks on Linda's bedroom door one day after church. Linda has already been back for two months and hasn't bothered to come see Paige in Kalamazoo, hasn't visited Paige's wife or son or seen Paige's house. It's really kind of ridiculous.

It's been a while since Paige has visited home, so it feels like a holiday. Paige lives a forty-five-minute drive away. Not that far, really. But she's busy, too. She has a young son, and she stays at home with him while her wife, Diane, goes out and works. It's nice to be out of the house today, to be interacting with adults.

Paige remembers hanging out in Linda's room when they were girls, having impromptu slumber parties, and watching her sister primp before school dances. As early as middle school, Paige knew she liked other girls, that there was no point in getting dolled up for the attention of boys. Still, she always loved to watch Linda get ready. She used to wish she could have even a sliver of Linda's confidence.

Today, Linda is lying on her bed, her eyes closed even though she's awake. The weather is hot and dry and still. It annoys Paige to see her sister looking so deflated, but then, that's Linda for you: never one to appreciate how good she has it.

"Can we come in?" Paige doesn't wait for an answer, but enters the room and sprawls on Linda's carpet. Skyla's not far behind her. Skyla used to play in here all the time when she was younger, whether Linda was at home or not. It feels simultaneously familiar and foreign, a forbidden space she usually slips into only when nobody is around. With Linda and Paige in there, it feels somehow altered, cramped and stuffy.

The room is a little worse for wear. The carpet hasn't been vacuumed in months. The rose-patterned bedspread, faded from too many washings, is thrown on the floor, taking up most of the space in the tiny room. Pushed partway under the bed are Linda's Barbie dolls, their hair matted like steel wool, their clothes half-off. When Linda went to college, she had tucked them into boxes, stacked them in the closet, but Skyla rummaged through all of Linda's abandoned belongings. The bookshelf holds copies of all the *Baby-sitters Club* books, old *Seventeen* magazines, a large spiral-bound book that was meant to store recipes. Linda filled only one page.

"We know," Skyla says from the floor, never one to waste time on niceties.

"Know what?" Linda doesn't open her eyes.

"You're preggers," Paige says, trying to keep the annoyance from her voice. Paige has been trying to get knocked up at the clinic for months, has been struggling to catch up to her wife, who birthed their son. And here Linda is, accidentally pregnant.

Linda sits up, panicked. "How'd you find out?"

"We didn't *know* know," Skyla says. "You just confirmed it."

Linda took the pregnancy test a few days ago, and in that time, she hasn't figured out what to do. She slides down from her bed and joins her sisters on the carpet. Paige has to scoot over to make room. Skyla kicks the bedspread into a wad in the corner.

"Does Grandma know?" Linda asks. She hasn't even told Ernest yet, although she thinks he must know, the way he keeps feeding her. But what if he doesn't? What if he breaks it off with her when he finds out? What if Dinah doesn't approve and kicks her out?

Both Linda and Paige look to Skyla, who shrugs. Lately Grandma Dinah has had a knack for training her eyes on Linda's face when they speak, refusing to look past her neck, or else patting Linda on the head as if she were still a little girl, making comments to the effect of, "A woman should have a little meat on her," misinterpreting Linda's weight gain.

"Oh God. Does Dad know?"

"Doubtful," Skyla says.

"His head hasn't exploded, so I'm guessing he doesn't know," Paige says.

"He's never home," Skyla says. "I bet you could have the kid and he still wouldn't know."

Paige pulls a Barbie doll from under the bed and tries to detangle its hair with her pinkie nail. Linda starts to cry. Paige eyes her from across the room. She isn't sure how to react. She never knows what to do when women are crying, and so she freezes and looks down at her own boyish flatness. She's always envied Linda her curves. Paige thinks of when her own wife, Diane, was pregnant, and the way her body filled with hormones and fluids and all the bits that make up a new person. Not that Linda knows any of this. Linda hasn't even thought to ask what's going on in Paige's life. When they were teenagers, they were so close. All they had was each other. Paige can't pinpoint when they grew so distant.

Skyla stops flipping through a copy of *Seventeen* dated 1997 and crawls over to Linda to hug her. "It'll be okay," she says, but even to her own ears, she sounds unsure.

"Grandma said *you* were the one who'd get knocked up," Linda says, blowing her nose.

"I love *other* people's babies," Skyla says, wise beyond her sixteen years.

"Babysitting is the best way to keep a girl from getting pregnant," Paige says.

"You going back to Nathan?" Skyla asks.

"Nathan sucks," Paige says, setting the Barbie aside.

"Ernest DeWitt is the father," Linda says.

"Ew!" Skyla says.

Paige hits her in the arm. "Keep your voice down."

Skyla kicks Paige in the shoulder. "What? He's literally a million years old."

"He's not that old," Linda says quietly.

"Bet he's twice as old as Dad," Skyla says.

"Dad's older than you think," Paige says.

"Bet his daughter's older than you," Skyla adds.

"Eliza DeWitt? She's about the same age," Linda says. This is a lie, and they all know it. Eliza babysat Linda when Linda was a girl.

"Linda DeWitt," Skyla says. "Gross."

"What are you going to do?" Paige finally looks up from her lap. Her sister is hurting, she knows. Paige has been butt-hurt that Linda didn't tell her she was leaving her husband, that she hasn't taken the time to visit, didn't tell Paige when she found out she was pregnant. But now that she thinks about it, Paige could have taken the time to visit, too. She will take the time, she decides. She'll be there for Linda. She gets up from the floor and picks her way around Barbies and magazines to hug Linda.

This sets Linda off crying again. She's missed her sisters over the past few years; she'd failed to realize they were no longer children. They, too, have grown into women. As much as Linda has, at any rate. As much as anyone ever does.

.   .   .

Ernest DeWitt isn't exactly what Linda likes. First of all, if she were honest with herself, he's far too old for her, a fact she has a hard time reconciling with his looks. His body is thick, his arms still strong, although his skin has lost its resilience. He has broad shoulders that, though they show signs of having once been sturdy, are now bony, tan, and freckled. His hair is more salt than pepper. His eyes aren't as clear as a young man's, and the skin around them pouches. There's gravel in his voice, a car crunching along a dirt road. She doesn't know how to explain: It isn't the physical fact of him. It's something in the calm she feels when she's with him, an unburdening, a resting. He makes her whole body feel like a sunny, grassy field. He smells like a grassy field. Like laundry hung to dry. Like a warm breeze gathering in the disused corners of her body, places that have been dark and stale a long time.

"Maybe you have daddy issues," Paige says the next week, while she and Linda are having coffee at the Hudson House. True to her resolution, Paige has been calling Linda every couple of days to check in. Linda even visited Paige, Diane, and Sage in Kalamazoo, brought a bottle of rosé and a bucket of colorful plastic dinosaurs from the dollar store. Diane threw out both as soon as Linda left; she was worried about phosphates in the wine, and synthetic materials in the toys.

"Maybe you have mommy issues," Linda says, pointing her mug of cocoa at Paige.

Paige curls her lip and thinks how right Linda is. Ever since Diane had Sage, Paige has felt like she needs to catch up, to spit out a kid of her own to prove she really is an adult. She sighs. Suppresses. She doesn't want to lay all this on Linda right now.

"I don't even understand what women see in men," Paige says instead. "They're awful. Like that man they arrested at the beginning of the summer. Thurber. You never hear of women doing stuff like that."

Linda shakes her head. "What about Gilmer's sister? She's not blameless." She feels herself getting annoyed. The Thurber business is awful, but she doesn't understand why everyone has to keep bringing it up.

"At least tell me Ernest is good to you," Paige says now. "Because he'd better treat you like a queen."

They both know from town gossip that Ernest DeWitt is *experienced,* the word always spoken as if it were dirty. Linda recalls women at church shaking their heads, making chicken noises at the sight of Ernest DeWitt's latest *tramp*. At times, he's gone around with single mothers and women from the trailer park, or women who were knocked up in high school, and on at least one occasion, with another man's wife. It's *disgraceful*. Thinking back, though, Linda now recalls another tone to those voices: a note of longing. *Those biddies were bored,* Linda thinks. Bored and scared, wanting the romance, but terrified of the impact.

There's another thing, an unspoken thing, and that's the matter of Ernest's ex-wife—a black woman. As if River Bend were still stuck in the sixties.

Even as she thinks this, she knows she won't yet tell her grandma or stepdad about Ernest. It's all too much: leaving Nathan, getting pregnant. She'd been careful in Texas, so strict with her birth control—in part, she thinks now, because somehow she knew she was going to leave Nathan. And maybe this is okay, now, with Ernest, because he feels right in a way that Nathan never did. *Maybe this will all work out,* she thinks, but she doesn't yet know.

And so she sneaks around with Ernest, visits him in the

middle of the day, goes to his house through the alleyway, knocks on the back door. In his yard, she can slip into the shadow of the old mulberry tree, which deposits her onto the stoop. She feels much more comfortable here than standing on his front porch, the western-facing facade of his house bright in the sunlight, framed by the small yard that drops off onto Main Street. She always knocks on his back door softly—there's no doorbell—and even with the lightest of touches, he answers quickly, as if he's been waiting for her.

Linda soon learns that *experience* is anything but a dirty word. Ernest loves her lingeringly, and when they're together, she's the sole focus of his attention. He loves her in the daylight, with the blankets off the bed. He loves her completely nude, and takes his time in a way that makes her feel treasured, so different from the distracted pawing she grew used to with Nathan. Ernest's love makes her question the wisdom of virginity, of saving yourself for marriage, of entering into a lifelong union with someone who barely knows himself, and doesn't know you at all.

And when the sun comes in through the thin curtains of Ernest's bedroom windows, when she uncurls from his side and tells him—two weeks after admitting it to her sisters, her heart beating behind her eardrums—that she's pregnant, he kisses her collarbone, the space between her breasts, her still-flat belly, then pulls on his shorts and goes down to the kitchen to make her an omelet. He isn't a good cook. He hacks at vegetables with a dull knife, cooks them in too much butter until they're overdone, layers slices of American cheese on top of eggs that are still a little runny. And he brings her that god-awful coffee. But Linda loves the food he makes for her, because the gesture is so novel.

"Eat up," he says. "I want my boy to come out big and strong." His boy, he thinks. He'll get things right this time, with this child.

In the back of his mind, though, he wonders how Elizabeth will respond. He's spent so long convincing her to move back home, and now she's coming in mid-September. Maybe he won't tell her about this development just yet.

"What makes you think it's a boy?" Linda asks. She's so relieved by his response that she's giddy.

He doesn't answer, just winks.

"I shouldn't be drinking coffee anymore," she says, but drinks it anyway.

Back in his bed after the sun sets, Ernest loves her so well she almost wishes she could loan him out. Every woman should experience this at least once. He loves her so that, afterward, it takes her a moment to remember where she is, who she is, and she stretches on his sheets, her arms over her head, her abdominal muscles pulled lean, her brain quiet, her body the warmest it has ever been.

At the end of August, a postcard from Paula is delivered to the farm, addressed to "The Williams Girls." As if Paula can't remember each of their names. Which, Linda figures, might be true. She's had no contact with them for fourteen years.

"Her handwriting isn't very feminine," Paige says, always one to nitpick in hopes of keeping her feelings at bay. She's more like Paula than she knows. She'd dropped by the farm today to visit her sisters, and then Linda sprang the card on her.

"And her spelling kind of sucks," Linda says.

The sisters huddle together on Grandma's couch to read it, Linda in the middle, holding the postcard because Paige and Skyla seem reluctant to touch it.

"How close is Utah to Vegas?" Skyla says.

"You don't know where Utah is?" Paige says.

"I know where Utah is," Skyla says. Paige is always on Skyla's case about her grades, bemoaning her general lack of knowledge about the world. As if Paige were so wise.

"Who does that?" Linda says. "Who sends a postcard out of the blue? It's just, random."

On the front is a picture of Arches National Park, that blue-blue sky behind those red-orange rocks. The back says, "Thinking of you all."

"It's kind of shitty of her," Paige says.

"She's thinking of us," Skyla says.

"She *wants* something, more like," Paige says.

"New theory," Skyla says. "Mom is a secret agent. She's been surveilling the house. How else would she know we're all here to receive her postcard?"

"A secret agent in Utah?" Paige says.

"Isn't that where Area Fifty-Six is?" Skyla asks.

"You mean Area Fifty-One?"

"Maybe she wants to reconnect?" Linda says.

"Yes. But," Paige says, "a postcard has no return address."

Still, it's a starting point. A much narrower search than *somewhere in the world,* or *maybe still in the U.S.*

Skyla gets online and accesses public records, telephone listings, newspapers of local towns. The sisters gather close, trying to see her phone. She finds a Paula Williams named in a newspaper clipping, an interview asking residents about a drought around Moab. This Paula Williams is quoted as saying, "So we can't water our lawns. No skin off my nuts."

"That's Mom," Paige says. "That's so Mom."

Elizabeth DeWitt

7

A lady from the school visits the house to talk to my mom. They're worried because the babysitter sent me to school in a diaper.

"Your seven-year-old should be potty trained," the lady tells my mom.

"What do you mean?" my mom says. "Of course she's potty trained."

"Why was she in a diaper?" the lady asks.

"Why was she what?" my mom says.

When the lady has gone, my mom asks me if it's true. When I tell her yes, she doesn't believe me. She checks my butt and finds it covered in diaper rash. After that, I don't have to go to the babysitter's anymore. My life before quickly blurs—the house, the babysitter, the girl child, the man child, the other Beth, even Mikey. They become like something dropped over the side of a boat, sunken to the murky bottom of the lake.

BALANCING

The air surging through the window is sweet and dusty, vibrating with heat. Ninety degrees outside, not bad for the end of August. Paula can't bring herself to turn on the air conditioner. She stretches in bed, her back damp with sweat, and listens to the coffeepot gurgling in the kitchen—Jorge making breakfast. There's the pop of a tube of crescent rolls, the slide of a cookie sheet into the oven. They have nothing to do, nowhere to go. Last night, they had a fight: Paula wanted a quiet night at home, but Jorge wanted to go out. She had to remember that was the danger of dating a guy twelve years her junior; his stamina for social events, hikes, even sex, is so much greater than hers. In the end, he went without her, and she went to bed angry.

She's glad he's making breakfast, that he brings two cups of coffee back to bed with him. Both of them have the weekend off work—a rarity, since Paula works in a restaurant that's always busy in the summer. Labor Day is next week, marking the end of the tourist season. It can't come fast enough. But today is a day of rest, and the time opens before them like a wide canyon. They negotiate their options while crescent rolls rise in the oven.

"We could fix the porch," Jorge says, curling next to her. His body is hot, but it's a nice feeling. In the backyard, they have a stack of lumber salvaged from a friend's house before it was torn down; their own porch needs to be ripped out and replaced, the lumber sanded and varnished, a project that's been on their list for months.

"We can work on that separately any old time," Paula says. "We don't both have to be here for it."

"We keep putting it off."

Paula sighs, stretches. Yawns. She's worked twelve days straight. She just wants to take it easy. She runs her fingers through his hair. "We could take Lola for a hike? Or drive down to the reservoir?"

He smiles, but only with one side of his mouth. He's always so busy doing, making, repairing, improving. She wants him to take a moment and just be with her. To feel the hot dry air pushing in through the open window. To smell the dust and yellow grass.

He touches his nose to hers. "Whatever you want."

Jorge lets her drive. She likes to lose herself in the altitude, the juniper shrubs and mounds of shale. In her truck, she has an altimeter salvaged out of an old Cessna fixed to the dashboard with Velcro. She tracks the correlation between its movements and the pressure in her ears. Even after fourteen years here, she still feels dizzy from the elevation changes. She pushes the accelerator and waits for the lag before she downshifts. She also notices a slight wobble, a rear tire off balance, but can't tell if it's the driver's or passenger's side. In the pickup bed, Lola gambols from one end to the other, her tongue lolling out, as she tries to figure out which side smells better. The truck climbs out of the shadows of the sheer cliffs bordering the road.

Jorge drums on his knees. Paula can barely hear the rhythm over the roar of wind through open windows. Ahead of them, the road appears to drop off into pure blue, but as she crests the hill, the downside reveals itself, a long, dark slither of road. Her engine startles a crow, and it takes flight, clutching part of a dead animal in its beak, the red meat of which is exposed, a bit of backbone dangling. A piece of raw flesh flops back onto the road.

At the reservoir, Jorge is restless. The fish aren't biting, but the buffalo gnats are. There are too many boats out, all cruising around in aimless circles, making waves that slide up the boat launch, lap the pier. Every time a boat passes, Lola barks and leaps up like she's headed into the water, and Paula has to grab her by her collar. Dogs aren't allowed in the reservoir.

"Maybe you're right," Paula says after an hour. "Maybe we should build that porch."

"We came all this way," Jorge says, skewering a worm on his hook.

But it's no use. Neither of them wants to be here. Even Lola is antsy, running up and down the pier, snapping her teeth at clouds of gnats. Jorge casts and reels, casts and reels, a mechanical motion. A father and his young son come down the pier with fishing poles, but at the sight of Lola, barking and snapping at seemingly nothing, the son turns his blond head into his father's leg and cries. Lola is an eighty-pound golden retriever, a bit pudgy, but hardly a monster. The father tries for a few minutes to convince his son that it's fine, the dog won't hurt him, but the son is having none of it.

"Nothing's biting anyway," Paula calls after him.

Jorge reels, reaches the pole back, casts again. He's quieter than usual, his movements jerky. Paula worries he's angry with her, about the porch, about the fight last night. She puts a hand on his arm.

"What's up?" she says.

He reels. "Nothing." He isn't even twitching the rod like he felt a nibble.

"No, really."

"Everything's fine."

In her heart, she feels this is it: the end of something lovely. She should have expected it. He's breaking up with her. She stares at the pier, its rotting wood, the end slimy with algae.

Paula steels herself for the news. In her mind, too, she begins calculating. She'll have to find a new place to live; there's no way she'll be able to afford the mortgage, unless she can swing a second job. Cooking down at the café is nice—relaxing even, in its own harried way—but they need her for so many hours. And hell, she's forty-eight. How much longer can she keep up twelve-hour shifts? Can she really manage a whole other job on top of that?

Beneath this is an issue Paula doesn't want to think about. She won't date again. She doesn't want to start over. She told herself this was it, that moving to Utah was a new leaf. And then she went and attached herself to a man twelve years her junior. Twelve years! Almost young enough that she could be his mother, at least in River Bend. She knows his leaving is her fault entirely. She isn't a romantic woman; she rarely says that she loves him, she doesn't like to hug and kiss unless it's going to lead somewhere. When they first started dating six years ago, Jorge was always trying to hold her hand at the store, kiss her neck in restaurants. It took her nearly a year to break him of this habit. Maybe she should have indulged him a little.

He reels his line in all the way, until the hook catches on the eyelet at the end of the rod. Then he sets the pole down on the pier. He sighs. His hands are shaking as he reaches into his pocket.

"This is stupid," he says. "I'm stupid. I wanted to do this last night. But then you wouldn't come out with me, so I thought, *Why not today?* I imagined us building the deck, hopefully finishing by dinner. Maybe grilling out. And when the sun was going down . . ." He pulls a little velvet box from his pocket.

Paula stares at it. Now she's stupid. His hands shake as he fumbles with the box, and before he can pry it fully open, the box snaps shut and pops out of his hands. It splashes into the reservoir.

"Shit," he says. The box floats on the water. He reaches over the edge, but the box bobs under the pier. "*¡Carajo!*" he says, and dives in after it.

And while he's dog-paddling, Paula reimagines her life with him. Even if she could get remarried, she doesn't want to. Not again. It isn't that she doesn't love Jorge, but sometimes she feels like people aren't meant to be together forever. Still, she knows theirs would be a good life. They'd keep busy with home improvements and gardening, fishing trips and camping and hiking with Lola. They'd have dinners for Jorge's kids from his first marriage. There would be barbecues and birthday parties and football games. Graduations, weddings. Grandkids. And she would be tethered here, to these rocks and this sky, for the rest of her life.

When Jorge hauls himself back onto the pier, he opens the box up at last. The look on his face is triumphant, until he sees the look on Paula's.

"Shit," he says. "I've ruined it."

"No," she says. "No, it's just—you know I can't."

He shakes his head. "Don't you think it's time you got a divorce?" He holds the box open with both hands, a sacred offering. His hair streams water into his eyes. A puddle forms around his feet.

"It's not that simple," she says.

He pulls the ring from the box, slips it onto her finger. "Sure it is," he says. "We'll go over Labor Day. We'll get him to sign the papers."

When she started dating Jorge, he seemed to be of the impression her husband had denied her a divorce. In truth, she'd never asked. The ring is wet and briefly cold on her finger. She looks at the way light blazes in it when it catches the sun.

They barely speak on the ride home. Her ring keeps twisting around so that the stone juts into her middle finger, her pinkie. It's hard to watch the road; she keeps looking at the diamond.

"Let's say we went to Michigan," Paula says. "Let's say he won't sign the papers. What then?"

"Why wouldn't he?"

My daughters, she thinks. But she shakes her head, looking at the ring.

Her husband had been good enough to marry her, to take care of Linda and Paige like they were his own, after her first husband left. When Skyla was born, he paraded her around town like she was heir to the throne. Skyla would be, what? Sixteen now? Which would make Paige nearly thirty, and Linda thirty-two. Almost the same age as Jorge. Oh Lord.

Paula feels her stomach drop, and she realizes she's going about twenty over the speed limit. Her truck catches air as it crests a hill, and Lola stumbles in the back. The wobble she felt on the way to the reservoir is getting worse. She really needs to balance her tires when she gets home.

"You're awful quiet," Jorge says. He reaches over to take her hand, and Paula downshifts unnecessarily. He settles for resting his hand on top of hers. Out of the corner of her eye, she can tell he's watching her. She takes his hand, gives it a little squeeze, and then adjusts the rearview mirror.

The sun slants through the hackberry trees in their yard. From the driveway, Paula can see Jorge along the side of the house, selecting the best pieces of lumber from the pile. Paula's truck is up on blocks. Even though she's getting dirt and tire grime on her hands, she still has on the ring. She doesn't own a jewelry box, and she's terrified of losing such a small, expensive object.

She knows her truck can wait, that she should help Jorge. She can hear him prying up the old porch. The sun isn't so low that they can't still salvage the day. Yet even as she tells herself this, she keeps balancing her tires. She has three of them done when she smells charcoal and lighter fluid. Soon, Jorge comes around the house with a plate for her.

They eat burgers, dry inside and charred on the outside, while sitting on the front steps. Paula tries to eat without tasting.

"I haven't had a vacation in years, and business has been slow," Jorge says. "I could probably take two weeks, no problem."

"I can't," Paula says. "Not during peak season."

"We'll hire a lawyer, then."

"We can't afford that," Paula says.

Jorge sets down his plate. He breathes audibly through his nose. "So, what? We just carry on like this forever?"

"What's wrong with *this*?"

"We're a little old to be playing house, Paula."

"Who's playing?"

"And I want to know you're not going to run off on me." As soon as he says it, he looks down at his plate. She leaves her half-eaten burger on the steps and goes back to her truck. Lola barks behind the fence, her nose whistling as she eyes Paula's plate.

"I didn't mean it," Jorge calls after her.

She lifts a tire, heaves it onto the axle.

"At least let me help you," Jorge says, coming up to the truck.

"I got it."

"God, Paula. You're going to throw your back out."

"It's my business. Why don't you go fiddle with the porch?"

He circles around to the other side of the truck and lifts a tire onto its axle.

"Put that one on back," Paula says. "You got to rotate them."

He pulls the tire off, rolls it to the back of the truck, and lifts it on.

"Careful not to rock it," Paula says.

"It's stable," Jorge says.

"I don't want my truck falling."

"It's fine," Jorge says, screwing the lug nuts on.

"Because if you break my daddy's truck—"

"Jesus, Paula. I don't give a shit about your truck." He throws a lug nut into the grass. "I want to marry you. Stop. Talk to me."

"You really need a piece of paper that says I love you?"

"It's not—it's just—no, I'm not saying I need a piece of paper."

"Yes, you are."

"I'm saying, why not make this legit?"

"Because my word isn't enough?" She's bent low to the ground, searching for the lug nut Jorge flung. "Because you think I'm just toying with you? How long have we been together?"

"It's not that—Paula, stop." He comes up behind her, places a hand on her back. "I want to build a life with you. I want to take care of you."

"Do I look like I need to be taken care of?" She finally finds the lug nut. She straightens, faces him. He looks little standing before her. His shoulders hunched, his eyes darting away from her face every few seconds. "Because what you're talking about is just some bureaucratic bullshit. It's a way for the government to keep tabs on you, to make sure you settle down and take a job and be a good little capitalist. Is that what you want? A desk job? A bigger house? A new truck? Because what's the point?"

"Marriage isn't a fucking conspiracy, Paula."

"We're not twenty-year-olds with college degrees. We're not starting a family."

She turns from him again, finishes screwing on the lug nuts. From the corner of her eye, she can see she's knocked the wind out of him. Good. Someone needs to bring him back down to earth. She begins jacking her truck down, removing cinder blocks, one corner at a time. Jorge just stands there. Watching her work. He doesn't offer to help. She can feel him watching. It takes an enormous amount of concentration not to look back over her shoulder, to keep working. When she does glance at him, he keeps standing there, his eyes small and watery red, dark pouches under them like bruises. She should go to him, she knows, she should put her arms around him and apologize. But she can't bring herself to do it.

"Why don't you go get me my torque wrench?"

He huffs off to the garage. She can hear him slamming around in there. When he comes back, Paula is jacking down the last corner of her truck.

"It's not in there," he says.

"What do you mean it's not there?"

"I mean it's not in there," he says.

"You used it last week. Didn't you put it back?"

"Will you wait a moment? Will you talk to me?" He stands behind her. "I want to spend my life with you."

"Did you put it back or not?"

"I don't know. It's not in there."

"Dammit," she mutters. She goes into the garage herself. It's not in the drawer, it's not on her workbench. She settles for a long socket wrench.

"Marry me," Jorge says when she comes back.

She tightens the lug nuts by hand as far as she can, then uses the socket wrench. "Because marriage worked so well for you last time?"

"Least I bothered to end it before I walked away."

"The fuck's that supposed to mean?" She's balancing all of her weight on the wrench. Her knuckles are going white, but she keeps tightening.

"Be honest. You don't want to get divorced, do you?"

"We're not having this conversation again," she says, snapping on a hubcap.

"I sent a postcard," Jorge says. "To your girls."

"You—what?"

"A couple weeks ago. I sent a postcard. I signed your name."

Paula can't even imagine Jorge meeting her family. She doesn't think they would be inhospitable to him, but she doesn't know.

You never can be entirely sure about people these days. "Where do you get off?"

"It's crazy that you've had no contact."

Jorge comes around the truck, tries to wrap his arms around her. "I want to know your family, Paula. I want to be a part of their lives."

"You had no goddamn right." She wriggles out of his arms.

"I'm your family, too," he says. "They're my family by extension."

"I need to test my tires."

As she pulls out of the driveway, he calls after her, "Yeah, run away. It's what you're good at."

Sunlight flares pink on the canyon walls. The air is already turning cool. A cloud of dust rises in Paula's rearview mirror. Her tires are still off balance; she could have figured that out just by going around the block. But almost without realizing it, she found herself driving out of town, headed toward the mountains.

Why can't Jorge be content with the way things are? She secretly believes that their relationship has lasted as long as it has because it hasn't *had* to last. There's no complication, nothing binding them together, so that each day they spend with each other is a choice. She wants to continue choosing him. She wants that freedom. But she knows that if she told him this, it wouldn't make any sense. Shit, it doesn't really make sense to her.

The truck bumps and rattles as she drives, and Paula realizes she's on a seasonal road. When did that happen? The mountain falls sharply to her right, and she can see way out over the valley, all the way back to town. Green patches mark the river and the lawns watered by sprinklers. She imagines those yards, too distant to see clearly, are filled with play sets and bicycles. Her own neighborhood has a lot of young parents, people who don't seem to want to bother getting to know Paula and Jorge, the only couple without young children. Deep down, she blames those parents for Jorge's insistence on getting married. When they moved into their neighborhood, Jorge told her he'd always wanted to live in a place where people watered their lawns. Where children played outside. Where neighbors came over to grill out. No doubt Jorge assumed getting married would allow them fuller access to that community.

Paula's truck pulls to the right, the tire wobble somehow worse now, making her steering wheel jump. Maybe the tire is going flat, or maybe she hadn't tightened the lug nuts properly. She hopes the road will widen and she can find a good place to pull over, but as she drives, the steering wheel jerks even harder, and before Paula can stop, something gives way and the rear passenger's side drops, pulling the truck sharply to the right. Paula stomps on the brake pedal, feeling something in her foot crack, a pain shooting up her leg. The cliff edge comes closer, a sheer drop into open air. Her mind stops, the air around her freezes for an instant, and then her heart is pounding in her head, her hands cold and damp on the steering wheel. There's the sound of crunching gravel and scraping metal. A loud clunk, the rear tire slipping over the cliff. Then the truck plants itself into the ground.

She's okay. Her truck is stopped, and she's okay. In front of her she can see the open air, still and blue, the green lawns of her neighborhood in the distance. She wonders briefly whether the noise of her truck was loud enough that Jorge heard it, a distant wail telling him what he had to lose, what she was losing.

Her daughters. She has trained her brain to shy away from the family she left behind, but it occurs to her again that Linda and

Paige are grown. They probably have children of their own. They probably have careers. Shit, Skyla would be driving by now; she, too, might have babies, if she'd gotten started as early as Paula had. That was the way with her husband's family: Jared had his son, Derek, when he was seventeen; his sister, Deb, had her son, Layne, when she was nineteen. She'd had her kids with Steve Brody, too, a guy who'd been fired from every decent-paying job in town. Last Paula knew, Steve was working odd jobs, and although he was good at it, he was still a drunk and a womanizer. A lot of people in town didn't want him in their houses. By getting knocked up by Steve, Deb had pretty much assured she'd be stuck in River Bend forever. That had shaken Paula.

The day Skyla was born, Paula was out working on her truck. Jared was forever on her case to take it easy, to stick to more domestic tasks, but Paula was never content to play housewife. She needed to be outdoors, needed to feel the sun on her face. She was in the driveway at the farm, the hood of her truck propped open. This truck had been her daddy's, and she remembered him working on it when she was a teenager. He was a quiet man, like her husband, quiet and stoic as she'd always thought men were supposed to be—men and women, for he demanded she control her emotions, too. She had every intention of keeping his truck running long enough to pass it along to her daughter. Paula stood to the side of the truck, one hand on her aching back as she angled herself to lean inside. Her belly was huge, bigger than she thought possible, and yet she had another month to go.

Paula pulled the dipstick from the oil well. The levels were good. She wiped the dipstick and was hanging the cloth from the hammer loop on her overalls when she felt a kind of pulling inside her belly. It was like a tug-of-war deep in her core, a child's game that she was losing. When she screwed the cap back on the oil well and lowered the hood, she felt it again, sharper, more urgent. And then she was doubled over, on the ground, her arms wrapped around her belly. Something, someone, was wrenching her baby from her. She knew what was happening, what needed to happen, and she worked herself out of her overalls, then nested on the fabric.

"What on earth are you doing?" Dinah said. Paula's mother-in-law had ridden up on her tractor, and Paula had been so focused on the pain in her body, she didn't even register the sound of the engine.

"This baby's coming," Paula said.

"Here? Like hell," Dinah said, and, leaving her tractor in the driveway, hauled Paula up by her armpits and deposited her in the passenger's seat of the truck. On the ten-minute drive to the hospital, Paula complained the entire time that they wouldn't make it, and that Dinah was going to be the one to clean the mess out of Paula's truck. But they did make it, with time to spare; Skyla was born after thirteen hours' labor.

"Your problem," Dinah said later, "is that you give up without really trying."

Right now, Paula is okay. She checks herself; nothing broken, nothing bleeding. She's okay. She clicks the door open and steps out of the truck, and as she places her right foot on the ground, her ankle gives way. Shit, but it hurts. She sits down on the road, her back against her truck, and rolls up her pant leg. Already her ankle is swollen. She tries moving it; it doesn't seem broken. Just twisted, maybe. Or fractured. She's never broken a bone, so she doesn't know. She pulls her cellphone out and holds it in her hand, and as she moves, her ring catches the sunlight. She doesn't want to call Jorge, to have him come rescue her. She's gotten herself into this mess; she should get herself out. She could wait here and hope someone comes by, but it might be days, weeks even, before someone passes on these roads. She could call a tow truck. And how much would that cost?

On hands and knees, she crawls around the back of the truck, hugging it as close as she can without touching it. She doesn't want to push it over the edge, but she needs to know what went wrong. She has her body contorted around the wheel well, a circus-level balancing act, and she can see that one of her wheel bolts has been sheered off, like a weed plucked from its root. The bolts on either side of it, unable to support the load, have snapped, too. She should have taken the time to find the proper wrench. Or left the job for another day. She knows better than to work angry.

The sun dips behind the mountains, leaving Paula in shadow. She dials Jorge, tells him approximately where she is. After he hangs up, on his way to rescue her—and isn't that some shit, her needing to be rescued?—she realizes she's right by the antenna farm at the top of the mountains. She calls him back, to give him this landmark, but her call goes straight to voicemail. He must be up in the mountains already, where their cut-rate phone plan can be a bit dicey.

She waits on the road until the sky grows dark, the first stars piercing the night, until the sliver of a moon rises above the mountains. The land around her seems both crushingly close and infinitely expansive, darkness consuming the trees, the rocks, the road, smoothing the world into a wide expanse of night as soft as old suede. She's dozing when her phone rings.

"Where are you?" Jorge says. He sounds frantic.

"Up by the radio towers," she says. "West of town."

"I don't see you," he says. "You have your lights on?"

"I do now," she says. She pulls herself to her feet and leans in through the open window to turn on her headlights, illuminating the space around her, the road bordered by spikes of grass and gray boulders. She finds herself shivering, and all she wants at this moment is for Jorge to get here. She's so tired. She wonders if she hit her head in the accident, but her head doesn't hurt, just her ankle.

"I still don't see you."

"Hold on. I'll see if I can't send a map pin."

While she fiddles with the app, her phone rings again. She doesn't recognize the number at first. Then she remembers the area code and freezes, unsure what to do for a moment, before she answers it.

"May I speak to Paula?"

"This is her."

"Oh. I—this is Linda. Williams. Your daughter?"

"Shit," she says. Her phone is beeping, her call waiting. "I know who you are."

A long pause. Paula feels something welling up inside her, something she's struggled for too long to keep down.

"Where are you?" Linda says at last.

"I'm at home," Paula says. Her throat tightens.

"Where's home?" Linda asks, her voice growing angry.

"That some kind of existential question?" Paula says.

Linda sighs. "The postcard was from Utah. Is that where you live?"

And before Paula can respond, she finds herself laughing. She tries to suppress it at first, tries to cover it with a cough.

"Nice. That's nice," Linda says. "Look, I just wanted—I just thought—"

But Paula is laughing too hard to keep it quiet now.

"You're going to be a grandma. Again. I just thought you should know."

And Paula laughs so hard she snorts. So hard her stomach hurts.

"Fuck it," Linda says, and she hangs up.

Paula is crying from laughing so hard. Then she's just crying. Then hiccupping. Her phone rings again, and she takes a few desperate gulps of air before she answers.

"I'm sorry," she says. "I'm so sorry. I don't know why I laughed."

"What? No, I'm sorry," Jorge says. "Are you okay? I still can't find you."

"Look," she says, hauling herself to her feet. "I'm flashing my lights. Anything?"

"What about that map?"

"You didn't get it?" she says. "I'll send it again."

"This phone service," he says in disgust.

She sends him a pin. Before she hangs up, she says, "I love you."

She leaves as soon as her truck gets out of the shop. Her ankle, which was just sprained, is mostly better by then. Jorge wants to go with her, doesn't want her making the trip alone, but she convinces him it's something she has to do herself. She drives three days from Utah, and when she gets to Michigan, she stays at the no-tell motel on the highway north of town. There are cheaper places, but not many. This motel is where people live when their credit is too poor to get a lease. It hunches across the street from the diner where more than one of the motel's inhabitants wash dishes for a living.

Paula calls Linda and asks to meet her at the motel; it's the least Linda can do, since Paula came all this way. Paula waits for

Linda at the window, holding aside moth-eaten curtains. The motel parking lot is pocked with potholes patched and repatched too many times. Rainbow puddles band every parking space, and dead grass borders the blacktop, even though the lawns in the surrounding businesses are still green. Paula sees the car pull up, hears the engine through the single pane of glass. She sees Ernest DeWitt in the driver's seat. He gets out with Linda and offers to come inside with her; Linda insists that she'll be fine. In the intervening years, his voice has gone gravelly, but Paula still recognizes it, still remembers him. Before returning to his car, Ernest gives Linda a quick kiss and tells her to call if she needs anything. Then he drives off.

What is Linda doing with that man?

Before Linda knocks on Paula's door, she pauses in the parking lot and stares at Paula's truck. Paula wonders whether Linda recognizes it. What is she saying? Of course Linda knows it's Paula's, what with the Utah license plates.

"Someday, this'll be yours," Paula had told her, the hood popped, her face bent close to the engine. "I'm just making sure it'll still be running for you." She'd meant it, too. She'd always had every intention of giving the truck to Linda, up until she left Michigan.

Linda knocks, and Paula has a moment of panic. It's not too late, Paula thinks. She could refuse to answer. There's so much she needs to say, to apologize to Linda for. The whole interaction seems hopeless.

"Took you long enough," Paula says when she finally opens the door. She moves aside to let Linda in the room.

"Really, Paula?" Linda doesn't enter. She stands in the doorway, peering inside as if the room is infested. As if, by entering, she, too, will become infested.

"Well? Get in here. You're letting the mosquitos in."

Linda steps inside. There's nowhere to sit except a ratty chair, so stained Paula can't guess its original color. The room reeks of the kind of horrid disinfectant institutions use to clean up all manner of sins. Beneath that is the smell of old cigarettes, even though the sign on the door claims this is a nonsmoking room. Most likely, it had been a smoking room for so long that now everything in it is permanently saturated. The walls are a dingy yellow. The bedspread is a dingy brown. The carpet is a color that Paula can't name, although it's surprisingly bright, as if the whole thing has been bleached. She suddenly wishes she'd sprung for a better hotel, that she had something more welcoming to offer Linda. She feels like she should apologize to her daughter for the motel, but she doesn't know where to start. Instead, she turns defensive.

"How was the drive?" Linda asks, rigidly formal.

"Oh? We're doing this?" Paula eyes her. "Fine. It was fine. The weather was nice."

"Here's the thing," Linda says. "You don't get to be belligerent. *You* left *us*."

Paula puckers. Nods. "Want to go get some coffee?"

Paula hasn't been back long enough to know where the coffee shops are. If there even are any. Maybe coffee shops are too hoity-toity for this area. So she drives them into town, to the bar at the Hudson House. Linda lays her purse on the bar. Paula lays her keys.

"Why are you here?" Linda asks. She looks at her mother with her eyes narrowed, like she isn't sure what she's seeing, but whatever it is, she doesn't much like it.

"I wanted to see you," Paula says, eyeing the back of her hand, her ring. "I wanted to see how you were."

"Pregnant. You didn't need to drive here to see it."

"You're barely even showing," Paula says, her eyes sliding down Linda's tummy. When the girls were growing up, she worried about Linda's weight. Paige was always thin. Skyla had been a chubby baby, but only slightly. Linda, though, was forever battling her weight. It shouldn't matter in this world, but it did. Paula knew how people would look at Linda, how they would treat her, how people always treat women whose bodies don't conform. Paula guesses Linda couldn't be much more than two months along.

"You look good, though," Paula says.

When the bartender asks what they will have, Linda orders root beer. Paula has coffee.

"You married?" Paula asks.

"No," Linda says. "Well, maybe."

"What do you mean, 'maybe'? Either you are or you aren't."

"Are *you* married?" There's so much anger in Linda, and it keeps bubbling to the surface before Linda can manage to put a lid on it.

Paula takes a long drink of her coffee. It's still too hot, but Paula keeps sucking at it anyway, coffee roasted too dark, to the point of burning, and made too weak. It looks watery in the cup, a thin sheen of grease on its surface.

Paula says, "That's why I'm here. I'm getting remarried."

Linda leans back on her stool. Paula eyes her ring again, the stone glinting even in this dim bar. Linda looks, too.

"At least he has good taste in jewelry," Linda says. "Good for you."

"Don't be like that," Paula says.

74

"How should I be? You want me to hug you? Should I throw you a bridal shower?"

"I thought you'd want to see me," Paula says. "I didn't think you'd come if you didn't."

"I don't really care anymore. You've been gone so long, I don't even care." Linda gets out of her seat, gathers her purse. "This was a mistake," she says. "Take me home."

They ride back to the Williamses' farm in near silence, and when Paula drops Linda off, she doesn't try to come inside, for Jared is there, quickly getting into his van, pulling out of the driveway to avoid Paula, and Paula is torn between wanting to make things right with her daughter and wanting to follow Jared where he's going—the hardware store where she's still part owner, or the bar maybe—to try to convince him to end their marriage. This is what she came here for, after all.

In the end, Paula hesitates too long. Linda has gone into the house. And Jared is just plain gone.

Elizabeth DeWitt
11

I'm invited to a sleepover. Bonfire, hayride, hot apple cider. We TP the house down the street, then stay up late talking, a conversation that turns serious fast. She tells me her parents are divorced, too, that she seldom sees her father, that he raped her when she was eight, and I can't even believe it, that there is another girl out there with my damage. How can this world be that messed up?

We both lie in the dark, she in her bed, me on the floor in a sleeping bag, staring at the ceiling. After a while, I tell her my story. Even though we have so much in common, I still feel like I might throw up, just saying the words out loud.

NURSE DEREK

I usually avoid the bar, mostly because the bartender, Slick Hudson, likes to give me a hard time for being a nurse. Slick is the name he gave himself. Jerry is the name his mother gave him, long before she died to get away from him. Well, okay, she died of cancer, but I really think if her son wasn't such a dick, she might have fought harder.

The first time I came into the Hudson House bar, I was twenty-four. I ordered an O'Doul's, not knowing it was nonalcoholic. Slick let me pay, tip him, and drink the whole thing before he told me through his guffawing face that I'd ordered kiddie beer. Ha-ha, Derek Williams is a pansy. And a *nurse*. True, nursing is not as manly a vocation as tending your father's bar, but it pays the bills.

A couple of months ago, Slick came into the ER with a certain fashionable plastic doll inserted, feetfirst and waist-deep, into his anus. The arms of the doll were raised above her head, and she was bent at the waist so that her bare torso hugged Slick's back.

Slick was blackout drunk, and his brother Mike brought him in in the back of his police car, not because Slick was under arrest, but because he needed to lie down in the back. I imagine, if Slick had been sober, he wouldn't have wanted his brother to help him out of this predicament, but then again, if Slick had been sober, maybe he wouldn't have had a Barbie doll in his ass. Maybe.

I had to wrestle Slick into the stirrups. He had vomit—presumably his own—on his shirt. Once he was lying down, another nurse had to hold his head to the side in case he puked again. When we got him still, he slurred, "I juss tripped goan downa stairs."

"Naturally," I said. "I see this all the time."

The best part? Slick doesn't have kids. No doubt he purchased a Barbie doll with the intention of having it in his ass. I removed the doll from Slick's anus, packed him with gauze. We sent him home with a hefty bill for the imaging we did to make sure he hadn't ruptured something, and a reminder that they do make adult toys specifically for prostate stimulation; he doesn't need to improvise. And now I hope I never again have to utter the words *slick* and *anus* in the same sentence.

I walk into the Hudson bar this evening, and when Slick sees me, he slaps the counter and shouts, "Well, if it isn't Nurse O'Doul!"

"Give me a Bud, Barbie," I say. Slick instantly quiets, his leather-tan face going pale as a cinder block as he fumbles to pull me a beer.

The bar is packed with Mumbly-Joes and witch-haired women, all hunched over pints of light beer. A few parents and their children are having dinner. This is a real Michigan bar, complete with roughhewn walls, mason jar light fixtures, benches in which people have carved their names, and smoothly grooved wood floors. The walls are crowded with memorabilia, like so many sit-down chain restaurants, but the Hudsons have missed the mark. Instead of kitsch, the decor announces a kind of insanity. On a six-foot stretch of wall, there's a hockey mask, a dirty Cabbage Patch Kid, a child's tutu, a poster for KISS, a coconut that's been carved into a monkey head, a backlit stained-glass window. It's the kind of place where the occasional Chicago couple, lost on their way to Detroit, will stop in for lunch and deem it "quaint," the wife pulling a pack of wet naps from her purse to clean the table, the husband rolling up his shirtsleeves as he orders a pint. Michigan has some great microbrew, but this is not the kind of place that keeps any of it on tap.

To give a real sense of the Hudson House, Gilmer Thurber used to cook here, right up until he was arrested in June. When Mike Hudson joined the list of people willing to testify against Thurber, the Hudson family was astounded. Somehow, they'd had no idea what that man had done to Mike when he was little. Now the Hudson House has a permanent HELP WANTED sign in the front window; they can't seem to hire and keep cooks. This place is a job of last resort.

Which I understand. Who would want to work here? It's tainted. I know it's wrong, but I look at Mike differently now. Like, don't they say hurt people hurt people? And what if the guy's so fucked now that he has no business being our sheriff? And his parents—what kind of person hires a man like Thurber? When Thurber was first arrested, the Hudson House's business dropped like the place was peddling plague burgers. Business picked up again, though, since this is the only bar in town.

I wouldn't be here tonight, but it's the easiest way to track down my dad, and my dad, I figure, is the person most likely to give me information on my stepsister Linda. I tried Grandma, but she wasn't talking. She never approved of how close Linda and I are. Well, were. Grandma wouldn't stay and chat, said she was on her way out to the fields, working way too hard for early September, when the corn isn't even ready for harvest. No doubt she's avoiding Paula, who, I hear, is also back in town. Which makes sense—why my dad's making himself so scarce.

Over in a corner, I find him shooting pool with Uncle Steve. Neither of them noticed me when I came in, or heard my exchange with Slick. It would have been nice for my dad to have witnessed me holding my own. My dad owns a hardware store. Uncle Steve is a handyman. Jared and Steve, the best of buddies. They still go hunting together every November. They probably hunt bear. Once they get out in the woods, I'm sure they take off their flannel shirts and find the fall chill exhilarating. My dad's beard is so thick, it keeps his whole body warm. My uncle drinks extra to make up the heat. They hunt armed only with a flask of whiskey and a bowie knife each. They feed their families all winter on bear meat. So I assume. I wouldn't know. I'm not worthy of bear meat.

My dad calls a ball into the corner pocket, and shoots it straight in. When Slick hands me my beer, I intentionally forget to tip him.

"Thanks for nothing, jackass," Slick mutters behind me.

"Who's winning?" I ask when I get to the pool table.

"I am," Steve says.

"You wish," my dad says, missing his next shot.

"Check the table," Steve says.

"You might win this game, but I'm three games up."

"I'm making a comeback," Steve says.

"We're all winners here," Bobby-Jo, the waitress, says, bringing

Steve another beer. He has it half drained before she even leaves the table.

"How you been, Bobby?" I ask.

"Woof. My dogs are barking," she says. Another table waves to her, and she adds over her shoulder, "Business is good, though, so I can't really complain."

Steve lines up another shot, and misses.

"Maybe you want to play Derek," my dad says, and he and Steve both laugh. "What're you doing here?"

"Just thought I'd stop in and say hi. You practically live here."

My dad circles the table, weighing his options. When he shoots, it looks like it's going in, but it hits the edge of the pocket and bounces back.

"A man needs a place he can relax," he says.

"You can't do that at home?"

"The farm has been a little crowded since your sister came back," my dad says.

"Stepsister. Have you talked to Linda?" I do my best to keep my voice casual, but I feel like I'm being obvious, that any second now he's going to call me out.

"Why would I?"

"You haven't noticed she's never at home anymore? At least not when I stop by. Where does she go?"

My dad leans his pool stick against the wall. "This is news to me."

Of course it is. He's never at home, either. I'm sure he only sleeps there. He did this when we were kids, too, started spending all his free time at the bar when my stepmother left. With Paula back in town this past week, he's been making himself even scarcer. My father's a champion of avoidance.

"You haven't heard from her?" I know Linda and I haven't been as close since she got married to that dickbag, but when we were teenagers, we were practically best friends. We had a lot of the same classes in school, we ate lunch together, we ran with the same crowd. She always talked to me when something was on her mind. So it's weird that she didn't call me when she left her husband, or when she got back into town. She knows I'm here. She has to know.

"I don't keep tabs on her," my father says.

"If you see her before I do, tell her she can come stay with me."

My dad takes off his glasses, rubs the bridge of his nose. "You only got one bedroom."

"I'll make room."

Steve looks up from the pool table. "She's over at Ernest's. Even had a toothbrush in his bathroom. I was there for a clogged drain this afternoon."

"Ernest?" I say.

"He always did like them young," Steve says.

"Can it," my dad says. Steve puts his hands up.

"Ernest DeWitt?" I say again. "The old guy?"

"He's not that old," my dad says.

"He's too old for Linda," I say, struggling now to keep my voice from shaking. This is what I was afraid of. I have, of course, seen her around town with Ernest, but I didn't know it was serious. I need to talk to her, to sort out what's really going on.

Steve is waving to Bobby-Jo for another beer, but she's purposefully ignoring him. He's so busy trying to get her attention, he misses his shot. "Loser plays Derek," he says, as if he just thought it up.

"We should go over to Ernest's and get her," I say, maybe too eagerly, because Steve squints at me like he's trying to put something together.

My dad lines up his shot carefully, but misses anyway. "She's a big girl. She can make her own decisions. Even if they are dumb."

"You going to drink that beer?" Steve says.

I'd all but forgotten it. I take a drink. "We should just let her know her options."

"Why would she want to live with her brother?"

"Stepbrother," I say.

Steve shoots another ball in. "Hey, Bobby-Jo."

"And why would she want to room with a stranger?" I say.

"I think it's romantic," Bobby-Jo says.

"What's romantic?" I say.

"Bring a pitcher."

"Starting over like that," Bobby-Jo says. "And now a baby."

"A baby?" my dad says.

"A pitcher," Steve says again, chalking his pool stick.

"Jared, hon," Bobby-Jo says. "We love your business and all, but maybe you should spend more time at home. How do you not know this?"

"Whose baby?" I say.

Bobby-Jo just stares at us like, *Duh.*

Steve laughs. "Ernest's going to be a father again?"

"Christ," my dad says, pulling on his beard; he must be really upset.

"How about that pitcher?"

Bobby-Jo runs a hand along my shoulder. "Anything for you, hon?"

"I'm good." I take another sip of my beer. Bobby-Jo leaves to get Steve's pitcher.

"No daughter of mine's going to have Ernest DeWitt's bastard child."

"Stepdaughter." She can't be with Ernest. I mean, when I saw her in town with him, she hugged me so tight, right in front of him. She said she'd visit, but then she never did. To think of Linda with *him*, to think of *them*—no, this has to be a mistake. Ernest was maybe the kind of guy who was good for a rebound. But to stay with him? To have his baby? For the love of God, his daughter Eliza is older than Linda! No doubt he'll dump Linda when he finds out she's pregnant.

But what if he doesn't? What if they stay together? Ernest would be about eighty at the kid's graduation, with Linda sitting next to him. I imagine him in a wheelchair, a blanket in his lap, FDR-style, as the kid walks across the stage to get his diploma. The fuck is Linda still doing with him? He doesn't help her raise his son, who's kind of a handful, sneaking out of the house to carouse with his buddies. A month before graduation, he even wrecks the self-driving car Linda worked so hard to scrape together enough money to buy him. He was drunk while not-driving it, joy-riding, I dunno, and probably banging some girl who was also drunk. Their tangled legs knocked into the control panel and hit the manual override. And now Linda's got to testify in court as to the character of her son; the girl's parents are suing for damages to cover the hospital bill. Linda already works three jobs in order to save for Jr.'s college, and to pay for Ernest Sr.'s Lipitor. And seriously, Linda? You should treat yourself better.

What kind of stepbrother, what kind of *friend*, would I be if I didn't at least try to prevent this?

"That's game," Steve says.

My dad scowls at the pool table.

Bobby-Jo brings Steve a pitcher of beer. She should have

brought it to him with a straw. He's already pouring himself some as he asks me, "You ready to lose?"

I lose three games of pool. The first game, against Steve, my dad tries to coach me.

"You got decent aim, but you need to hold the pool cue like this," he says, his hand low on his cue, his pinkie looped around the end. Even with his tips, I keep scratching, so that Steve loses interest after the second game. He takes to downing pitchers and chatting up the barflies.

My dad plays me, reluctantly, savagely. He roundly wallops me in a few shots, then wanders away, up to the bar. I've taken the fun out of pool for him.

"Slick, get my son a beer."

Slick places in front of me a beer that's all foam.

"I said get my son a beer, not a pint of air."

The second beer is better. Even though it's light, it hunches in my stomach like a cold hunk of fur, a yeti of a beer.

"You don't look so good," Bobby-Jo says. She sidles up to me and rubs my shoulders. She's skinny, but she has a strong grip. I'm not tall, but I'm not a small guy, either. I've put on a few pounds since starting work at the hospital. I don't have the energy to hit the gym on days off. Plus I drink way too much pop. I need the caffeine most days. Bobby-Jo manages to dig through my extra padding and work my sore muscles like it's nothing.

"You're wasting your time, Bobby," Slick says. "Derek wouldn't even know what to do with a girl like you."

"Why don't we settle up?" my dad says.

"No, stay," Steve says. "Give us a round of Jack. Neat. On me."

"I'm good," I say. I really don't want to be here. I didn't want to play pool, I didn't want this beer, and I really don't want a shot of Jack. What's the saying? Beer to liquor, throw up quicker?

"You got Mondays off. Stay and have a drink with your uncle."

"Yeah, stay awhile," Bobby-Jo says, giving my shoulders one last squeeze before dropping off a check at one of the tables. I've known Bobby-Jo since high school, back when she was a plump girl with thick black hair. Now she has a gaunt face and bleached hair down to her waist. Not really my type, but her jeans are so tight—something about the thinness of the fabric, pale blue, and the way it pulls taut over her crotch—

"You know, she broke up with her boyfriend last week," Steve says. "You should get in there while the getting's good."

And I have to admit, Bobby-Jo has a certain appeal. But she's so tiny. I'm pretty sure a big guy like me would break her. It'd be like riding a bicycle with no seat. At the very least, she'd have to be on top.

An hour later, the bar is starting to clear out. Steve has queued up the jukebox with every Rush song ever. Bobby-Jo keeps making eyes at me like she's going to have to carry me out of here, and like she won't mind it at all. My dad has disappeared.

Steve bought me three rounds of Jack. He's probably spent half his paycheck tonight. Aunt Deb's going to let him have it when he gets home, so he's in no hurry to leave.

"Dance with me," Bobby-Jo says, and for some reason my body's working faster than my brain. I find myself holding her in my sweaty palms and swaying to "Time Stand Still."

"I love this song," she says.

"Really?" I say. "I hate that guy's voice."

"What? Geddy Lee rocks."

"Who?"

She's so close, her breath on my cheek. She smells like cigarettes and fruity perfume. I let my hand slip down—I want to know if any of her is still plump—but when I stoop enough to feel her ass, the room tilts.

"Easy there," Bobby-Jo says, pushing me back on my feet. Her voice has changed. She sounds unsure, guarded. She takes a step back from me, and I try to regain the lost ground. She looks better than I had thought she did. What's the saying? A hand in the bird—no, wait. A hand in the bush is worth flipping the bird? Her hair looks somehow softer. Her eye makeup is soft. The hard angles of her face are soft. Too soft. She's doesn't seem solid to me.

"Why don't I call you an Uber?"

"S'all right. I walked here."

"You sure?"

But I'm already on my way to the barstool. I just need to sit down for a second and get my bearings.

"Should've known you couldn't handle your liquor," Slick says as I try to get up on the wobbly stool.

"Not as good as you can," I say.

"Why don't you get out of here?" Slick says. Which I had been meaning to do, but now I don't want to leave.

"Maybe I want another drink," I say, leaning over the counter to better look at the bottles.

Slick smirks like I'm joking, but I stare him down until he pours me another shot. And I realize, as Slick pours, that he keeps sneaking looks at Bobby-Jo.

"Oh shit," I say. "You want to hit that."

"Shut the fuck up, Nurse O'Doul."

"Slick wants to hit it," I say, doing a little barstool dance, all crossed-wrists and bouncing shoulders. Slick leans across the counter and pulls me toward him by my shirt.

"Listen closely, because I'm only going to say this once," he says.

"Oh, big man."

"Shut. The fuck. Up."

"Sorry? Didn't catch that."

"Slick, let him go," Bobby-Jo says. I'm drowning in his cologne. He must have hooked the bottle up to his showerhead this morning.

"Let him go," she says again, placing her hand on his. He releases me so fast, I have to hold on to the bar to keep from falling backward.

"Really," she says, and stomps back into the kitchen.

"Get the fuck out of my bar," Slick says.

"Anything you say, Barbie." I hop to, because he looks like he's going to come over here and fight me. As I leave, he calls after me, "And learn how to treat a woman."

Out on the sidewalk, I try to button my coat against the wind, but then I remember it's only September and I'm not wearing one. I've gone a block and a half before I realize where I'm going. Of course I am. The only logical way to crown a night like this is by paying Linda a visit. At Ernest's. Where she keeps a toothbrush. Fuck.

It takes a while to ring the doorbell, because the damn button keeps sliding around the doorframe. When Linda answers, she's wearing a bathrobe. Her hair's uncombed like she's been sleeping fitfully. She can't have been asleep, though, because all the lights are on in the house, and when she opens the door, the TV is blaring in the other room.

"Derek? Are you okay?"

"Hey, Lin. Nice place you got here."

"Are you drunk?"

"Are *you*?"

She grabs my hand and pulls me into the house. Her hand is

so warm. Soft. When I get inside, it occurs to me how homey the place is. It smells like pot roast. It smells lived-in in a way that my house never has.

"What are you doing here? Is everyone okay?"

"Oh, Linda," I say, and nearly fall on her as I go to hug her. The floor in this house feels uneven. Shifty. It's like being in a fun house, if your idea of fun is trying to walk on a floor that won't stay put.

I lean against the wall. "Why are you here, Lin? This house is all woogity."

"Who's at the door, babe?" Ernest appears at the top of the open staircase.

"'Babe'?" I say. "That's a pig's name."

"It's just my brother."

"Stepbrother."

"Hey, Derek," Ernest says. He comes down the stairs gingerly, picking his way like he's off balance. Of course he is—the stairs are all sliding from side to side.

"You okay?" Linda asks. And why is she worried about him, when I'm the one who's wrecked? He's wearing pajama pants and no shirt. Dude has the soft remnants of a six-pack and well-defined pectorals. He's probably sixty and in better shape than I've ever been, all muscle and tan skin, big hands that he gets to put on Linda. His cock's probably bigger than mine, too. I bet he's uncircumcised.

"Everything okay?" he asks. The drawstring of his pajama pants is untied.

"Everything's great," I say. "My stepsister finally leaves her jerk husband, but now she's pregnant with Ernest DeWitt's baby." I watch him, waiting for him to get angry, to show that this is news.

"Why don't you sit down?" he says. "Have some water."

Which is really very kind of him, considering the next thing I do is puke on his shifty-assed floor. Even nicer, he lets me lean on his muscly arm and helps me navigate those floors on my way to the living room. It's hot in their living room, and there are too many Ernests in there. There are like four or five Ernests, and all of them are taller than me as they help me to the couch. They're all leaning over me, moving me onto my side in case I puke again, laying a trash bag under my head. Their faces are too close to my face, and they're smiling, a lopsided smile—only the right side of the mouth, only the right eye, as if the left side is grimacing. Something inside me reacts to this with warning bells, but I can't put it together. Instead, I close my eyes to block out all the Ernests. I don't want him here. I will him gone, and then it's just me and Linda in the house. She hands me a glass of water, and I take her hand without opening my eyes. Her hand's so big and rough. I try to fit it into the pocket I make with my hands, but it's too big to contain. She pulls away, leaves the room, slow footfalls too heavy for the weight of her. When she comes back to wipe my face with a warm washcloth, she sounds like she's composed herself. She treads lightly. She wipes my face with all the tenderness of a mother.

In the morning, I wake up on Ernest DeWitt's couch. I'm hoping I'm up early enough to slip out before they wake. I find my shoes by the front door. Someone's already cleaned up my puke in the hallway. I barely remember being guided to the couch, Linda wiping my face with a washcloth.

Before I get both shoes on, Linda appears in the doorway to the kitchen.

"Stay for breakfast? Ernest's making waffles."

And what can I do? I mutter an apology when he puts a plate of bacon on the table, and again when Linda brings me coffee. I eat the man's waffles, soaked in warm, real maple syrup that he's melted butter in. I eat like it's going out of style. I train my eyes on my plate to keep from looking at Linda. I'm eating not only to soak up the poisons my body is making as it processes the booze, but also as a way of taking what little Linda can offer me.

Ernest doesn't eat with us. He says he needs to do some work on Linda's car, and takes his plate and his coffee into the garage with him.

Linda and I eat in silence for a while. It's kind of nice, just Linda and me, until I wreck it by saying again that I'm so, so sorry.

"Oh, Derek. I told you last night, you don't have to be sorry."

"We talked last night?" As if I don't remember. Of course I remember.

"Why Ernest DeWitt?" I'd asked her, while lying on his couch.

"Don't do this," she'd said.

"Why not? I never do this. That's the problem. Maybe if I'd done this sooner, you wouldn't have married Nathan. Maybe you wouldn't be here now."

"I like here," she said.

"I like you."

"Don't," she said.

"I love you."

"I know," she said.

It's a full week before I see her again. I stop by Grandma's farm on Sunday, all casual, holding a huge bowl of mashed potatoes like I'm there for supper and not for Linda. Grandma isn't in the kitchen when I get there. Instead, Linda is pulling cornbread from the oven.

"It's one of the few things I can manage to keep down these days," she says, cutting us each a wedge from the cast-iron skillet. She puts them on tea saucers, a little pat of butter on each.

"Where's Grandma?" I ask. I can't believe my luck, to find Linda here alone.

"Probably out in the fields. Because why not?"

"I should have brought ham," I say, scooping mashed potatoes onto my plate next to the cornbread.

The windows in the kitchen are all open, letting the cool air breeze in. The day has turned rainy and cold, the September sky the color of fireplace ashes. In Michigan, they say if you don't like the weather, just wait five minutes.

The farm is quiet, the bulk of the chickens having been sold recently, and the only sound is a distant whinnying from the fields, a goat's bleat, the tractor's engine, the wind pushing the smell of damp leaves and fresh-cut hay across the hills. From the picture window, I watch a truck pull up in the drive, blocking my car in. Paula is inside, just sitting there, both hands on the wheel. I'd forgotten how tiny she is. She looks like a child sitting in her daddy's truck. The look on Linda's face says she's not surprised to see her mother. This must be why Grandma's not in the house. She never misses Sunday supper.

"Mommy Dearest is here," I say. Linda huffs. I watch Paula get out of the truck and stand there awhile, one hand on her hip, the other hand holding a dish of something orange covered in plastic wrap. I came here wanting to talk to Linda, maybe smooth things over after last weekend, but now my stepmother is knocking and

Linda is staring Paula down through the picture window. I go let her in.

"Derek," she says, surprised. I'm sure she hasn't thought about me in years. "You've grown." She looks pointedly at my waistline.

"You've aged," I say with more bitterness than I mean. I don't really hate her; I just hate what she did to Linda, to my dad, to Skyla and Paige.

"Dinah's out?" Paula asks. "She never misses Sunday supper."

"Nobody invited you," Linda says.

"I'm sorry," Paula tells Linda, setting her dish down on the counter. "I really am. I didn't come here to fight. I came to put things right."

"You got a time machine?" Linda says, glancing out the window at that truck in the drive. It somehow manages to catch the light, even on such a dreary day.

"Let's start this over," Paula says. She makes Linda tea and seats Linda in the living room. Ordinarily, I would take this as my cue to leave, but today I follow them in. I'm keeping an eye on my stepmother, because she wasn't here, she didn't see Linda—or Paige, either, for that matter—after she skipped town. Her daughters were broken, and I'll be damned if I'll let her break Linda again. After Linda devours the first piece of cornbread, I bring her a second, this time drizzled with honey. Paula watches Linda eat and, I swear to God, the woman is sneering.

Linda has to be about eight weeks into her pregnancy and her face has gotten rounder. Of course Paula would be disappointed. Growing up, Paula had always preached manual labor as a means of weight control. She would gossip about Aunt Deb, who'd grown plump in the years since she married Uncle Steve, even though she chain-smokes instead of eating.

"Tell me about this guy you're marrying," Linda sighs.

"Marrying?" I say. I can't help myself.

"Can we talk in private?" Paula says, eyeing me, but Linda ignores her, so I do, too. She has no claim to this family. She relinquished that years ago, when she walked away.

"Why didn't he come meet the family?" Linda says.

Paula's gaze falls to the floor. "He couldn't get the time off work," she says. "Can I get you anything? Another cup of tea?"

"I'm good," Linda says.

"Well, hell's bells," Grandma says from the doorway. "I'd taken her for dead." She's in a pair of faded frayed jeans and a flannel shirt. She has hay in her hair.

"Hey, Ma," Paula says.

"You brought her here?"

"Not really," Linda says.

"I came on my own," Paula says. "I wanted to see my daughter."

"You came for a divorce," I mutter. Of course she did. What else would she have come for?

"'Bout time," Grandma says.

"I don't want to start trouble," Paula says. "I just thought maybe it was time we reconnected."

"Why?" I say. "You caught wind of the baby?"

Linda face-palms.

Grandma crosses her arms over her chest. "What're you talking about? There's no baby here."

It hadn't even occurred to me that Grandma wouldn't know. I would have to go and open my big mouth. I came here to smooth things over, but I've made them a million times worse. I rack my brain, trying to figure out how to back out of this, but there's just this low-level buzzing instead of thoughts. I'm that much of an idiot.

"Well, shit," Grandma says, eyeing Linda now. "I thought I was just feeding you too well." She comes into the living room, but refuses to sit on the couch where Paula is.

"How far are you?" Grandma says.

"Eight weeks," Linda says.

"No," Grandma says. "You've been back longer."

Linda stares her down.

"You been to the doctor yet?"

"They put it at eight weeks, Grandma."

Grandma is quiet while she considers. Then she turns to Paula. "This is your fault. I tried to raise 'em better than this, but there's only so much I can do."

"Hold on a minute," Paula says.

"No. You don't get to talk," Grandma says. "You tricked my son into marrying you, and then dumped him with your children. Who gives you the right?"

Linda rubs her belly like she already feels movement in there. Paula leans forward on the couch. "What can I get you, baby?"

"I think it's time you left," Grandma says.

"She's okay," Linda says.

"I was talking to both of you," Grandma says.

"That's a little much, Grandma," I say.

"You think I'm raising a third generation? No, sir. I am not."

"Where do you suggest she go?" Paula says.

"Back to her husband? Let him sort it out."

"That's just like you," Paula says.

"Or better yet, back to the man who did this to you. Ernest, right? Ernest DeWitt? You've been spending an awful lot of time with him."

"You can always come live with me," I say quietly.

"Oh, for fuck's sake, Derek," Linda says. "Shove a sock in it."

"Don't you dare talk to my grandson that way," Grandma says.

Linda tries to get up from the chair, but she isn't fast enough. She leans over and throws up cornbread all over the hardwood. She keeps heaving until her stomach is empty, until only strings of mucus and saliva come up. No matter how long I work in hospitals, I will never get used to watching someone puke. I can clean it up, no problem, but watching it in the process of coming up—I can't. It's all I can do not to puke, too. Grandma seems to waver, to want to comfort Linda. She has her arms crossed over her chest, her fingers gripping her forearms. Instead, I go to Linda's side, hold her hair and rub her back.

Paula and I both help Linda pack what's left of her belongings. It takes only about an hour. She didn't bring much with her from Texas, and hasn't acquired much since coming home. She's called Ernest to make sure he'll take her in.

"Let me drive you over," Paula says.

"No," I say. "Let me." I still need to talk to her, still need to make things right.

Linda turns to her mother. "You've done quite enough," she says, and I watch a flush spreading up Linda's neck to her face. I try to put an arm around her, to comfort her, but she shrugs out of my grasp and goes to pack boxes into my car.

"I got those," I say. Some of them are heavy, and she needs to take it easy. I start stacking boxes. Linda turns back to her mother.

There are fewer than a dozen boxes, but the last one won't fit in my trunk. The backseat is already full. I'm struggling to find space while Paula is having the heart-to-heart I need to be having with Linda.

"This is silly. Let's just put them in my truck," Paula says.

"Fine," Linda says.

That's it, I think. *I've lost. I've lost Linda.* I unload the boxes and pile them in the pickup bed.

"I'm so sorry," Paula says, taking a step toward Linda, her arms raised a little like she's going to hug her. "If there's anything else I can do . . ."

"I'll be fine," Linda says, taking a step back. "I've made it this far without you."

"Is he at least nice to you?" Paula says, her shoulders slumped. "I remember Ernest. He had a reputation."

"Yes, well," I say, cutting her off and opening Paula's passenger's-side door for Linda. "So did you."

Elizabeth DeWitt

13

In eighth grade, after one of our classmates gives birth to her second baby, my friends and I start the V Club. We even have a hand sign, which is just a peace sign, and we flash it at each other while pledging allegiance to our club.

Gloria is our first member. She's a slumpy girl who won't look you in the eyes when you talk to her, and she stares at her feet in the showers in gym class.

That fall, Gloria starts dating a guy who doesn't go to our school. In fact, I don't think he goes to school at all. I meet him at a football game. He has a bowl cut and a beer belly and an old letterman jacket that the leather is cracking on. He buys hot chocolate for all of Gloria's friends.

Soon, Gloria stops returning the V sign when we flash it at her. She starts biting her nails, chews them away to nothing. She no longer talks to us, or anyone else in school. She's always been quiet, easy to overlook, but now she's somehow transparent, folding silently into herself. I am able to miss her, even when she is sitting in the desk in front of me in class.

Within a few weeks, she stops attending school altogether. She disappears so gradually that I don't notice her gone, not at first, until all at once one day I remember she used to be there.

SMALL WAYS

B eth experiences every pothole, every dip in the road, as if
it were a personal insult. Her back hurts, her head hurts,
her butt is numb, and she feels like there is water sloshing
the length of her legs, just beneath the skin. It doesn't help that the
U-Haul trailer seems to be weighing her car down, pulling at the
back end and forcing it to ride low on the tires. Doing permanent
damage, she just knows it. Even less helpful is the fact that this
move is not Beth's choice. Her financial situation hasn't been good
since the divorce. Now, after being fired from the restaurant where
she cooked for the past eleven years, after deciding to move and
waiting all summer for her house in Charlotte to sell, she finds
herself with very few options.

Her son, Dan, so attuned to other people's moods these days,
tries his best to occupy her mind, to get her to stop fixating on
the negative. He really is such a sensitive boy, especially for a
fifteen-year-old. Beth often wonders where he gets it from. His

father isn't like that. And Beth certainly isn't, either. Dan DJs for her, favoring nineties artists he knows she likes: Mariah Carey, Salt-N-Pepa, TLC, Destiny's Child. Not a very creative list of faves, but then he knows she grew up in rural Michigan—the same place they're headed now. Probably, she didn't have much exposure to anyone else.

In the backseat, his sister, Jeanette, gives their mother the silent treatment. Occasionally Dan's cellphone will buzz, Jeanette asking him to ask their mom for a rest area or a hamburger. When they stop, Beth notes how urgently Jeanette runs for the bathroom, how ravenous she is when she digs into her food. Jeanette holds grudges silently, but thoroughly, like a true DeWitt.

"Rest area?" Beth asks, eyes on the rearview mirror where Jeanette pretends to be asleep. Dan hesitates, swiveling in his seat to check on his sister.

"Jeanette, I saw you looking at your phone," Beth says. "Yes or no? Rest area?"

Jeanette's eyes pop open. She doesn't glare at her mother. She holds her face blank, nodding at Dan. When Beth pulls into the rest area, she no more than gets the car in park before Jeanette is out the door. Beth tries and fails to remember being twelve, tries to summon the extreme loathing, directed both inward to the self and outward to family, classmates, teachers, strangers at the mall, grocery clerks, the guy who takes tickets at the movie theater—it's as if Jeanette hates other people for not being her, but she also hates herself. A Gen-Xer stuck in an iGeneration body.

Jeanette is mature for a twelve-year-old, with hips and breasts and piles of natural hair. Beth knows the pressure Jeanette already feels, simply because she's at that age. And it'll only get worse from living in River Bend, where the default is Dutch. She knows Jeanette will feel like she's supposed to be tall and slender, with long legs and blond hair. Beth can also remember, all too vividly, the isolation of never seeing anything of yourself in your classmates. Never seeing other people of color, never seeing black hairstyles. Not having a store that carries good black hair care products. Never finding clothes at the local shops that flatter your figure. Why is she bringing her daughter to this town? Why couldn't she just shut her mouth at work and carry on the way she had for years? None of this would be necessary if she could only remember how to be complacent.

A few days ago, Beth found on Jeanette's computer a listicle of pencil tests you can do to find out how attractive you are. It included things like placing a pencil under your breast; if the pencil didn't drop, it meant your breasts were too saggy. Or holding a pencil against your chin and nose; if the pencil touched your lips at all, it meant your lips were too big. That's how they get you: It's all the small ways they tell you you're not good enough.

"You spend too much time online," Beth told Jeanette that evening. "It's getting in the way of your school."

Jeanette stared at her blankly.

"You only get half an hour a day."

"What about school projects?" Jeanette demanded.

"Half an hour of recreational use."

Beth hadn't even wanted Jeanette to have a computer, but her father bought it for her for Christmas. Beth considered devising her own tests, skewed in favor of black girls everywhere: Place a pencil in your unbound hair; if the pencil drops, your hair is too straight and stringy.

"How are you doing with all this?" Beth asks Dan. He shifts in his seat, seems to be choosing his words carefully.

"I'll be fine," he says. Not *It is fine,* or *I am fine.* The wording is not lost on Beth.

"It'll be nice to see your granddad, right?"

Beth will never assuage the guilt that she drove away her children's father. The kids will see him in the summers, but she doubts that's enough. She watches Dan not know how to act on a daily basis, not know what to say, and she wonders how he would be different with a male role model. Someone to teach him some semblance of confidence. Dan is a fragile-looking boy, with pale brown skin and hair cut too short—he doesn't like to fuss with it, although she has heard him say he wishes he had dreadlocks. She's noticed that, when he talks to people, he refuses to meet their eyes, instead wielding a paperback novel like a shield. If only he were outdoorsy, he might have that gold-russet skin like his sister. And he might lose some weight. He's not fat, exactly, but doughy. He prefers libraries to football fields, and it shows. Jeanette is on her way back from the bathroom now, and even with her face in her phone, she moves with more pep, more confidence than Beth can ever recall seeing in Dan.

They arrive in River Bend around midnight. Beth had wanted to avoid driving at night, but they'd gotten a late start and made more stops than she anticipated. And now here she is, returning home to the town that, once upon a time, she couldn't wait to leave.

The way back isn't quite as she remembered—the new highway bypass throws her for a loop. It's as if River Bend wants to be left behind, forgotten. Even in the dark, Beth can tell the town has changed only for the worse. Somewhere in the intervening years, the village installed lampposts that look like gaslights—someone's kitschy idea of sprucing the place up. The new lights sort of resemble the Gaslight Village at the Muylder Museum in

Kalamazoo, her favorite exhibit when she was a child, a life-sized diorama of how River Bend would have looked in 1850. The museum, however, had flickering lights that looked like real flames; the static bulbs in the lights along Main Street are stubbornly unchanging, like the village itself.

The potholes on Main Street are like trenches she has to rumble the car over, and most of the storefronts downtown are boarded up. River Bend was never a booming place, but now it's just the skeleton of a town. As she pulls into the alley behind her father's house, the trees and garages lean close, bearing down on her. Beth finds herself taking great gulps of air, and is glad her kids are both asleep, that she can have a moment to pull herself together after parking.

The house had blurred in her mind over the years. In the darkness, it seems to have grown larger. She knows it's painted pale yellow, but for the life of her, she now has trouble making it out against the sky. There is no moon out tonight. The alley behind her is dark, the streetlamp burned out. She stares at her father's house, trying to discern the pitch of the roof, the stairs leading up to the back door, anything.

She should be able to find a happy memory of it—this is the house where she spent her early childhood, the house where they lived when her family was still whole—and yet, even as she strains her mind, all she can come up with are memories of Gilmer Thurber here, in this house, his presence in every corner, filling the house like dark water.

The longer she stares, the harder it is to see, so that she finds herself turning away, giving the house the side-eye, trying to trick it into materializing. Next to her, Dan snores quietly. Jeanette shifts in her sleep and gives an unhappy whimper. Beth knows the house stands there, yet the lot seems to be full of stars and space, with distant planets dotting the wall facing her. The Milky Way is folded into the roof. Her eyes are sore and dry. She finds herself dozing, her head drooping onto her chest, and then her eyes blink open. She could close them, just for a second, if only her mind would quiet. Instead, she stares at the house until its eastern-facing wall grows pale, until the sky around blues and brightens. At first she thinks it a trick of the light, but as the dawn comes on stronger, the house looks blue, and stays blue. It's been painted recently, she realizes. It's only the third week in September and the mulberry tree in the backyard is a sunny yellow, its leaves dropping to the grass beneath. A light goes on inside the kitchen, and she can see her father, Ernest DeWitt, through the gauzy curtains, poking around in the fridge, the pantry, making coffee. At the sink, he pauses, tilts his head, then reaches out and pushes the curtains aside.

"Wake up," Beth says quietly, and when Dan stirs next to her, she adds, "we're here." She has to tell herself, *Get out of the car; go inside the house.* She shakes her head. Dan wakes his sister, and Jeanette comes briefly to life in that moment when her body is awake, before her brain has booted up.

"It's morning," Jeanette says. "I slept in a car all night." She seems proud of this fact, like it's the kind of bohemian lifestyle she's always longed for. Even as her kids open doors and stretch in the new sun, even as Beth's father greets his grandchildren for the first time since they were little, Beth has to keep telling herself, *Get out of the car.*

Jeanette walks right up to Ernest DeWitt and hugs him, and something inside Beth stirs violently. She spills out of the driver's seat and onto the driveway.

"Eliza," her father says, and just hearing her childhood name makes her bowels turn to ice. He has his arms held open to her.

She doesn't want to forgive him so easily. She doesn't want to hug him, doesn't want to be here, yet here she is, standing dumb and tired in the driveway as the smile he wears grows strained around the eyes. His face sags at the jowls, his glasses are crooked on his nose, and she finds herself staring at him. She'd forgotten the details of his face, and she wonders briefly whether he really is her father. They look nothing alike, and not just because he's white. The round, upturned nose, too small for his face, and the fleshy jaw. His arms, those strong, tan arms, go heavy, they droop, and Beth inserts herself into them to prop them up.

"It's good to see you," he says, and kisses her forehead. "When did you get in? I was waiting, but I fell asleep on the couch."

"You painted the house" is all Beth can say.

"It was Linda's idea," he says, and turns as the back door claps shut. There, standing on the stoop, is a girl Beth recognizes immediately. Dirty blond hair, a little too much makeup smudged from sleep. Linda Williams. When she was in high school, Beth used to babysit the Williams girls. Linda would have been about ten, old enough to stay home alone really, except their mother seemed keen to foist the girls off on anyone else.

Beth wonders what her father is doing with this child, but it occurs to her that, as creepy as it is, their relationship makes a kind of sense. There's something of the child in Ernest's gaze, something that feels like a game of hide-and-seek: When you look into his eyes, you might catch a glimpse of a shoe or a pigtail disappearing around a corner, but when you follow it, it's gone. Speaking with Ernest, it's easy to lose all track of the present, you're so focused on seeking out the child, hiding.

This wouldn't be noteworthy in a man of twentysomething; you could pass him off as a late bloomer, but Ernest is in his early sixties, and so the game of hide-and-seek will forever catch Beth off guard. Yet women love him, and men yearn to be near him in hopes that some of the child will flit into their gaze.

Beth has always hated this about her father; she has only ever wanted him to grow the fuck up. A bit of a hypocrisy, really, given that she, too, has a child inside her, that she had felt the child stirring, shifting in sleep, when her father called her Eliza. Her anger at her father is, in part, anger at her own inner child, whom Beth can't seem to shake.

"So nice to see you again," Linda says, sidling up next to Ernest, inserting herself between father and daughter. Beth remembers Linda as a horse girl who always smelled like hay and manure. Now her hair is unusually full and glossy, and her fingernails are too long for a farm girl's. None of this is to be overlooked; even so, Linda stands with her hands on her belly, still flat like a twenty-something's. Beth notes Linda's rosy cheeks, her pudgy face.

Beth closes her eyes. Her father has put a child in this child.

After unloading boxes, Beth leaves to return the trailer, but her car is on empty. She stops at the only gas station in town. A truck pulls up to the pump in front of her, with a man, woman, and child all sitting on the bench seat. When the man gets out, it takes Beth a second before she recognizes him; he's older, yes, his hair retreating from his forehead, his skin wilted with sun damage, but once she notes the round blue eyes, the thick lips, it's not hard to find Steve Brody in this face, worn past its years.

More startling is realizing the woman in the truck is Deb. In the decades since Beth last saw her, all the color seems to have drained from her, so that she's not only old, but old-fashioned, like she's stepped out of a 1950s television program: She's gray in a Technicolor world. Deb doesn't look at Beth, and Beth decides not to linger. She'll fill her car halfway and leave.

She slides her card into the reader, and when she withdraws it, the reader beeps loudly. A message flashes on the display: Her card has been declined. She tries running it again, and again it is declined. She knows there's money in the account; the bank probably put a hold on it because she didn't tell them she was moving. While she decides whether to try again or drive around the block until the truck leaves, a car pulls in behind her, waiting to use the pump.

"Pump three," a voice calls over an intercom, "please see the cashier inside."

Beth looks up to find she is pump three. Steve also looks up. Beth doesn't like the expression on his face when he recognizes her.

The man in the car waiting behind her scoffs. He has his window open, his arm draped out, and when Beth looks at him, he honks for her to get out of his way. He's scowling at her, not a look of annoyance, but of hatred. Beth knows this look. He assumes she's a deadbeat, a stain on society.

Worse, now Deb has seen Beth. Beth can tell because Deb's cheeks have colored, and she stares out the side window so as not to look at Beth again. And while Steve won't look at Beth, either, he's puffed his chest out, and he's smiling.

She can't deal with this. Not right now. As she walks inside to prepay cash, the driver waiting behind her throws his arms up in disgust and squeals his tires as he maneuvers his car to the other side of the pump. Once inside, Beth browses the aisles of canned goods, the off-brand frozen pizzas, while she waits for both Steve and the other driver to finish pumping and leave.

. . .

The bedrooms in Ernest's house smell like they've been locked up since Beth was a kid. She strips bedding, ashy with dust, and replaces the linens with her own. It makes no sense to her that he kept this big old house all these years. He never remarried. What use had he for three bedrooms, other than to collect dust? He hasn't even stored anything in them. The house is furnished, but spare, as if waiting for people to come and live in it again. *Well, here we are,* she thinks.

Despite how much space there is, it's not enough. When Jeanette found out she would be sharing a room with her mother—Beth had withheld this information until the last possible moment—she went into Dan's room and shut the door. She hasn't been seen since. Dan brought her lunch in his room. As patient as he is, even he is beginning to show signs of strain; he's no longer quite as accommodating with his mother, and instead of helping unpack, he has plopped himself down on the couch in the living room with a book and has budged only for meals and bathroom breaks.

Beth takes the same bedroom she had as a child. Inside, she's flooded with memories. They weigh on her so that she's exhausted, and she takes to bed within a week of moving home. In here, there isn't much to occupy her mind. A worn wood floor, mostly covered by a beige Berber rug. And that gaping wound of a window, dressed in gauzy curtains. Today, she lies in bed, staring outside, looking down on the yard of the empty Thurber house. Without warning, she's back inside those walls, where too many adults live. Her babysitter, the white-haired witch. She remembers the walls hung with crucifixes and the portrait of blond Jesus in white robes, both his hair and his clothes tainted by cigarette smoke. And her babysitter's middle-aged son, Gilmer, walking around in various states of undress. Gilmer and his sister are in jail now, awaiting trial for the horrible things that went on in that house. A trial won't be enough, though. Corporal punishment wouldn't be enough. Castration would be closer, but still insufficient.

And what of Mrs. Thurber? Dead probably. And oh so many children there, all of them affected. She wonders where they are now. Who were their parents, even? There were the Hudson boys, grandchildren of Mrs. Thurber. Jerry and Mikey. Are they still in town? She seems to remember her father saying Mikey was a cop now. She isn't sure, though, because she hasn't gone out much, and when she has, she's wandered about town in a protective fog. Even now, her instinct is to freeze, to close her eyes, in order to shut out the memories. But that won't do. To keep from looking, she pulls the curtains.

It takes a week for Jeanette to finally come out from her confinement in Dan's room. She spends a day exploring the house. Such as it is. She would have much preferred moving in with her father, but her stepmother, Mara, said that children needed their real mother. Translation: Mara had no desire to raise another woman's kids. Jeanette's father had a chance at a do-over, and Jeanette knows she shouldn't begrudge him that. Still, she does.

So this is to be her exile. A frigid, rambling house. A living room where the ceiling sags. Dingy shag carpet, tangled and matted, the color of muddied toffee. A bathtub that takes so long to drain that you stand in someone else's dirty water if you shower in the morning—which is why Jeanette showers at night, or, worst case, takes a bath in the basin tub upstairs in the morning.

Her granddad's house has a mustiness, a clamminess, that

Jeanette can't stand. She longs for the small, tidy house they left in Charlotte, the bright, sunny windows, the smooth tiled floors. Their house had been painted in pastels, a buttercream kitchen, a lavender bathroom. Her granddad's house is white on white, the walls repainted so many times over the years that the surfaces look thick and wavy. The washer and dryer are old and clunky and take forever to finish a load. There is no dishwasher. The television is a monstrous box, like the house itself, with wires sprouting off the top, and nobs to pull and turn for power, volume, and channel selection. The bark-brown couch smells of pets, but there are no pets. When she asked her granddad how old the couch was, he said, "Someone left it on the curb on trash day," with a note of bragging in his voice. "That must have been ten, fifteen years ago?"

The only nice thing about the house is Linda's coffeepot: brushed metal, with a mesh filter basket. Jeanette coaxes a cup of coffee out of it one day when Linda isn't there, but she does something wrong. The coffee comes out gray and translucent. But oh! The dark, smoky taste of the coffee Linda makes, the exhilarating jolt when it hits her blood! Jeanette tries it black, like her mother takes hers, but it's too much. She's been drinking it with milk and sugar for maybe a week now—not in secret, exactly, but she isn't going to advertise it to her mother.

Dan dares Jeanette to go into the basement one Saturday morning. He comes up from there with a handful of Indian-head pennies, dark and worn and metallic-smelling, like blood. Tempting, but when Jeanette opens the door of the basement and sees the light from the hallway quickly dissolve into blackness, and the cool breeze lifts the odor of dirt and mushrooms up to her face, she reconsiders.

"Who cares about a bunch of old pennies?" she tells her brother.

She can't shake the cold after that. It settles into her body to stay. She takes to rising early in the morning and standing over the floor vent in the kitchen, letting the hot air fill her flannel nightgown and blow life back into her frigid limbs. She shares a bedroom with her mother, whose sleep is fitful and irregular. Her mother thinks Jeanette doesn't hear her crying at night, her breathing willfully even, the subtle splash of tears dropping onto her pillow. Worse yet is when her mother does sleep, and talks incoherently. Her mother looks sicker and more tired by the day.

Jeanette has always heard that Midwestern winters were brutal, but nobody ever warned her about Midwestern fall, the feeling that the world outside is shutting down, the ache in her spine that tells her to sleep, too, sleep for months. It's already bad, and it's only the end of September. She's put on five pounds, has to check herself from snacking all day. She's hungry and lethargic. This morning, on her way downstairs to stand over the floor vent, she contemplates whether she'll make herself eggs or Cream of Wheat for breakfast, fantasizes about having both. She can imagine what her new friends at school would say. The smart girls in town don't want to be friends with her, and she doesn't have much patience for the Beckies on the cheerleading squad, who are unbearably bubbly, so she's befriended a couple of horse girls, the first kids who would talk to her, girls who battle constantly to keep their slight frames slight. Allison, she knows, doesn't eat meals. And yesterday, Jeanette went into the bathroom after lunch and heard someone throwing up. Caitlyn came out of the stall, smiled at Jeanette, and started talking about fifth period as if everything were fine. And now it makes sense: Caitlyn has sick breath, every morning and every afternoon. When Jeanette eats lunch at school, Caitlyn makes comments like, "I wish I could eat like that, without facing the consequences." Jeanette isn't sure whether Caitlyn thinks Jeanette's eating doesn't have consequences, or Jeanette doesn't face them. She wishes she hadn't quit band. All of her friends at her old school had been band kids, like her brother.

When she gets to the kitchen this morning, Linda is already slouched in a chair next to the floor vent, wearing a bathrobe and sweatpants, fuzzy socks on her feet. She clutches a mug of coffee in both hands, and alternately presses it to one cheek, then the other. Jeanette hesitates in the doorway, feeling despair bubbling inside her. Her feet are so cold she wants to cry.

"Want some coffee?" Linda says, and Jeanette blanks her face. "Right. Cocoa?"

"I'll try some coffee."

Linda smirks. Does she know Jeanette's been drinking her coffee? And will she tell Jeanette's mother? But no, Linda goes and pours Jeanette a cup, and Jeanette steals her place over the vent. The rush of warmth is bliss, her nightgown ballooning with heat.

"Smart," Linda says when she returns with a steaming mug. She's added milk and sugar; she knows how Jeanette takes it. "I need to get a nightgown."

"How old are you?" Jeanette blurts out, then quickly checks herself. She takes a sip of the coffee and mutters, "Thanks."

"Thirty-two," Linda says. Her tone of voice suggests she is not offended, but rather amused.

"Younger than my mom," Jeanette says.

"Yeah. It's a problem."

"It doesn't have to be," Jeanette says, even though it does weird her out a little when she sees Linda and her granddad kissing. Warm now, she joins Linda at the table.

Linda runs a thumb along the rim of her mug. "How are you settling in at school?"

Jeanette can't help but roll her eyes. Her mother hates it when she does this; she tells Jeanette not to sass. Linda only laughs.

"It's okay. You don't have to be excited."

Jeanette pulls her feet up onto her chair. When she sees Linda looking at them, she tucks them underneath her, inside her night-gown. Her skin has gone ashy since moving here; River Bend doesn't have the humidity she's used to. She checks the weather app on her phone, hoping for rain, and is relieved to see that it's supposed to warm up next week.

"Let me get you a pair of fuzzy socks," Linda says, "and then I'll make us breakfast." And she goes upstairs to her dresser.

When Linda is gone, Jeanette counts the months. She heard her mom say something to her granddad about Linda being ten weeks pregnant. Next spring, there will be a baby in this house.

Jeanette doesn't want to think about it.

Beth needs a job. She's been looking for months, since before the move, but nowhere in this godforsaken town is hiring. She gets desperate, to the point that she even applies to be a line cook at a rinky-dink country club up in Kalamazoo, a forty-five-minute drive away. She used to be a sous chef. She used to run a kitchen with twenty people working beneath her, a kitchen that cranked out 280 covers on a Saturday night. A nice place, too, the kind that would loan a man a jacket if he showed up in his shirtsleeves.

As September winds down, she finally manages to find a job cooking down at the Hudson House, where they do a lot of meatloaf-mashed-potatoes-canned-peas dinners. The only sea-soning they believe in is salt, and that they use sparingly. Their pies come in frozen from Gordon Food Service. Their whipped cream squirts out of a can. And, too, Beth feels a tightness in her chest when she learns that she was hired to replace Gilmer Thurber. She can almost smell him in the kitchen. She tells herself this is temporary, that she'll keep looking, but she quickly settles into complacency. She doesn't have the energy to job search when she gets home in the evenings.

When she arrives home tonight, though, Jeanette has the table set, a salmon in the oven. She's mixing black currants into couscous. She's somehow managed to procure asparagus in the fall. Beth has taken to leaving her money for groceries. She'd love to go with her daughter, she'd love to see where she gets her ingredients, but she knows Linda must be taking Jeanette up to Meijer in the next town north. The family sits to eat, Beth and the kids, Linda and Ernest all crowded at the kitchen table, five people squashed in at a table meant for four. Meals are always tense for Beth: Dinner table conversations leave so much unsaid.

After they finish eating, Jeanette produces a German chocolate cake she'd stored in the microwave. It's on a plate, frosted sloppily, but it's the most tender, moist cake Beth has ever eaten. Beth's recipe is good, but not as good as this.

"You made this?" Beth says.

Jeanette shrugs.

"Where'd you learn to bake like this?"

"Food Network." She's licking the last of the icing off her plate.

"Since when do you have a sweet tooth?"

Jeanette shrugs again. "I'm on the rag," she says.

Beth hadn't known her twelve-year-old daughter had gotten her period. Her stomach hurts when she realizes she's just as distant, just as self-absorbed, as her own mother had been.

Ask Beth about her mother on any given day, and you might get a variety of answers: She died three years ago, so suddenly nobody knew what to do. Or she lives in another state, far enough away to still count as an absence; she and Beth haven't spoken in years. Or she still lives in-state, holed up in a house cluttered by hoarder tendencies; Beth can't visit her mother, can't even get a foot in the door. All of these have the ring of truth, the feel of it, but here's the reality: Gretchen's physicality is far less potent than the thought of her, the ways in which she and Beth have hurt each other over the years. As such, Gretchen is there, always there, a hunched bundle of nerves lurking in the corners of Beth's mind.

Years ago, Beth's family disintegrated. Her mother is always mad at her auntie (who lives down in Indiana, where people haven't yet realized she ain't Miss Thang), and her auntie won't talk to Beth, who's guilty by association. Beth's grandmother spends most of her time abroad, since she has the good sense to keep some distance between herself and the rest of them. Beth hasn't seen her whole family together in nearly two decades.

When Beth told her mother about losing her job, about potentially losing her house, Gretchen's reaction was much the same as when Beth told her mother she was getting divorced: "I could have told you this was going to happen."

Her mother had never approved of the marriage in the first place. She never visited her grandkids, didn't even talk to them on the rare occasion she called Beth. She skipped Beth's wedding, although she did send a gift, a leaded crystal vase, in lieu of her presence. The vase was already broken when it arrived, a chunk from the rim rattling around in the bottom, and Beth hadn't bothered filing an insurance claim with the carrier, or even notifying her mother. Instead, she used the vase broken, filled it with cheap bouquets bought at the grocery store and left too long to wilt, and then rot, Beth never bothering to change the water. When Dan was seven, he broke the vase for good while throwing a football in the house, and while neither Beth nor Greg were angry, Dan felt terrible. Come to think of it, maybe that explained his aversion to sports.

Beth is surprised by how few memories she has of her mother in this house. She tries to imagine her in the kitchen, making dinner, or hanging laundry in the backyard. Did she garden? After Beth's parents divorced when Beth was four, Beth moved with her mother into the Section 8 housing in town, but within a year, Gretchen was remarried. Beth's first stepfather was rich, or at least appeared to be rich. Turned out, all of his trappings of wealth belonged to his company—his car, his house. All of it went under with the company a few years later. No doubt Gretchen had hoped to strike it rich with this divorce—her own mother had set herself up quite comfortably by divorcing a rich man—but Gretchen took very little. There wasn't much left to take. She'd had to move Beth back to the Section 8 housing.

"Serves you right," Beth had told her mother.

Ever since the move, Dan's father has called daily to check in on him. At first, Dan wondered whether this was his father's real reason for buying him and Jeanette cellphones, except his father doesn't call Jeanette every day. According to Dan's father, Dan's problem is that he doesn't form relationships like his sister does. And it's true; Dan doesn't get attached to people in the way he thinks he should, and it sort of worries him. Actually, he never noticed it before, never thought to worry about it, but one night just before the move, he heard his parents fighting. His father had come to pick them up for the weekend. He heard his mom tell his father that yes, they really were moving, and no, there was no reconsidering, and then his dad asked if his mom really thought it was a good idea, and his mom said it was a little late to start this again. And then his dad said it: "He's not like other kids. He's not going to be able to just start over like that."

Well, (a) Dan's not a kid—he took driver's ed this summer; and (b) Dan is kind of on his mom's side: His dad was always trudging up old, already-settled conversations. Dan had been through months of counseling, at his father's behest, had learned strategies to get out of his own head, to be present in the moment. Of course he could start over. He was even looking forward to it.

The truth is, Dan has a girlfriend now, or pert near, and even though part of him knows to keep it to himself—he can't imagine his mother would invite Kelli Brody and her family over for dinner or anything like that—another, more primal part of him wants to climb onto the roof of his granddad's house and shout to passersby. Not about Kelli per se, but about the general natures of attachment and physical magnetism. But he hasn't climbed, hasn't shouted, has he? See there? Impulse control. He's successfully navigated a social setting with a fair amount of decorum, and emerged on the other side with a great feeling of accomplishment. This is surely a mile marker: Dan is now an adult. Ergo, his dad needs to lay off him.

And anyway, it's not like Jeanette isn't also affected by the move. At her new school, Jeanette is so far ahead of her classmates that soon she's falling behind. She doesn't want to do her work—it's boring—and so she doesn't.

"You only have to give the idiots what they want," Dan says when she brings him a letter from her history teacher, Mrs. Schwartz, detailing Jeanette's failure to live up to her teacher's expectations. Jeanette asks him to add their mother's signature. In the month since they moved here, their mother rarely comes out of the bedroom, except for work. On her days off, she doesn't emerge at all, not to shower, not to eat. A sour bodily smell permeates the air, so that Jeanette often sleeps in a sleeping bag on the floor of Dan's room, or on the couch. She does her homework in the dining room—when she does it at all.

"It's just so boring," Jeanette says, rolling her eyes. For emphasis, she places both of her hands on her cheeks, pulling down her lower eyelids until the red inner parts show.

"Well, no wonder. Look at your classes. Reading development? You already read at a high school level. Have Granddad go in and make them switch you."

"Why would I do that? They'll just give me more boring work."

But Dan talks to Granddad, who has Jeanette switched wherever possible. There isn't another history class, though. When Beth learns this, she acts like she's the one who's been wronged. "You can always come to me," she tells Dan, and Dan wonders whether she misunderstood, whether she thinks he was the one who had her classes switched.

In her new classes, Jeanette is behind for the semester, having come in a month into the school year. She doesn't know anyone, and these kids aren't too eager to talk to her. They look at her askance and whisper among themselves, giggling but falling silent when they see her watching. After school, she doesn't have time to catch up with her horse-girl friends from her old classes; she has too much homework now.

Dan comes home from band practice to find her sprawled out on his bedroom floor with textbooks everywhere. She's wrestled her hair up into a tight bun on top of her head, the only way she wears it anymore. She looks like a librarian.

"Thanks a lot, ass face," she says, indicating all her homework.

"My pleasure," Dan says, feeling very grown up indeed at having ruined his sister's life.

. . .

Beth is washing dishes one day, staring out the window into the backyard, when Dan comes into the kitchen and nudges her aside.

"You should go chill," he says, taking the sponge from her.

He's a good kid, and she's grateful for him. She's not really sure where he learned to be so sweet. Not from his father, surely. As much as she wants to take his suggestion, her mind is restless. She decides to get caught up on the laundry instead. She goes around the house, gathering clothes—there's a half basketful of Linda's tunic shirts and yoga pants in Ernest's bedroom, and for Christ's sake, can't the girl do her own laundry?

The laundry room is tiny, with barely enough space to close the door behind her. The washer and dryer, the rack for detergent and fabric softeners, they take up almost the entire room. There's a window above the washer, and when the afternoon sun shines in, the room grows as hot as the inside of a mouth. Today, the sky is overcast, a dreary day to usher in the second week of October, and the room is cold. The door behind Beth stands open, yet the room still feels too small. Beth can't wait to burst back out of it.

There was a time—how old had she been?—when Gilmer Thurber was here, in this house, this room, with Beth. She can't remember how or why, but she seems to think it was at her father's invitation. He was here, in this house, and where was her father? In the house, but not in the room. And Gilmer grabbed Beth, pulled her into the laundry room. He had her up on the dryer, her clothes on the floor beside them. She could hear the shower running. Gilmer smelled like sweat and engine oil. He'd been teaching her father something about cars—she'd forgotten that, willfully: He and her father had been close, a mentor/mentee relationship, and he had been here, in this garage, and then this house, frequently. Beth's parents divorced when she was four, and she moved in with her mother. She must have been no more than four when Gilmer had her up on the dryer.

Of course, her father didn't know. Under threat of violence, she never spoke about it, instead accepting it as just a part of life: Sometimes her father would be unavailable, and then Gilmer could put her on the dryer.

Beth leaves the laundry unfinished, backs out of the room, and shuts the door. She'd thought moving back to River Bend would be okay now, with Gilmer gone, but she has her work cut out for her, damming these memories up again. It takes her the rest of the day, in her bed. Over the next few weeks, she finds more memories resurfacing, in the ill-lit recesses, on all the flat surfaces, the tables, the counters, in every room but the bedrooms, never the bedrooms, so that these rooms—especially *her* bedroom—become the only safe spaces. If she finds herself in one of the other rooms, she has to back away, pull herself up the stairs and to her bed, where she breathes deeply, concentrates on this room, its sunny wallpaper, the way the smooth wood floor creaks as she crosses it, the smell of the pine tree outside floating in through the open window. She finds her fingers in her mouth, scraping the undersides of her fingernails clean on her lower incisors, and this becomes a part of her ritual, the cleaning of her nails. She takes comfort in the fact that her hands often retain the taste of garlic and onions, or the flowery soaps Linda placed by all the sinks, or even the taste of dirt. Even this helps to calm her.

Downstairs, Linda makes coffee every morning. Ernest will have three cups, Linda half a cup, her pregnancy cheat. If Beth isn't around, Jeanette will also pour herself a cup. She drinks only half, leaving a half-full mug in the sink. Linda doesn't mind. She herself drank coffee at Jeanette's age; she needed it when she would wake in the dark of winter and head downstairs, the kitchen cold before Grandma made breakfast. Linda would drink coffee as she pulled on her snow boots, her coat, and shuffled outside wearing a head-lamp, huffing her way through the snow to the barn, her breath puffing in the glow of her lamp. She kept a mug of coffee with her as she fed the horses and cows before school.

Linda is a little annoyed, though, by the amount of sugar Jeanette heaps into her coffee. Linda buys coffee online—the local shops don't carry her brand—and it doesn't need anything but a splash of milk. But Linda reminds herself that Jeanette is twelve, a new coffee drinker.

Sometimes Beth, too, comes down for coffee, standing in front of the window over the sink and sipping it while watching the squirrels in the yard. At the first sip, Beth's face will lift into something akin to a smile. She doesn't talk to Linda, who is usually sitting at the kitchen table, her feet on the heater grate, but she'll do the almost-smile, and sip half a cup at the sink before refilling and heading back to bed or to the bathroom to get ready for work. Linda had always thought black people were so loud and lively; she doesn't know what to make of Beth's silence.

Linda doesn't mind, though. She's accepted that she and Beth will not be friends, that Beth cannot bless Linda's relationship with Ernest. If Linda had a say, she wouldn't even be here. She'd never have chosen to fall in love with a man so much older. And yet, here she is, the acting stepmother to a woman seven years older than she, a woman who can barely stand to be in the same room with her, a woman Linda has no idea how to read, how to coax out of the soft womb of depression she's curled inside. But

Linda can take care of Beth in this one small way: She can make her a cup and a half of coffee in the morning.

From her bedroom, Beth smells something burning. It's a faint smell, scarcely detectable. *Probably someone burning leaves,* she thinks. She lies there, trying to ignore it. She tries concentrating on this space, but the smell intrudes. There's no choice but to get out of bed.

On her way down the stairs, the smell grows stronger, and it occurs to Beth that it may be inside the house. She finds Linda cross-legged on the couch, with Jeanette sitting on the floor in front of her. Linda wields a curling iron and is using it to press Jeanette's hair, which is so long, it piles into Linda's lap. She's pressing it dry, too, no leave-in, no oil. Nothing. Jeanette's head pulls back each time Linda drags the iron through her hair. Jeanette doesn't look bothered by it, but watching this scene, something inside Beth breaks. She makes a grab for the iron, and it touches Jeanette on the side of her neck, right along her jawline. Jeanette yelps, jumps away from her mother. Beth jumps, too, and ends up with the iron against the crook of her arm.

"What do you think you're doing?" Beth says.

Linda says nothing. Just pulls herself up from the couch and leaves the room.

"Did she hurt you?" Beth asks once Linda is gone.

"Did *she* hurt me?" Jeanette says.

Beth inspects the burn on Jeanette's neck. It's purple-brown. She goes to the medicine cabinet, rubs Jeanette with aloe. She thinks the skin will flake, but it probably won't blister. Her arm is another story. There's already a great gray blister forming on the inside of her elbow.

"You can style your own hair," Beth says when she finishes rubbing Jeanette with aloe. She inspects Jeanette's hair, the ends now dry, singed, the white tips ready to fray.

"What's wrong with you?" Jeanette demands. Beth has gotten to her daughter; for once, Jeanette's voice is on the verge of real emotion.

Beth goes and gets a pair of scissors. Jeanette doesn't speak, doesn't move, as Beth cuts her hair.

"It has to be done," Beth says, as if Jeanette had asked her a question. "She's burnt it."

Clumps of hair fall on the couch, cling to the front of her. They stick to the blistering burn on Beth's arm. Jeanette freezes. Closes her eyes. Beth cuts it to Jeanette's shoulders, but it's uneven, so she cuts it chin-length. It's still uneven. She gets the clippers she normally uses on Dan's hair, puts the longest guard on it. When she's done, Jeanette's hair is less than an inch long. It curls into little corkscrews. Her scalp is pure white, visible where the curls pull away from it.

Jeanette still doesn't move, doesn't open her eyes, a reaction Beth can't understand. Beth's worked her whole life to protect her daughter. Even during the divorce, Beth and her husband were careful never to raise their voices, to always treat each other with respect. But this immobility. Somewhere along the line, Beth has failed.

Your hair," Ernest says from the doorway, and Jeanette opens her eyes. She looks so much like Beth at that age, it's alarming. Those wide, dark eyes, so distant, focused on something beyond here. When Beth was twelve, she was acting out in school, and Gretchen would call Ernest, would ask him what he was going to do about it. But what could he do? He didn't know how to reach Beth, hadn't known for years, not since he and Gretchen were called into the school when Beth was in second grade. The questions that school counselor asked, and the way she'd eyed Ernest. He and Gretchen both realized the school suspected some kind of abuse, and Ernest felt they were accusing him personally.

"Can I talk to you?" Ernest says to Beth, and Jeanette wastes no time. She's up and headed for the doorway, her back unnaturally straight, brushing hair from her shoulders and chest as she turns the corner.

Ernest sits down on the couch next to Beth. He's not accustomed to living with other people, to maintaining familial bonds: He's been a bachelor for over thirty years. What he wants to say is *How can I help? What do you need from me?* It hurts him to see his daughter so visibly broken, and to be at such a loss for how to fix things. He blames her mother, for how Gretchen raised Beth after the divorce, because blaming Gretchen is easier than thinking too hard about things he doesn't want to think about. Gilmer Thurber. The trial. He'd been contacted by a lawyer. The questions had caught him so off guard, but since then, his mind has been working on it. He should call the lawyer back; he should testify, tell what he knows. But, God, the thought of that man, the thought of his own little girl. Ernest isn't sure he can do it; he's not sure he's strong enough.

He wants to make things right, wants to make up for lost time, but he doesn't even know where to begin, and so what comes out of his mouth is "Why can't you just be nice?"

Elizabeth DeWitt

14

My friend Deb and I play penis *in choir class. It goes like this: I say* penis, *and then Deb says* penis *louder, and then I say* penis *even louder, and in theory, we keep going until we get caught. We don't ever get caught, mostly because we end up giggling before we can finish our game. We're altos and stand in the back row, and we play while everyone else is singing. Also, our choir director is too busy mooning over Alexia, the blond soprano in the first row, to bother with much of anything else. He and Alexia are dating. It's supposed to be a secret, but this is a small school, and just about everyone has seen them at the mall holding hands.*

"It's so gross," Deb says, and I nod along. "I mean, he has buck teeth and wears those gay vests," she says.

I don't tell her that part of me signed up for voice lessons with him after school because I imagined being the student who got seduced. Like in a romance novel, I could be the student whose talents, whose beauty, had gone unrecognized until now. She wouldn't understand anyway. She's thin and white and redheaded.

A few weeks later, we find a heart drawn in pencil on one of the music stands, with "Alexia + Mr. Henley" written inside. You can see it against the black lacquer of the music stand only if the light hits the graphite just so. I find myself wondering whether she calls him Mr. Henley when they're alone together. I can't even imagine what his first name is.

HEAT

The kitten is in heat. Deborah thinks about letting the damn thing out in the middle of the night. For three days the kitten has writhed, slinking around the house, rubbing its sides on everything, purring and yowling and whipping its tail around. Now it rears up on its hind paws and scratches at the back door, leaving ragged wounds in the screen, its moans lewd and low.

It's too hot for October, a late-season heat wave, and the house is crowded, with all of Deborah's girls indoors. Hannah, the youngest, follows the kitten around, scratching it just above its tail to watch it roll on the floor. Deborah's older girls, Kelli and Mandy, are currently grounded. Plus there are the two dogs. And Steve's bird, that damn African gray parrot he got ages ago from a friend whose toilet he fixed even though the guy didn't have any money to pay him. The bird speaks mostly swear words and bad French. Mandy always corrects its pronunciation.

131

Mandy is the one you have to watch out for; even though she's fifteen, younger than Kelli by eleven months, she's the instigator, the sassy one. Kelli is quiet and shy, would have been bookish in a different environment. The girls are both teenagers, *Irish twins* their grandma likes to joke, because they were born less than a year apart. They got grounded for breaking curfew. Deborah might have gone easy on them, if Mandy hadn't compared the household to a concentration camp. So. No phones, no computer, no leaving.

Deborah thinks it's only fair, considering how strict her mom had been when she was their age. All of her mom's strictness didn't matter; Deborah still got married in haste at nineteen, just before her son, Layne, was born. She would be damned if her daughters were going to live that life. Deborah was seventeen, only a year older than Kelli is now, when she started dating Steve. And then she found out her friend Eliza was dating him, too. She'd seen Eliza—she goes by Beth now, according to Facebook—at the gas station, and has heard she's back in town with her two kids. Deborah shook her head; that woman had better stay away from her family.

Deborah is well aware of the threats in a town like this. River Bend is full of men who want to take and take. Just last June, that horrible man Gilmer was caught hurting children in his basement. Deborah can't even imagine the terrible things he did to them—young children, too, some four or five. There are times when she hates her husband for his insistence that she needs to stay home with the kids, but other times, she's thankful. Who knows what might have happened to her own kids if she had a career, if she had to leave them in someone else's care? Their house may not be big and fancy, like the houses she'd always dreamed of living in, but inside, she and her family are safe.

Even so, today the house seems shrunken, its walls pressing in on the family. Mandy stood in the kitchen with the refrigerator door wide open for a good ten minutes, yelling across the house to Kelli, telling her sister what there was to drink. Now the girls hang in the open front doorway, shouting to some neighborhood boys on the sidewalk, thinking they have their mom on a technicality. They keep pushing the dogs back as they try to nose between their legs and out the door. If the kitten should sneak out, it would be their fault. How many times has Deborah talked to them about letting out all the air-conditioning?

Hannah sprawls on her belly on the concrete floor in the living room, the kitten rolling around next to her. She's coloring in a book—not a coloring book—with one hand, and stroking her kitten with the other. Deborah can hear its unholy purring from the kitchen. Hannah likes to lie on the floor, which is bare because the dogs messed it so much that Deborah pulled up the carpet and threw it out on the curb a few months ago. The slab underneath is discolored in the spots where the dogs had most often gone, and no amount of bleach can remove the stains. Deborah has scolded Hannah time and again for lying on the dirty floor, but it's hot in the house even with the window unit blasting, and the floor, Hannah says, is good and cool.

"The cat's being silly," Hannah giggles. As she scratches the kitten, it squats down low to the ground and begins pumping its butt like that Nicki Minaj in those music videos Mandy always watches.

"Knock it off," Deborah says. She picks the kitten up by its scruff, drops it in the bathroom, and shuts the door. The simple act of moving around the house has dampened the underside of her bra. Sweat trickles down her back. What she wouldn't do for a cigarette right now, but she's out and it's three days until payday and she needs her last few dollars for laundry.

133

When she leaves the bathroom, she realizes the front door is closed, and Kelli and Mandy are nowhere to be found. The girls' bedroom is empty, the backyard is quiet; Deborah begins to fret when she hears thumping on the roof. She pokes her head out the front door and hears her girls. When she steps outside, both the dogs bound past her and jump around in the driveway, hoping to greet visitors. She finds Kelli and Mandy lying on beach towels on the roof. The girls are always saying the grass is too pokey to lie in the yard. On a day this hot, it takes commitment to lie out on a black-shingled roof in a bikini, especially for Kelli, who inherited her mother's red hair and fair skin. Still, at least the boys they were talking to are no longer in sight. Deborah herds the dogs and chains them up.

"You aren't supposed to leave the house," Deborah calls up to them.

Kelli raises herself onto her elbows, removes the washcloth from her eyes.

Mandy, without moving, calls back, "We didn't leave the house. We're *on* the house."

Back inside, the damp air smells like dogs. They have just the two, a bitch and the one puppy that didn't die directly after being born, and didn't wander out into the street and get hit by a car, and didn't get adopted when Deborah put an ad on Craigslist. The puppy isn't really a puppy anymore; it's two years old and has long since grown into its paws. Deborah likes the puppy, but part of her doesn't want to get attached. So she tells herself. If she were honest, she'd have to admit that she already is attached, that she really should get rid of the dog and the puppy since there isn't room in the two-bedroom house for two dogs, three children—four, if Layne ever comes home—a husband, and herself, and now the kitten the girls found behind the dumpster at the gas station when they walked down last week to buy pop. And the damn bird, half-bald because it's always pulling out its feathers. Deborah lived in constant hope that her husband's parrot would die, until Mandy informed her that some African grays live to sixty or seventy years.

Yet for the moment, the house seems almost sufficient, with Steve working, and the dog and puppy chained up in the yard. Hannah has fallen asleep on the couch with the air conditioner dripping on her, even though Deborah has told her a thousand times not to, that sticking her face in that thing or sleeping in its breeze is why Hannah's always got ear infections.

Deborah shuffles from room to room, gathering up laundry. The space around her shifts, the walls swell; the house expands in the afternoon heat. Deborah stands up a little taller, and the air moves in and out of her lungs with less effort on her part.

The Laundromat is just across Main Street. When she steps outside, a basket on her hip, she has trouble finding Kelli and Mandy. Their towels are still on the roof, a ladder leaned against the house. In the backyard, the lawn chairs set up next to the kiddie pool are empty. Back around front, she sees the girls standing on the sidewalk, talking to a boy who has to be Eliza DeWitt's son. He has a nappy head and dark knees, just like his mother. Mandy giggles and punches the boy in the arm, and the dogs strain at their chains, barking, egging each other on. So much energy for such a hot day. The boy doesn't seem to notice Mandy's flirtations; he's fixated on Kelli, whose bikini, Deborah realizes, no longer fits right; her breasts, though small, are all too visible through the fabric and on the verge of oozing out around the edges of her top, which is old and thin and downright indecent.

Deborah feels her face heat up and pinch into a frown. A hard bulb grows in the pit of her stomach. Kelli must be aware of how she looks, too, because she crosses her arms over her chest. A line of sweat darkens the back of her bikini bottoms.

"You need to answer me when I call," Deborah says. Had she even called to the girls? She can't remember.

"God, we're just talking," Mandy says. "It's not a *sin*."

Deborah sizes the boy up. Those dark eyes. He's a full head shorter than even Kelli, who's shorter than Mandy by a couple inches. "I never seen you before," Deborah says.

"Dan Hansen," the boy says, holding out his hand to shake. Then he adds, "Ma'am."

Even the way he moves his mouth looks like his mother. Deborah feels the hard bulb in her stomach sprouting, sending up creepers. Eliza DeWitt has been back only a couple of weeks, and already her boy has found Deborah's girls. The only black family in town. They don't belong here.

Deborah eyes her oldest daughter. "Go in and watch your sister. Both of you."

Kelli now has her legs crossed as well as her arms. She looks like she needs to use the bathroom. She's staring down her own long, pale legs at her toenails with their chipped blue polish. It's been a long time since Deborah was young enough to wear shorts, when she seldom felt cold even when the snow fell, even when her pinkie toes had worn through her canvas shoes. When she was Kelli's age, she had no money to buy a winter coat and instead wore layers of cardigan sweaters in pink and green and yellow, always Easter colors, all year long. But she was smart, her teachers had said so, and she showed promise. That was before she met Steve, when she still thought she was getting out of this town, when she could still imagine herself wearing heels to her office job. But what are her kids' options, really? Even if her girls get grants for college, their grades are poor. Hannah is always in trouble at school, for fighting with the other kids, for refusing to do as the teacher asks. And God only knows what Layne will do when they let him out.

"*You* watch her," Mandy says, and without thinking, Deborah slaps the girl. Dan's eyes widen. He opens his mouth like he wants to say something, and then thinks better and shuts it. He turns and walks away up the sidewalk.

Mandy narrows her eyes and her lips, her bottom jaw shifting to one side, a look she learned from her dad.

"I'm washing laundry," Deborah says. "Get inside. And put on some clothes."

"It's too hot," Kelli whines. "Stupid Indian summer." She reaches an arm up to wipe the sweat from her brow, and when she pulls her arm away, the hairs on it are plastered to her skin.

"You don't need to be sitting around the front yard half-naked for all the world to see. Get inside and make Hannah a snack."

That night, after Steve comes home and pulls his dinner from the oven, while he eats on their bed in his dirty work clothes, Deborah brings the last of the clean laundry home.

"I saw that DeWitt boy today," she says.

Steve sits on the edge of the bed, his plate in his lap, hunched over his food.

"God," she says. "The DeWitts have been back what? A month? And he's already met the girls."

"Hansen," Steve says with a mouth full of potatoes.

"What?"

"The kid's name is Hansen."

"Whatever, Eliza DeWitt's boy."

"Beth," he says.

As soon as he says it, he realizes his mistake. He knows she goes by Beth only because of social media, but doesn't want his wife to know that he's been keeping tabs on Beth. When he was younger, he was better at juggling these interactions, better at keeping straight in his mind who knew what. Somewhere along the line, though, his brain grew fuzzy, and he lost his knack for compartmentalizing. The best he can do now is hope Deborah didn't notice.

Deborah did notice, though, and she wonders how he knows. Has he visited Beth? She remembers their encounter at the gas station—the way Steve looked at Beth—and her stomach feels watery. She wants to find out, but she's aware she's already pushing it. She takes a deep breath, sends the creepers back down into the bulb. What's done is done; it's her daughters' futures she's worried about tonight.

"You're getting the bed all dirty," she says, brushing sawdust off the blanket.

Elizabeth DeWitt
15

I know how to break apart frozen beef patties with a quick tap on the flat-top griddle. I know how to crack an egg in each hand and deposit them without shells into the silicon rings. I've mastered the art of squirting condiments in the dead center of a bun, of evenly distributing the two pickles on a Quarter Pounder, of making sure the processed cheese food droops evenly over the sides of the burger. My manager nicknames me the Grill Goddess.

I've learned everything I can in this kitchen, and I'm bored. I dream of the day when I'll work in a real kitchen, in the kind of place they feature on Great Chefs *on PBS. I'll learn to sauté and braise, to sear meats with a perfect crust, to bake soufflés, sauced with dollops of compote or crème anglaise. But for now, this job helps me save for college, save for the time when I'll get out of this cow town.*

My manager moves me to the second drive-through, where I have to bag the sloppy work of other cooks. My coworker Earl, who's taking orders in the first drive-through, uses the opportunity to hit on me over our headsets. He's cute enough, his floppy hair and olive skin, but also maybe a little skanky. He just broke up with Lila, who smelled so bad in gym class the other girls were whispering that she had a yeast infection—we all smelled it when we were in the showers, and doesn't that mean she's a slut? He seems tainted by that smell, and I can't tell if I'm grossed out by him now, or excited. He's probably experienced. He might know things. Regardless, I'm a good girl. I tell him I can't go out after work. I have to wash my hair.

After work, while I'm waiting for my mom to pick me up, he says we should go out after I wash my hair. I tell him I have to clip my toenails. He asks how long that will take. He's cute enough, but boy is he dumb. I tell him it will take all night, all week, it will take as long as he's interested in going out with me.

He offers me a ride home, and I'm scared. He's standing too close to me, close enough I can smell his fabric softener, and I'm frozen here on the concrete. My mother has told me about getting into cars with boys. I wish she was here, I wish I was getting into her car right now, but she's late, and when she does arrive, when I point out how late she is, she says, "You're the one who wanted this job." She shakes her head and humphs. "So hell-bent on going to college."

DINNER SHIFT

The Hudson House isn't what it once was. When Slick and Mike Hudson's parents ran the place, it was a clean and efficient kitchen serving simple, wholesome food. Now, with Slick as the owner, the kitchen is understaffed, Slick trying to cut labor costs. To compensate, he buys canned vegetables and instant mashed potatoes, precooked chicken for salads, factory-made dinner rolls, pre-breaded frozen shrimp. Anything to speed up prep time.

Beth is embarrassed to work here. She misses the country club in Charlotte, regrets that she took it for granted while she was there. There was an energy to that kitchen, a hustle that is utterly missing at the Hudson House, where she and her coworker—who seems to change every week—putter around a too-small kitchen, plating mostly fried food, greasy because the fryer is set too cool. Slick seems to think that turning the temperature up to 375 would increase his electric bill exponentially.

Worse yet is the fact that Gilmer Thurber used to work here. There's something about stepping into Thurber's role that makes Beth feel nasty. She thought when he was arrested, that was it, he was gone, but now she can't help but think about the fact that he must have touched everything she touches: the pans and trays, the spatulas, the fryer baskets, the plates. She can almost feel him permeate her skin, and when she goes home in the evenings, no amount of soap and hot water can scald away his residue.

Today, a Saturday in mid-October, is the first time Beth has had to work a dinner shift. One of the reasons she took this job is because she was hired to cover breakfast and lunch. Today, though, Slick scheduled her for the dinner rush because all of his night cooks have been fired or quit. She feels like she should be home with her family in the evenings, even though in some ways, it's nice to be at work. Her father's house may be big, but it feels small with so many people living there.

Around about three o'clock, Slick comes into the kitchen, already with a five o'clock shadow, his hair excessively gelled and a little too long so that it's bordering on a mullet. His upper lip is shiny even under the stubble. It looks wet, with sweat maybe. Beth feels repulsed by it.

"Beth," he says. "Meet your new coworker, Paula."

Linda's mother. Beth used to babysit for this woman, bless her heart. She looks exactly the same as she did when Beth was a teenager: still thin and tan, still just as blond. She seems almost fragile, she's so slight, and Beth doubts she'll be able to keep up in the kitchen. Paula and her husband used to hang out with Steve and Deb. Beth was always jealous of their friend group, having nothing similar for herself.

"What happened to the other guy?" Beth says. He worked there for such a short time, she hadn't even learned his name. Paula is the third coworker Beth has had since she started the job two weeks ago.

Slick just rolls his eyes, doesn't even bother answering. No doubt the guy has quit. Of all people, Slick would go and hire Paula Williams. The way Paula looks at her, though, Beth doesn't think Paula remembers her. Paula's ignorance of Beth's existence is almost as hurtful as the memories she brings up.

"I wasn't expecting to have help tonight," Beth says as Paula ties an apron around her waist. She never really liked Paula. Come to think of it, Paula is a lot like her daughter Linda. Both women act like the world owes them.

"What'd you think?" Paula says. "Slick was going to leave you high and dry back here?"

The nerve of her, Beth thinks. As if Beth can't handle a dinner rush in this dumpy little greasy spoon.

What Beth doesn't know is that Paula hates it here as much as Beth does, and for many of the same reasons. She hates the kitschy decor, hates the bland food, hates the feel of the restaurant. She hates that her life has come to this. The restaurant where she worked in Moab is one of those places the travel magazines feature for their amazing pancakes. As much as Paula hates to admit it, she doesn't fit in this town anymore. She misses her dog. She misses her boyfriend. Or, well, fiancé. She misses him almost as much as she missed her daughters over the years, which surprises her. She didn't think she would.

She should have just taken Jorge's advice and hired a lawyer. She wants to go home, back to Utah, but she still hasn't had a chance to talk to Jared. She wonders how he's managed to avoid her so well in such a small town. He never seems to be at the hardware store when she stops in, and she suspects that he may be home more often than it seems, that Dinah and Skyla are covering for him. She's a little ashamed to see how much like Dinah Skyla has become. Not just in her mannerisms, but in her loyalties. She doesn't begrudge Skyla this. She knows she's brought it on herself.

In the kitchen together, Beth and Paula are so wrapped up in their own issues, neither can manage to fall in sync with the other. When the orders roll in, both try to command the grill; neither wants to run the fryer, or worse, the salad station.

"I've got these burgers," Beth says, wielding a spatula like a weapon. "If you want to grab those apps."

Paula shakes her head, watching the grill flare up around the burgers. "You've got it up too high," she says. She's thinking now of Jorge, of the burgers he made the Saturday before she left for Michigan, the dry meat, the bitter char. The proposal. The fight.

Beth doesn't bother to respond. She's not sure what kind of Podunk restaurant Paula worked at previously, but clearly, the woman doesn't know her way around a grill.

Paula fills a fryer basket with jalapeño poppers and lowers it into the grease. Beth shakes her head when the grease barely sputters at the frozen hors d'oeuvres. When the waitress, Bobby-Jo, places the next order, Paula pounces on the burgers, leaving Beth to make the salads.

"Did you wash this lettuce?" Beth asks from the salad station, holding a fistful of dripping iceberg lettuce.

"Lady," Paula says, "I got here after you."

"Slick did dinner prep tonight," Bobby-Jo says. She's standing on the other side of the line, holding her stomach and looking at the floor.

"You all right?" Paula asks.

"My stomach is off," she says, traying the appetizers to take them out to the dining room.

"She's probably been eating here," Beth mutters when Bobby-Jo leaves. She slops together some dinner salads. What's the point in making them look nice when the ingredients are so lousy? When she sets them in the window and calls for Bobby-Jo to pick them up, Slick comes in instead.

"Beth, I'm going to need you to cover the dining room," he says.

She stares at him blankly, Jeanette's stare. She doesn't want to look at him and his wet lip.

"Did you hear me?" Slick says. "Bobby-Jo got sick. You'll need to freshen up the bathroom, too, before taking her tables."

"And there's nobody else you can call in?" Beth says.

"What?" Slick says. "Are *you* too good to serve?"

Unbelievable. She literally cannot believe it as she takes off her white chef's apron and switches it for a black server apron. She almost tells him that she *is* too good to serve, that she didn't go to culinary school to wait tables. A few months ago, she would have, but then losing her job at the country club is what brought her to this godforsaken town in the first place. And so Beth swallows her pride, goes into the bathroom that smells like an outhouse—Beth reminds herself again not to eat the food—and sprays copious amounts of air freshener. She checks the stalls to make sure the poor girl hadn't exploded in there. She hadn't. Thank God for small favors.

Beth hasn't waited tables in almost twenty years. She wasn't good at it then, and she's even worse now. She doesn't want to talk to these people. She has no friends left in town. Once upon a time, Deb Williams had been her only real friend, but then Steve

Brody got in the middle of it. It hurt to sacrifice her friend, but she'd thought she was in love. At the time it seemed a fair trade. Now she not only has no friends, but no man.

Even worse, Slick's words echo in her mind: "Are *you* too good to serve?" The emphasis on *you*, like there's something particular about Beth that makes her the logical choice. She's always found serving to be humiliating; somehow, it's even worse to serve people in River Bend.

She remembers a time in culinary school when a group of young professional men came into the restaurant and sat in her section. She served them bisque and salads and lamb chops and individual soufflés. And so much wine. Toward the end of the night, one of the men grabbed her ass. All evening, he'd been eyeing her in a way that made her feel like she was on the menu, and then he grabbed her.

At least nobody has grabbed her yet tonight. They complain about how slow her service is, and when she brings their food, they send their burgers back for being undercooked. (And oh, the righteousness she feels making Paula turn the grill back up.)

Along about eight o'clock, a couple comes into the Hudson House. The guy looks familiar to Beth, though she has trouble placing him, with his glasses and thick beard. The girl is young, maybe still in high school, with long honey-blond hair. She bears a striking resemblance to Paula. And then Beth puts it together. Paula's husband.

"Jared," Beth says.

Jared looks up at her, pushes his glasses higher to take her in.

"Eliza?" he says. "I haven't seen you in ages."

"I go by Beth now," she says, cringing at her old name.

"What's good tonight?"

No pleasantries. *That's fine,* Beth thinks. *Let's get this interaction over and done with.* After taking his order, more memories click into place: Jared is not just Paula's husband, but Deb Brody's brother. She wonders whether he knows about her past with Steve. He was pleasant enough with her, so she doubts it, but then again, you never can tell with Midwesterners. He could very well be seething deep down. By the time she makes it to the kitchen, she's already forgotten his order and has to go back out.

In the kitchen, Paula almost wishes Slick had asked her to wait tables instead of Beth. She would ask him to switch them, except she knows it would be a wasted effort. Beth had already argued with him, and he'd had to remind her who's boss. No way would he change his mind now, even though Beth is no doubt costing him money with the number of orders she's messing up.

In a way, Paula feels bad for Beth. She recognizes her as a bit of a kindred spirit. No doubt Beth hates schmoozing guests as much as Paula does. It probably doesn't come naturally for her, either. When Beth enters the kitchen and flat-out forgets the order she just took, though, Paula feels less sorry for her.

"Get your head in the game," Paula tells Beth. "Your fuck-ups are putting me in the weeds."

"Don't blame me because you can't keep up," Beth says.

"I could keep up fine if you'd only tell me the right orders."

Beth pulls the latest order from the window and huffs back out into the dining room.

Paula doesn't need this grief. What she needs is to find Jared. Get it done and get on home. Maybe she could try a sit-in at the Williams farm. The man has to come home to sleep, right? She isn't sure, though. She was never good at reading her husband; he's a master at keeping himself to himself. She tries to think of ways to get Dinah to let her in, and it occurs to her that she's been working the wrong angle. She should be hitting up Skyla.

By the end of the dinner rush, Paula is ready to scream. Beth stands on the other side of the line, counting her tips.

"These cheap-ass West Michigan Dutch," Beth mutters. Then she looks up and gives Paula a shitty grin. "Speaking of, Jared Williams sent his compliments to the chef."

Paula's stomach drops. "Jared is here?" she says, halfway through taking off her apron.

"He left maybe five minutes ago," Beth says.

Paula stops. It's an enormous effort not to reach across the line and slap the woman. "And it never occurred to you to tell me my husband was here?"

"Oh yeah," Beth says, grinning even worse. She tucks her tips into her back pocket. "Y'all are married, aren't you?"

Paula takes a deep breath and a step back, away from Beth. "Seriously?" Paula says, tying her apron back on. "Fuck you, Beth."

And really, Paula and Beth could have been friends; they have enough in common. Instead, Beth realizes she's made an enemy of Paula.

Elizabeth DeWitt

17

I take a second job in Kalamazoo, working at an erotic bakery, busting my ass to save enough for college. Most of our business is for bachelorette parties. The first project I'm given is an erection cake, a three-foot-high sculpture. It's so long, we have to special order dowels to thread down the length of it. The testicles are ridiculously bulbous, or else the whole erection will topple over. Its head is almost as large as my head. I spend hours draping it in pristine white fondant, sculpting veins with royal icing along the shaft. On top of the baker's table, the cake is taller than me by a couple of inches. I have to crawl up on a chair to sculpt the urethral opening.

"It's not a vampire's cock," my boss tells me. "Paint it with the skin-tone food coloring. Put some hair on those balls. Make the veins a throbbing purple."

But it pains me to ruin its perfect white. I want to dust it in powdered sugar. I want to cover it in wedding frosting. White, it still looks like a cake.

MEA CULPA

Beth pours her coffee, and instead of drinking it over the
sink, she takes it out to the back porch. She's been pushing herself to get out of bed more; the porch isn't far, so it
seems less overwhelming than going out. The only other person
who uses the porch is her father. There are such gaping holes in
the screens that mosquitoes crowd it in the summer, and earwigs
weave their way around the floor. One lone folding chair sits by
the door. Mostly the porch holds bags of garbage, fly-strewn and
stewing in the sun, until somebody, usually Dan, gets sick of the
smell and hefts them out to the bin behind the garage. But this
morning is trash day, so all the bags have already been removed.

If this were Charlotte, she would sit on the front porch. Neighbors would wave as they passed, walking their dogs or going for a
jog. She might not have had a lot of close friends in Charlotte, but
people were friendlier there. At least the black people were. She
misses that kind of low-stakes human interaction. Though the

heat wave has broken, this morning is still warm for mid October, and the putrid sweet stench of trash lingers. Beth brings out a kitchen chair, better for her back than the folding chair, and sits with her coffee held up by her face, watching the steam condense on her eyelashes.

She doesn't notice her father when he comes up from the garage, where he'd been replacing the catalytic converter in Derek Williams's car. These automotive repairs are his sole financial contribution to his growing household. He sees Beth sitting alone, so self-contained that she appears to be in deep thought. *No sense bothering her,* he thinks, and continues on his way. This is the same thought Linda often has, and Dan and Jeanette, when Beth comes down from her room. *She looks busy.* Even when Beth is doing nothing at all: *I don't want to disturb her.* So when Beth sits on the porch, or at the kitchen table, or in the living room, when Beth moves through the house, washing the dishes, cooking a meal, vacuuming the carpet, or dusting the bookshelf, her family often scatters, to give her space; Beth may have gotten out of her room, but she still has trouble getting out of her own head.

It's not that Beth is oblivious to the effect she has on the family. More like, she feels perversely empowered by it. Simply by entering, she can clear a room so effectively that it seems like she has her own house. She knows her children are fed and clothed, that they leave for school each morning. But the details of the feeding, the clothing, the getting ready for school, these tasks belong to someone else. This must be how her ex-husband feels, when he calls to check in on the kids. Checking in is more like checking off: Yes, the kids are still alive. Check.

When Beth finishes her coffee, she has a second cup, and then a third, emptying the pot, bringing each cup out onto the porch to drink alone. As the fall has settled into Michigan, Beth has grown more and more tired, needing caffeine for all her waking hours. She doesn't want to make coffee, doesn't want to fuss with Linda's imported beans or learn how to use her fancy coffeemaker, with its filters and temperature gauges and extraction times. She feels bad for having finished the pot, but instead of making more, she switches to tea, brewing a cup of dishwater from an old crinkled bag she finds at the back of the cupboard. She kind of likes it. She buys more at the dollar store: It's her own silent protest, her refusal to buy anything nice. Linda won't drink Beth's tea. Beth offers it to her anyway, if Linda is slow to leave the kitchen when Beth enters. Soon, it seems to Beth that tea is the only thing in the house that is truly hers.

Beth is in the kitchen one day, making tea, when there's a knock at the back door. She knows who's on the other side. She thinks, *He must know I'm alone in the kitchen, that I alone will hear him knock.* And how easy it is, how naturally she goes to the door to find him there, standing on the back stoop.

"Thought you could maybe use some company," Steve says through the screen. She hasn't seen him since she ran into him at the gas station. Up close, he's older, of course—they both are—but the years seem heavier on him. His face is hard and tight, as if time has compressed it. There is visible sun damage on his bare scalp. Beth glances down to see that the screen door is locked.

"How's Deb?" she says.

"I just want to talk," he says. He's studying her face, trying to match his memory of her to the woman before him.

"Like hell."

"Who's at the door?" Dan calls from the living room.

"Nobody," Beth says. "He's just leaving."

"I swear, I just want to talk," he says, his hand going for the doorknob. He slumps when he finds it won't turn.

"There's nothing left to say." Twenty years ago, Beth would have flipped the lock and grabbed hold of him as if he were a life preserver. She should close the door and dead bolt it. Instead, she stands there, staring at the screen. He jiggles the handle like it's stuck.

"Go home to your wife, Steve." She can't make herself close the door.

"Uncle Steve," Linda says in the doorway to the living room. "Come on in."

"He can't stay," Beth says.

"I can stay a little," Steve says.

"God, Beth, don't be rude," Linda says.

Beth wants to smack the girl, wants to teach her how to speak to her elders, but a part of her knows that she, Beth, is the one who's superfluous, the one who moved here out of necessity, not because Ernest wanted her here. So instead of fighting with Linda, Beth opens the door.

"What brings you round?" Linda asks.

"I wanted to see if Ernest is free this weekend. The salmon are running."

"Well, come on in. Can I get you coffee? A beer?"

"A beer sounds good." And they go into the house together, talking, catching up. Steve seems to have forgotten Beth entirely, but then that's always how it was with him: Once he speaks a lie, he slips into it as if it were reality. He said he'd come to see Ernest, and now that's what he's here for. Never mind that he's left Beth holding the door.

Steve Brody has a talent, which is the ability to look into a woman's eyes and see her damage. It looks to him like a tiny silent version of the woman, crouching inside her iris. The position of the tiny woman dictates how he will react; for instance, if the tiny woman was bunched, ready to spring, Steve knew enough to move on. If, however, the tiny woman was hugging her knees to her chest, or if she was teetering, or if she was trying to sneak away—if any of these were the tiny woman's position, well, now, these were the women Steve liked best. The hugging woman was in need of comfort. The teetering woman needed support. The sneaking woman needed to be seen and acknowledged. And once you could determine what a woman needed, you could give it to her, even while taking everything else: her time and money, her breath and sweat, her love, her mind, her youth.

The problem with Beth was that, over the years, she has gone from a hugger to something else entirely. Her tiny woman is silently drowning, curled inside a pool of warm water. Steve doesn't know how to work her, and he needs to know how. He needs to have her, to scoop her up and apply her to his life like a balm. This new Beth unnerves him, so that he begins to doubt himself.

He doesn't like doubting himself.

As soon as Linda has delivered Steve faithfully to Ernest, she rounds on Beth.

"You have no right to keep my family from this house."

Beth wants to blame Linda's outbursts on pregnancy hormones, but part of her thinks Linda would be just as unbearable if she weren't pregnant. "I didn't realize anyone else was home."

"Bullshit," Linda says, her face reddening.

"I keep forgetting you don't have a job, or somewhere to be."

"And what's that supposed to mean?" Linda has her hands on her belly, which is just beginning to show. She arches her back, thrusting her belly forward. As her body has expanded, she's developed the habit of wielding it like a weapon.

"Nothing."

"I'm still looking for a job," Linda says. And while it's true that she has put in a few job applications around town—at the flower shop, at the dollar store—she hasn't been as proactive about finding employment as she should be. She mentioned this to Ernest, and he told her not to worry about it; she should focus on growing him a healthy boy.

"It's just, I've had a job since I was fifteen," Beth says. "But it's not for everyone."

"You mean like warming up food down at the Hudson House?"

"Better than being a financial drain on someone else's family."

"In case you hadn't noticed," Linda says, "I'm pregnant."

"That's not an exemption."

"And frankly, it's none of your business. Ernest wants me here. He wants me to take it easy."

For a moment, Beth imagines how her future will look: working multiple jobs to support this household, Linda never so much as changing a diaper or warming a bottle. Beth's father will still be tinkering with cars for cash, but it's not enough. Ernest may be okay with Linda not working, but he's sleeping with her, so he's well compensated.

"It must be nice," Beth says without generosity, "to be so well taken care of."

When Beth was a child, after her parents divorced, her father didn't pay child support. It wasn't that Ernest DeWitt didn't want to, but more that he couldn't. Beth remembers visiting him when she was a teenager. There would be only beer and bologna in the fridge, no toilet paper in either bathroom. There were times when he would have no electricity. Beth has no doubt that now, if she weren't here, he would be unable to support Linda or her baby. And Beth knows that if she stays here, she will always be the breadwinner.

And just like a child who's jealous of another's toy, Beth wants to bring Linda down to her level.

The next morning, driving down Main Street, when Beth passes Steve in his truck, she doesn't avert her gaze. She stares at him. He's never had a problem reading her—he always had a knack for interpreting her moods—but today, he comes up short. Steve sits stationary, waiting for her to pass so he can turn into his driveway. Beth is moving in the opposite direction—*the wrong direction,* he thinks. Her house, the grocery store two towns over, the restaurant where she works, all are behind her. As she passes, she slows, turning her neck to watch him. Her face is utterly blank, her shoulders slumped, both hands on the wheel, and her eyes meet his for long enough to unnerve him. Once she's gone, he hits the gas, and his truck lurches into his driveway so quickly he almost hits Hannah, who is crouched down in the dusty gravel, trying to pull her kitten out from a gap under the house.

The first time Beth meets Steve, it's in a motel on the highway, like the most clichéd of love affairs. They pay cash, or rather, *he* pays cash, and she feels more guilty about letting him pay than she feels about sleeping with him. She's driven by his house regularly since moving back home: It's as small and dingy as ever, the grass patchy and baked, the paint peeling, the gutters falling off, the sidewalk cracked. How many kids does he have living at home? Three? How do they all fit? She can't afford a motel, but she knows he can't, either. *How irresponsible,* she thinks.

The scratchy bedspread is patterned with all the same colors as bodily excretions, the motel itself part of the punishment for her transgression. In the sex, she thought she'd find him again, rediscover the Steve she'd had so much trouble leaving behind, but he isn't there. This is some other Steve she's never met, a Steve who takes his time, takes forever. She'd wanted a quick deal, over and done, but it seems like hours that she's in that motel room, staring at the piss-yellow ceiling and its water stains, breathing that old-cigarette air, kissing his old-cigarette mouth. He huffs out dust on top of her, prods her with his dick, and the whole time all she can think is, *I deserve this.*

And so she keeps meeting him at the motel room he can't afford, or meeting him between paydays on the dusty country road north of town to screw on a blanket in the back of his pickup, as if they're teenagers again. But they're not teenagers; her back can attest to that: It knots up from the grinding it receives against that blanketed pickup bed. *I am trash,* she now realizes. *I'm the kind of trash my mother always worried I'd be.* This thought makes her keep going, not even making love, but fucking. He's never made love to her. All those years of fucking. She'd always been trash. And every time they fuck, that girl inside her, Eliza DeWitt, ebbs closer to the surface. Eliza's attachment to Steve was never broken; her relationship with him kept her here, in River Bend, all these years. This is another reason Beth can't sleep at night: Since moving home, Eliza has been screaming from the dark well inside her. In there, Steve married Eliza instead of Deb. Eliza lives in that dirty shoebox of a house with him and too many kids and too many pets.

Sometimes Beth falls overboard into those darker places, and the person who surfaces into this world is Eliza. And why not? Eliza is nicer, having long ago accepted that this is all her life will ever be. No use fighting it. Eliza has the docility, the complacency, that comes from having lost hope. And when Eliza takes the lead, dripping wet and pruney from the time she spent underwater, she goes about Beth's life, cooking at the Hudson House, watching television at home, shopping at the dollar store, attending football games to see Dan march.

Dan and Jeanette welcome Eliza, ask no questions of her, although after a week, they talk between the two of them about how they hope she'll stay. Even Ernest spends more time in the house when Eliza is there, because she's a joy to him. Eliza never went to college—Steve talked her out of it—and so she doesn't have to struggle to remember how to relate to her father. Eliza doesn't really want to talk about the state of the country, about gender politics and the glass ceiling, about that topic most shunned in the Midwest: racism. Eliza isn't hyperaware of the ways her father is privileged, the ways in which she is not. She never went out and paid tuition and got her own kind of privilege as a countermeasure. No, Eliza had none of this, or if she did, these thoughts are submerged now with Beth.

In the meantime, Beth sleeps until she is stronger, floating in the amniotic waters, relieved by the respite, while Eliza enjoys the chance to stretch. And as Eliza sits in amiable silence with Ernest, and drinks canned beer on a Saturday afternoon, and watches the game on TV, she rather wishes Beth would stay submerged. Beth only makes a mess of things anyway. Eliza goes to motel rooms with Steve, and makes pot roast for dinner, and never thinks about the factory farms Beth drove by on her way home to Michigan, and the miles of stink, and the brown muddy pens with so many bodies crammed in together. She doesn't consider the carbon footprint of new potatoes in October. She's even almost pleasant with Linda—a fact that does not escape Linda's notice, does not fail to raise Linda's suspicion. And when Ernest comments on the change, Eliza looks mildly surprised, having forgotten how it was that she used to act.

After two weeks of this, Ernest is optimistic, although cautiously so: He's known his daughter too long to feel entirely comfortable. Jeanette moves back into the bedroom with Eliza. Dan seems happier. For a time, the DeWitt household is rather peaceful.

That is, until Beth manages to claw her way back to the surface, disoriented—disappointed—by the direction in which Eliza has taken them.

Steve never notices any change in Beth, for while he's accepted her new name, in his mind, Beth is no deeper than the outermost surface of her skin.

Ernest's house is overdue for remodeling. He should have expected the demands of an aging house, but dealing with a flooded basement hadn't really been on today's to-do list. It's already the end of October. He'd intended to clean out the garage back in September, before his daughter arrived, to get Linda's car out of the driveway so there would be room for Beth's. He also wanted to clear space in the bedroom closet and dresser, so that Linda could unpack the rest of her belongings.

Instead, Ernest is ankle deep in cold water, which smells strongly of rust from the old pipes. He goes outside to shut off the water to the house, then calls Steve to come take a look. Steve is finishing a job across town, but he says he'll be over right after. Ernest sloshes his way to the pipe, confirms that, yes, it is shot, and, no, there is no easy fix.

While he waits, he hauls a few boxes out of the basement—keepsakes Gretchen left behind that he hasn't thought about in years—and stacks them on the coffee table. There's an entire box full of Beth's baby clothes—tiny shoes and stained onesies and sundresses and blankets. He wonders if Gretchen even knows she kept them. She'd been reluctant to throw anything out, and would probably be considered a hoarder nowadays. There's a box of yellowing photos from one of their few Christmases spent together as a family. The sickly tree, the meager offering of presents beneath it. The photos are water damaged, and Ernest suspects the pipe has been leaking for a long time. One box is nearly empty. This is the one he most wants to rescue.

The bottom of it is sodden and sagging; he has a rough time carrying it up to the living room without its contents falling out. Inside are little gifts Gretchen had given him: a button-down shirt, now stained, and a framed photo of them at a church picnic. Set beside this is a lump wrapped in newspaper. He opens it. Inside is a pink tea set, the lid a little scuffed, but in good overall condition. The pot is printed with flowers and butterflies, curling ivy that spells out "Tea for Two." Two cups, both with flowers adorning their insides. He got this set for Beth's fourth birthday— the last birthday she had before he and Gretchen divorced. He'd seen it in the window of the flower shop downtown and brought it home, gave it to her without even wrapping it. She'd loved it. She sat him down and served him "tea" in it, which was really just warm Kool-Aid, the orange food dye a cloying contrast to the pink porcelain. Gretchen came home in the middle of the tea party.

She'd walked into the house, the kitchen, quietly, as she was apt to do in those days. She was always trying to sneak up on Ernest to catch him cheating on her; she thought if she caught him in the act, she'd have leverage in the divorce. But on this day, she'd only seen Ernest spending time with his daughter. This innocence seemed to make her even madder. She'd said with vinegar in her voice, "Isn't that sweet?" And Beth had been startled so badly she dropped her cup, spilling Kool-Aid on her dress and chipping the saucer. Then she'd started to cry.

All Gretchen said was, "What were you thinking, buying her something so breakable?"

He knows he should throw out all these keepsakes—the clothes, the photos, the tea set. If Linda should come in and find him sitting on the couch holding on to these things, how would that look? Still, he can't bring himself to do it. He packs the items away again and carries the sodden box up to the attic. The tea set he fishes back out, still unsure whether he'll give it to Beth or put it in the trash. He feels very tired. He should sell this house, he knows it. He has no desire to keep up with it anymore; it's been ages since it's been cleaned properly, though Linda has been talking about sprucing the place up, fixing the broken cupboard door, re-grouting the tub, replacing the upstairs toilet seat that scooches sideways when you sit down. She threatens to go through his clothes, too, and bag up the pants that he never wears, the shirts that have holes in them. The woman is out to overhaul his life.

On his way back downstairs, he has to catch himself. His entire body feels wrong. He grips the railing, which is loose, and wonders if it will hold. There's an immense throbbing behind his left eye, and then the room tilts and the tea set goes banging down the stairs, his body slumping after it. He spends some time on the floor at the bottom.

He feels himself expanding, like he could burst out of his skin, out of the house.

He doesn't know how long he's been down, but this is the second time in as many months that he's found himself on the floor. He can't see straight, and realizes his glasses have been knocked off. When he tries reaching for them, his right arm feels weak, tingly. He hears his back door open.

"Ernest? Hello?" It's Steve, tromping through the house with his work boots on. "Shit. You all right?"

Ernest fumbles with his glasses. "Yeah. Just slipped on the damn stairs," he says.

Steve offers him a hand, pulls him up from the ground.

"You don't look right," Steve says. "You sure you're okay?" His eyes seem to focus on Ernest's mouth.

"I banged my head pretty good is all." He gathers the tea set, now cracked. One of the cups is divorced of its handle. The other cup is oddly intact.

Steve leads him into the dining room, drops him into a chair. "You want some ice or something?"

"I'm fine," Ernest says. "Seriously. Fine."

Steve looks him up and down.

"Only, don't tell Linda." It's stupid, and Ernest knows it. His mother died from a stroke when she was younger than he is now. But if Ernest is going out, he's going out quietly. He's had enough women worrying over him in his life, and Linda has certainly been through her share of heartache already.

"Don't tell me what?"

He looks up to find her standing in the doorway to the kitchen, a bag of groceries slung over her shoulder.

"What'd you do to your glasses? They're all crooked."

"Me and Ernest were roughhousing," Steve says, without missing a beat.

"You two are like children," Linda says. She never even thinks to question it, but when Beth enters the kitchen and hears the story, there is a shudder and a whisper from Eliza, who's had plenty of practice being deceived. But Beth doesn't say anything.

She knows better than to call Steve out on a lie. Instead, she keeps an eye on him, lingering by the basement stairs while he fixes the pipe, and showing him to the door afterward. Whatever has actually happened, she doesn't want him to use it as an excuse to linger here. Once he is gone, she turns her attention to her father, watching him for any sign of change, but life in the DeWitt household carries on as usual.

Beth is watching television one night, the first time all week she's had the living room to herself. Whatever happened to her father last week has slowed him down; he's been spending more time sitting on the couch the past few days. But tonight, he is out in the garage, working. Dan is at band practice, and Jeanette is upstairs doing her homework. Beth flips through the channels, not really paying attention, until a news story catches her. Gilmer Thurber and his sister went on trial today. The screen shows a house, the Thurber house, sitting dark and empty in the October gloom. The shot switches to a reporter outside the county courthouse. In the background, Gilmer is led inside in handcuffs.

Seeing him again causes Beth's brain to grow fur. She grips the remote so tight it creaks. Too many memories crow at her; she shoves them down into the well with Eliza. Let her sort them out.

She changes the channel, but all of the local stations are covering this story. She turns the television off and sits in silence. The news is nothing but violence and depravity these days. She tries to remember a time when it was different, when the world was less messed up, but she can't. She just wants to sit in silence and not think. But she can't sit in silence; upstairs, she hears Linda talking, a low buzz that vibrates the ceiling. Jeanette laughs, and before Beth can think about it, she's on her way up the stairs. She finds Jeanette and Linda in the master bedroom, Linda's bedroom, bent before the old mahogany vanity. They each have an eyeliner pencil in one hand, an index finger pulling down their lower eyelid. Beth watches her daughter watching Linda apply makeup. Linda's hair is curled, thick from prenatal vitamins. She's having trouble seeing the mirror, careful not to lean her bump of a belly against the vanity. Jeanette runs the pencil along her own eyelid, her eyes flicking back and forth between her reflection and Linda's.

"Give that to me," Beth says, startling Jeanette so badly she pokes her eye with the pencil, tearing up. When Beth takes the eyeliner from her, she realizes she's still holding the TV remote.

"I was just trying it out," Jeanette says simply.

"You can wear makeup when you're in high school," Beth says.

"What, are you going to cut my eyelashes off, too?"

"Go to your room," Beth says. "And hand over your cellphone." As Jeanette slaps her phone into her mother's hand and huffs past, Beth says, "I don't want to hear your stereo, either." Beth waits for her door to slam, but of course it doesn't. Jeanette is too reserved for that.

"Leave my daughter alone," Beth says.

"She's been left alone plenty."

"You sure have all the answers, don't you?"

"Your daughter is lonely, Beth. I was just trying to cheer her up."

"Jeanette has lots of friends," Beth says, but the look Linda gives says she knows it's a lie as much as Beth does.

"She *had* friends," Linda says, "back in Charlotte. She feels isolated here. And she hates what you did to her hair."

Beth can't help but wonder how much time Linda has been spending with Jeanette. More than grocery shopping, it seems.

"Her hair is none of your business," Beth says.

"And her history teacher, Mrs. Schwartz, has been giving her a hard time again."

"We don't need you here," Beth says. "You can go back to your family."

"Ernest invited me to move in here. If anyone leaves, it should be you."

The TV on the nightstand turns on. Beth looks at her fist, still clenched around the remote. The same news story is playing, although on a different station. They show Gilmer and his sister being led out of the courthouse. A shot of their home, stock footage from last spring: a little blue box of a house, green trim, gingerbread up by the roof painted pink. Beth remembers him inside this house. Inside the laundry room. Staring at his belly, too close to her face.

Beth needs to sit down.

Linda pales. She's rubbing her belly down low, holding on to it like it might fall off her. "Stuff like this just doesn't happen in River Bend," she says.

And Beth really looks at her now. Linda's only seven years Beth's junior, but she seems a lot younger. Her face is untroubled, even as her eyes fill with tears. Beth remembers Linda as a child, out on her family's farm, remembers Linda on crutches, her foot in a cast because her horse had thrown her. Her hands and neck were always torn up with corn rash during the fall harvest. Beth almost wants to protect her, until she reminds herself that Linda is the enemy.

"Get your head out of your ass," Beth says.

"Excuse me?"

"This kind of thing happens all the time. No, I'm not buying it, your naive act. You know damn well how this town works. And it's people like you, people who turn a blind eye. You make me sick, all of you."

"The fuck's your problem?" Linda gets up to leave, but Beth blocks the door.

"No, you're going to listen to me. You need to stay away from my daughter. Go back to your own family. Such as it is." Beth can hear herself, can hear her voice getting higher, louder. From the dark well in her mind, Eliza yells at her, tells her to stop, that she's being cruel, but Beth won't listen.

"You think just because you opened your legs, you're a part of this family? I know you. I know where you come from, *what* you come from. Stay away from my daughter."

"Mom," Dan calls up the stairs. His voice sounds so distant, small enough to brush away.

"You don't believe that," Eliza says, splashing her arms and legs, making waves. "You're being nasty."

"Shut up. Will you just shut up a second?" Beth says.

"I didn't say anything," Linda says, her face pinched in grief.

"You think you can just sit on your ass here, that because you're having a baby we'll take care of you? We'll pay for your fancy coffee? And that's another thing. You know you're not supposed to have caffeine, right? You're not even growing a baby right. You're a mess."

"I'm a mess? Your own children can't stand to be in the same room with you."

"She's right, you know," Eliza says.

"Oh, hell no," Beth says.

"There's like this cloud of funk that follows you around," Linda says. "You can smell it."

"I'm not above smacking a pregnant woman."

"Mom," Dan calls again. His voice sounds urgent now. When

he appears in the doorway, he looks so small, so young. "Grand-dad fell."

Linda is out of the room and down the stairs in half the time it takes Beth to turn inward to Eliza and ask her to take this one. But Eliza only splashes harder. "I thought you didn't need me."

In the dining room, Beth finds the scene she doesn't want to face: Dan kneeling by his granddad, trying to shake him awake, Linda staring with a hand over her open mouth, and Ernest on the floor, not crumpled like Beth had imagined, but sprawled on his side like a child in sleep, one arm pinned under him. If it weren't for his quick shallow breathing, and his glasses crushed beneath his face, Beth could have told herself he was sleeping.

The third stroke leaves Ernest DeWitt speechless, vacant, hobbled, unable to go to the bathroom on his own. He can't get out of bed without assistance. If Linda has had an easy life, that's done for now.

Beth looks into a hospice facility but can't afford it. Instead, they rent a hospital bed and set it up in the dining room. A nurse comes and hooks Ernest to IVs. Nurses visit twice a day to administer his meds, monitor his vitals. Linda is at first reluctant to help, at least with the messier jobs. She'll feed him, bathe him, brush his hair, help him walk from one room to the next, but she doesn't want to change him when he's soiled himself. She can't go there, can't fully move her heart into the role of caregiver. This she leaves to Beth.

Today, Beth bathes Ernest, changes his clothes, and brings him out to a rocking chair she's gotten for the back porch. If she doesn't think of him as her father, she finds that she doesn't mind too terribly that she has to care for him, has to step into the role of mother or nurse. Her own children's infancies had been the moments of motherhood in which she felt most comfortable. Those years in which her children's lives were entirely hers. There was no reason to believe they had thoughts or experiences beyond their small worlds: the nursery with its blue bunny wallpaper, the kitchen, the shady sparse grass of the backyard, the car, the stroller. There was no way yet for her to have screwed them up too badly.

Ernest was like that now, his blue eyes showing no signs that he knew Beth, that there were irrevocable moments between them. Yet he is her father, and how weird to be changing his diapers. She wonders how often he changed hers, and how often he left it up to her mother. In her mind, Beth has an estimate and is keeping a tally, a kind of score, who has been better to whom. Beth feels like she's winning. And she holds on to this tally, because to address the way she really feels—the devastating knowledge she's never had a real relationship with her father, and now she never will—to look this grief in the eye would surely break her.

For the times Beth is at work, Linda calls her stepbrother, Derek, and Derek comes immediately, changing his schedule to work nights at the hospital. The first time Beth meets him, she thinks, *This poor fool's in love with Linda. He'd do anything for her, and she'd let him do it.*

After the third time, Beth tells Linda, "You need to let Derek be," and to her great surprise, Linda doesn't argue. Derek goes back to working days, and Linda takes over Ernest's care. Beth tells herself it's good practice for when the baby comes in six months, but she knows it's different. She can see it in Linda's eyes. Linda now walks around the house in a daze, her eyes set a hundred feet ahead of her.

When Beth is home, Linda uses the time to get out of the house, to go bother her silly sucker of a stepbrother at his own house. Good riddance, Beth thinks.

She, too, turns outside of herself for comfort. Her chosen diversion is Steve, and she grows reckless in her need. She calls him at home, talks to his kids like she's a telemarketer. She drives by his house to see if his truck is parked outside. Eliza shakes her head, but Beth ignores her.

When they leave the motel room, Steve always goes out before her, and she usually waits for his truck to clear the parking lot before she exits, but not tonight. Tonight, she walks out at the same time, hugging herself against the early November chill.

"I know it was you who called my landline the other night. What happened to being careful?" he asks.

"Fuck it," she says.

"Someone will see us," he says, and while his voice is even, his eyes hold the warning of real anger.

"Nobody's here," Beth says.

"I'm here," Paula says. She's such a tiny woman, neither Beth nor Steve noticed her in the doorway to the room next door. "Then again, I've seen you two coming and going from here all month. You've never been discreet."

Steve stops on the sidewalk. He towers over Paula, but the woman doesn't flinch. For the first time, Beth realizes how imposing Steve is, how threatening. She's never seen this before. When she was younger, when she and Steve were first together, she'd thought him quite dashing, romantic even, when he held doors for her, when he wrote her love letters in French. Only recently has she begun to see him clearly. Steve the redneck. Steve the drunk. Just another violent Brody. The magic was all in her head; Steve is a man incapable of magic.

THE HOUSE OF DEEP WATER

"What do you want to keep your mouth shut?" Steve says. He's seen Paula skulking around the bar lately, no doubt looking for Jared. He knows his wife's sister-in-law well enough to know there's a price, and it isn't likely to be monetary.

"You sure Deb doesn't already know?"

Beth watches Steve's eyes, those round hamster eyes, grow even wider. How had she never noticed it before, that rodent quality to him? She used to think he was smart, because that's how he thought of himself. But he isn't, not exceptionally so. Or at least, he isn't anymore. Perhaps he never was, or perhaps alcohol has taken his brain down a few pegs. Either way, she realizes it had never before occurred to him that he might get caught.

And how arrogant! She supposes he thought himself safe before, too, decades ago when he was cheating on her. His arrogance makes her want to carry on until they *are* caught; she wants to ruin him, even if she has to ruin herself in the process.

"Of course she doesn't know," Beth says, "or I'd have heard from her."

Paula appraises Steve. She doesn't even look at Beth. She sees more than enough of the woman at work.

"I want a divorce," she says. "Talk to Jared. Convince him. It's more than time he moved on."

"You yeasty little asshole," Beth says. "You're blackmailing us?" Part of Beth panics, lashes out, but part of her welcomes this interloper. Let her run to Deb, let her tell on them. Burn it all down.

"Beth," Steve warns.

"Yes, control your woman," Paula says.

"I'll do it," Steve says.

Paula nods, and without a glance at either of them, goes back in her room.

. . .

November settles in with pewter gray skies and brown leaves shushed on the ground. When the oak tree in the front yard is bare, its branches a tangle of black against the sky, Beth feels herself settling in for the winter, her body heavy and slow. Ernest sits on the back porch, watching everything and nothing. It's been almost two weeks since his stroke, and the family has settled into a new normal, a rhythm revolving around his care. Beth is keeping an eye on him while raking leaves into waist-high piles when Steve's truck pulls through the alley. Dan is in the passenger's seat.

"I thought you were at band rehearsal," Beth says when Dan gets out, lugging his backpack.

"He came home with my daughter," Steve says. He shuts off the truck, hops out, and walks toward Beth.

"Thanks for the ride," Dan says. He already has his phone out and is texting on his way into the house.

"Yes, thank you," Beth says to Steve. "You can go now." She won't look at him. She hasn't seen him since they ran into Paula at the motel three days ago, and she's weak with wanting, dizzy as she wrestles leaves into a bag. Most of them end up back on the ground at her feet.

"I'm sorry to hear about your father," Steve says. "Why didn't you tell me?"

She looks over at Ernest. She knows she should dismiss Steve again, but she's too tired. She wants nothing more than to let Eliza take over. In her twenties, it took everything she had to pull herself up and out of his life, to leave him alone with Deb. She doesn't have it in her to do it again. He takes the rake from her, lets her hold the bag. When he bends down to scoop leaves, she notices his sunburnt skin.

"I always knew you were a redneck," she says, touching him there. In a moment of panic, she checks on Ernest again, who still hasn't moved.

"You're going to do this here, in front of Father?" Eliza says.

Steve straightens, his face serious, and he kisses Beth gently, so gently, and Eliza whispers to Beth, "This is your fault, all your fault."

Elizabeth DeWitt

18

I have a secret boyfriend. Steve and I meet in an empty field behind my apartment, out of sight of my mom's bedroom window. When I get there, he's already sitting in the grass, his back against the fence. We've been meeting every night for a week, like something from a romance novel. Now, sleep deprived, I worry he's a fiction I've created. He turns to look at me, his features redefined by a moon bright enough to cast shadows. I touch his face to prove he's really there. My hand, dark, so close to his skin.

He's the only boy who has ever loved me, the only boy, I'm sure, who will ever love me. I'm dark and I'm sullied, but Steve takes my hand and kisses it.

We watch the moon roll across the sky. Eventually, he gets up and brushes the grass from his jeans. He wants to get home before the world wakes up, but I grab his hand, pull him back down.

"Let them wake up," I say. "Let them know you've been in a field all night."

He sits down with me for a few more minutes.

SETTLING

1998

S teve tried to steady his hand to shave. He didn't know why he was so nervous—maybe because he had a soft spot for Deb? She'd always reminded him of a small wounded animal. Like the baby bird he'd seen hit by a car, its head split open like a ripe tomato, or the raccoon his dad shot in the barn, not quite killing it. His dad couldn't be bothered to put another bullet in the poor thing. Steve tried to nurse the raccoon back to health. When he failed, he made himself end its suffering.

He kept nicking himself as he shaved, had to blot his face with toilet paper. By the time he left the house, he was already ten minutes late. He stepped outside to a cold, bright Thanksgiving morning. The night before saw the first snow of the season. Just a dusting, but the world was new and white, and when he pulled up at the Williamses' farm—the crumbling barn, the broken tractor parked off in the field, the horses whinnying in the paddock, the scrawny chickens pecking at dried corn sprinkled on the snow—he almost lost his nerve. He'd dropped Deb off here dozens of times, but he'd never been invited in to meet her family, not until today. He loved Deb, he really did. He was excited about the child growing inside her. Part of him wanted to step up, to be the man of this farm, to help make the repairs that required a little brawn.

The other part of him frantically needed to be with Beth.

He wouldn't see Beth today. She was up in Kalamazoo at school and wouldn't come home for Thanksgiving this year. She was fighting with her mother. He was to spend the entire day with Deb's cobbled-together family—her mother, who didn't approve of him and made no bones about it; her brother, Jared; his wife, Paula; and their collected kids. He and Deb hung out a lot with Jared and Paula, who were both a few years older. Steve always felt like he had to catch up with them. Jared was good people, chill, quiet, loved fishing as much as Steve did. Paula, though. He didn't trust her. When she looked at him, he had the unsettling feeling she saw right through him.

He took a deep breath before getting out of the car. To be honest, he didn't feel like he belonged here, in this family, on this farm. He'd been thinking about breaking up with Deb for about a year now, and Beth had decided today was the day. He knew it was what Deb's family expected of him. But he didn't like doing what was expected. Plus, there was the baby. So when Deb invited him to spend Thanksgiving with her family, he accepted.

Deb. She stepped outside, wearing a pink sundress and old work boots, a pale green cardigan thrown around her shoulders. His heart broke. She looked so skinny; even though she was six months pregnant, she wasn't showing much in that dress. Her legs were pale, with little goose bumps on them. He wanted to take her into his arms and kiss the warmth back into her. And what if he did it; what if he stepped inside that house with her and never left?

"My family's waiting," she said when he pulled her to him. She seemed a little standoffish. Had she been talking to Paula again?

"Am I late?" he asked, knowing full well he was.

"A little," she said on their way up the front steps. "You didn't bring a dish?"

It hadn't even occurred to him that he should. He kicked himself. He was surprised to realize he didn't want her family to think badly of him.

Inside the air was steamy with competing smells: cooked turkey and potatoes and cranberries and green bean casserole with those canned onion rings on top. Beneath that was a lingering scent of dogs and horses, a house that hadn't been cleaned in a while. When Deb's father died last March, her mother, Dinah, broke down. Steve had been planning on ending things with Deb then, but he stuck around to help her through her grief. Then she got pregnant again. And decided to keep it.

Dinah plodded about the kitchen, with Paula orbiting around her.

"I'll take a look at that tractor after dinner," Paula was saying.

"That thing is on its last legs," Dinah said. She wasn't even fifty yet, but she'd aged so much in the past few months she seemed seventy. She started hefting the turkey from the oven, and Steve worried she might throw out her back.

"Let me," he said, stepping in. He took the oven mitts from her and pulled the turkey out, its brown breast meat crackling hot, stuffing spilling lewdly from its nethers. He hated stuffing. It was always so mushy. He set the bird on the stove top while Dinah got a platter.

Paula skirted around him with an armful of water glasses.

"We were starting to wonder whether you'd chickened out." She was a tiny woman, with soft shoulder-length blond hair too girly for the way she dressed—mostly overalls or cargo jeans. When she came back into the kitchen, she helped him move the turkey to the platter.

"Don't stand there with your teeth in your mouth," she said as soon as the bird was in place. "You can help set the table."

That was another thing. If he stayed with Deb, he would have to put up with Paula. The woman was always so bossy, and frankly, it was wearing on him. He wondered what Beth was doing today. He imagined her in her dorm room, the window cracked because the heat was always too high in her building. She might be at her computer, typing up a research paper, or maybe she was reading a book in bed. He'd had plans of going to college himself, but he never managed to save enough money. Two years ago he'd gotten close, but that was when Deb got pregnant the first time, and he'd paid to take care of the situation.

In Beth, Steve placed all of his fantasies of life beyond River Bend. He imagined them at school together, maybe sitting in the same lecture hall or walking together under the fall leaves. Right now, starting a new job, he barely had time to visit her, let alone go to school himself. He figured she was a stronger person than he was. She'd gotten out of River Bend by her sheer force of will.

He hoped if he held on to her, some of her strength would rub off on him.

Dinah made them say grace. The entire time, Deb held his hand under the table. She wouldn't let go, not even when they started passing dishes. He found it difficult to eat with only one hand. Farther down the table, Deb's niece Linda eyed him. She seemed to be cataloging his body language. At twelve, the girl was a little strange, but then, in his experience, horse-crazy girls generally were. Linda and her sister, Paige, weren't actually related to Deb by blood; they were Paula's girls from her first marriage. Still, they were always around the farm. Jared's eleven-year-old son, Derek—also a little weird; Steve suspected the boy didn't bat for the right team—was Deb's actual relation. The boy watched his stepsister Linda like he was studying how to be a woman himself. Paige was the only normal kid of the lot, a sweet girl of ten, her hair still in pigtails.

Steve did the math and realized Paula would have had Linda when she was sixteen—three years younger than Deb. She was doing just fine. Jared would have had Derek at seventeen. It gave Steve hope. And for a moment, Steve really could picture it: him and Deb with their own farm, a big pretty house. Maybe they would raise goats. They'd have a few babies, and sell cheese, and sit by the fireplace in the evenings.

Sometimes he envied Jared: While Paula was bossy, she wasn't the kind of woman who needed constant affection for reassurance. Steve watched them together, and he thought, *If that's marriage, I could do it.* Their relationship was so different from anything he'd ever witnessed. His parents were certainly no role models; his dad's anger would rear up and spring on whomever was closest, Steve or his mother, it didn't seem to matter which. His mom ran around on his dad. But Jared and Paula were solid. They were a riot at the bar, hustling out-of-towners at pool, buying all the locals a round when they won big. He wanted what they had, but when he imagined getting married, he usually imagined marrying Beth. He knew his parents would forbid it, or at least his dad would. His dad didn't approve of him dating a colored.

"Which dish did you bring?" Paula asked. Steve felt himself go red. She'd seen him walk in empty-handed. He'd never been invited to anyone's house for dinner before, at least not as an adult; he hadn't realized he was supposed to bring something.

Under the table, Deb gave his hand a squeeze, but she didn't argue with her sister-in-law. He wished she would. Not that he needed her to defend him, but it would have been nice.

"What'd *you* bring?" Steve demanded.

Paula nodded to the table. "The sweet potatoes. And the rolls," she said. "And beer."

"It's fine," Jared said, putting a hand on Paula's shoulder. "There's plenty of food."

Jared was a man of few words, and that he would use some of them to defend Steve was touching. What a stand-up guy.

"Is it fine, though?" Paula said. She turned to Steve. "Because it'd be nice to know that you're going to provide for Deb, in her condition."

Dinah watched with interest, her hands folded in her lap. Paige's head ping-ponged between her mother and Steve. The way Paige watched him now, pushing her food around her plate and not eating, so interested in the conversation and yet so quiet, made him feel a little queasy. He was wrong. The girl was just as weird as her sister and stepbrother.

"Of course I'm going to provide," Steve said. He took a drink of his beer to try to cool the heat in his face.

"Really?" Paula said. "You got a job yet?"

"Steve works at the tool and die now," Deb said.

"That's a start," Paula said. "How is it? You like it enough to not mess this one up?"

Sometimes when people came at him like this, Steve felt the impulse to strike them. He wouldn't do it, though. He wouldn't go there. Instead, he stared at his plate, at the food that he didn't help make, at the beer he didn't buy.

"He starts on Monday," Deb said.

"Ah," Paula said. "Well, here's hoping you can at least stick it out a few months." She raised her beer bottle.

"That's enough," Dinah said. "I'm sure Steve's doing his best."

His best. He wasn't doing his best, and he knew it. But they didn't know it. They seemed to think this life was all he was capable of.

How could he have admired Jared and Paula? The woman was mouthy and moody and manly. Her kids were weird, the way they watched him. It occurred to him for the first time that Linda, who kept sneaking looks at him while she pretended to study her plate, had a little crush on him. If only her mother felt the same way, he could use it to his advantage. He wanted so badly to shut Paula up.

And before he could stop himself, he heard himself say, "I actually came today to ask Dinah's blessing." *Shit.* Now, why did he have to go and do that?

Silence at the table. Nobody ate. Nobody drank. Even Paige stopped pushing her food around. Deb squeezed Steve's hand so tight. He looked over, and there were tears in her eyes. He hoped to God they were happy tears.

"My blessing," Dinah said at last. "For what?"

"I want to marry Deb," Steve said. *Shit, shit.*

"And is that what you want, Deb?" Dinah said. She stared at

Deb like she was trying to read her daughter's mind, and Deb responded by going scarlet.

After a time, Deb looked up at Steve. The tears rushed down her cheeks. "Of course," Deb said.

"Then you don't need my blessing," Dinah said.

After dinner, after Steve hugged Dinah goodbye and kissed Deb good night, when he pulled into his driveway, he felt bereft. In just a few hours' time, he'd begun to feel like he was a part of the Williams family. Nobody had really welcomed him, but Dinah hadn't protested his intention to marry Deb, and wasn't that a start? Now, walking into his house, the place seemed so small and cramped, cold and dingy. Tonight hadn't gone at all as planned, and maybe that was okay. He could begin to see himself settling down with her someday. He could see the farm, the goats. Maybe they'd have four children, three boys and a girl, to share the chores.

He would have to think hard on how to proceed, but his reverie was cut short when he turned on his computer and signed into ICQ. There was Beth, asking how it went, whether he'd done it. He was in the process of writing a response—something delicate, to let her know there'd been a snag, but nothing he couldn't work out—when another message came in, this one from Sandra.

Sandra. His own secret refuge. Sandra, with her long legs and floral-patterned bodysuits. Sandra and her weed. Her brother grew it out back in the cornfield. She was only sixteen, but she seemed so much older. She was always teaching Steve things, like how to smoke from a bong, how to shoplift without getting caught. How to screw. Like, really screw.

She would have to be dealt with, too, just like Deb. But not tonight. Tonight, he was lonely, and Sandra was angry at her family after her Thanksgiving. She wanted to talk to someone. She needed comforting.

Steve remembered Deb as he'd pulled away from the farm, her white legs in the moonlight. Her long red hair. Her sweetness when they kissed good night. Ah, but Sandra. He typed his reply: *On my way.*

Elizabeth DeWitt
19

On more than one occasion, my roommate wakes me up in the middle of the night to ask if I'm okay.

"Whatthefuck does it look like?" I say. "I was sleeping fine."

"No, you weren't. You were screaming."

TAKING STOCK

Paula can't get her husband's attention. Since she got back into town more than two months ago, she's been leaving him messages, which he ignores, and stopping by his house, though he's never there. Today, she called Linda, who hasn't heard from her dad in days. He's been making himself awful scarce; she has no choice but to ambush him at their hardware store.

"You're a hard man to pin down," she tells him at the counter of Williams Hardware. They both still have the name in common, and joint ownership.

"I could say the same of you."

"You look good," she says. He stands behind the register, pulling on his beard while going through the inventory sheet. On a Friday afternoon in the middle of November, business is slow. No major home renovations are under way in River Bend; the only customers are those buying leaf rakes or turkey fryers. Store traffic is plodding, predictable, just the way Jared Williams likes it.

"I heard you were in town," he says. "I figured you'd up and left again."

A lie, of course, since she's left him messages daily.

"I suppose you know about Linda by now," she says.

"That she's pregnant? 'Course I know."

"That's what I wanted to talk to you about."

He eyes her suspiciously. He has every right.

"I'm going to level with you, Paula." He sets down his inventory sheet but stays behind the counter. The register, the glass display of pocketknives, the lighters and waterproof wallets, are all effective barriers. "I know you're getting remarried. I know you're here for a divorce."

"Christ," she says. "This town."

"What's the town got to do with anything?"

"I'm not even sure I'm getting married, but River Bend has it as gospel."

He nods at her left hand, resting on the counter, and the diamond that blazes on her finger. "So you're not here for a divorce?"

She takes stock of the store, the aisles of goods. Back when they ran this place together, she'd never been able to find anything. She couldn't get the hang of Jared's sense of organization. The cast-iron skillets are in an aisle with faucets and cabinet knobs and coffeepots. Now, why wouldn't they be shelved with the camping gear?

"That, too," she says. "After all this time, you had to know it was coming."

She's never sure how to read him. His face is always hard to gauge through his beard, but he also has a way of holding himself very still, perfectly erect, and he refuses to slump even now. He keeps the emotion out of his voice when he speaks.

"I'll buy you out of your half of the store," he says.

"Actually, that's what I wanted to talk about." She runs her hand along the counter. The knives in the display case look chintzy. They aren't the fine blades you'd find on display in a store in Moab, knives made to appeal to hipster vacationers—overpriced, with handles of bone or wood or marble. These knives are cheap, and they look cheap. Their handles are made of plastic, their blades so thick, it would be hard to get an edge and nearly impossible to keep it.

"I'd like to give my half of the store to Linda," Paula says.

"What?"

"She could use a little extra income."

"What about Paige?" he says, his fingers in his beard.

"What about her?"

"You don't think she could use the extra income?"

"Linda's going to be a mother."

"Paige already is a mother."

Paula rolls her eyes. Knowing Paige, she's more of a burden on her wife than she is a real partner, but who can tell?

"And Ma says things are shaky in that girl's marriage. A little extra money couldn't hurt."

"Fine, then. I'll split my half between the two of them."

"What makes you think there's enough income for three people?"

Everything in the store looks cheap now. The cast-iron skillets are rough, the Coleman lanterns rusty, the ice scrapers have blades that would snap at the first real cold, the screws and bolts and lug nuts all in their bins seem likely to strip. Even the display of tools—basic household sets of screwdrivers, hammers, wrenches, drills—look cheap.

"You said you were going to buy me out."

"I can't afford to lose half of what this store makes."

"Why not? You live with your mom."

"Yes," he says, removing his glasses and rubbing his eyes. "And you saddled me with our daughter, plus your daughters."

"You want me to take Skyla back with me?"

"That a threat?"

"She's not real keen on this town."

"You're not getting my daughter." His arms go rigid, and he grips the counter as if for support. It's satisfying, his shift in posture.

"What can we do to help Linda, then?"

"Linda's a big girl."

Paula crosses her arms like a man would, both hands tucked into the armpits. "You really think she'd have been better off with me around?"

"Girls need their mother."

"You can't say we were happy."

"Who is?" He replaces his glasses, and his eyes look small.

"We fought all the time."

"Don't pretend you left for them."

"I want to help."

"Yeah, get it done quick so you can take off again? Is that about the size of it?"

"Two months is hardly quick," Paula says.

"Two months out of the years you lost with your daughters," he says.

"Fuck you," Paula says.

The store grows emptier the longer they argue. Men in River Bend don't want to have anything to do with other people's affairs. If they had been arguing in the flower shop, there would have been women crowding near. It's true, though; part of Paula can't wait to leave. Her job has called to say they've hired her replacement. Jorge has been asking when she'll be home. He even "offered" to come to Michigan to "help out." Maybe it is time Paula left. She could send Linda money to help with the baby.

"You don't need to worry," Jared says. "I'll take care of things."

And because Paula is out of arguments, and because she never could sustain a fight with her husband, she leaves the store.

She shows up at his house that evening. Of course he isn't home, but her idea is to wait him out. The man has to sleep sometime.

"He doesn't always come home," Dinah says.

"What do you mean?" Paula says. It doesn't seem likely that Jared has taken up with another woman. He was never what Paula would call amorous, even when they were first married. On the outside, he projects the River Bend masculine ideal—the beard, the sloppy clothes, the handiness, the hunter's prowess—but Paula has always secretly wondered whether he couldn't be diagnosed with low testosterone.

Dinah doesn't answer, just raises her brows and looks at Paula sideways.

"What? He drinks himself stupid and falls asleep on the lawn?"

"That was always more your game," Dinah says.

Paula won't give up, though. Not this time. She knows she needs to move on, to let him move on. And, too, she needs to do this for Jorge, who has been so patient. She's been gone over two months, half expects ultimatums, but even though he calls her every day, he hasn't pushed her on this. Maybe a little distance has been good for them. But she also carries a suspicion that if she tries her luck, he'll get over her. No, she needs to settle this business and get on home, back to her own life.

And that is how she finds herself in the Hudson House bar on a Friday night, drinking a Coke, waiting for Jared. Even though it's well into November, the bar is still decorated for Halloween, with cardboard cutouts of jack-o'-lanterns and black cats dangling from the ceiling. Orange garland drapes along the bar, and she recognizes it from her own hardware store. It's the cheap kind that sheds like Lola does every spring, sheds so much that when she leans against the bar to get a refill on her Coke, she ends up with orange plastic shreds clinging to her clothes. A plastic pumpkin sits full at one end of the bar, and when Paula takes a rock-hard Tootsie Roll, she sees that the pumpkin isn't, in fact, full of candy. There's newspaper underneath, with candy laid on top.

"That's not for eating," Slick says. Paula puts the candy back.

"Another shot, Slick," Steve says. When he notices Paula sitting there, his first instinct is to duck out of sight. "Shit," he says.

"I take it you haven't talked to him?"

"I've been meaning to."

"We had a deal," Paula says, staring him down.

Slick pours a shot, but Steve has forgotten it. "Four dollars," Slick says, as if Steve needs reminding, as if Steve hasn't drunk thousands of dollars away in four-dollar shots at this bar.

"Can I buy you a drink?" Steve asks Paula, and she waves him off. Back when she lived here, when she, Jared, Steve, and Deb went out most weekends, she hadn't noticed how inarticulate Steve was. Maybe he wasn't back then, or maybe she was just too drunk to notice. But now, the man slurs something horrible, looping one word into the next. She wants to pat him on the shoulder, tell him it's going to be okay, even though it's not true. Nothing in this town is okay. For God's sake, she works *here*, where Gilmer Thurber used to work. She doesn't understand how the town is going about its normal business, when that man is on trial for the terrible things he did. If Thurber had hurt one of her family, she would be the one on trial today, because she would have murdered him.

"I was thinking about leaving," she says. It's bad enough she has to work here; she doesn't want to spend her free time in this pit.

"Naw, stay. You're here to see Jared, right? He'll be here."

So she plays pool with Steve instead. Even though he's sloppy drunk, he can still handle a pool cue, probably from muscle memory, the same way he fixes people's plumbing. The man could never get another job because he's never sober long enough to learn a new trade. He gives her a run at pool, though, until she whups his ass.

When Jared finally arrives, she spots him in the doorway, and he turns to leave. She calls after him, but he pretends not to hear her. So she chases him out.

"There's still the matter of the divorce," she says. Lake-effect snow floats down in great wet clumps that melt as soon as they hit the pavement. Cars shush by down Main Street. Paula left her coat inside, and shivers in a tee shirt and tennis shoes. She didn't bring snow boots with her to Michigan. She never intended to stay this long.

"Sure," Jared says, and gives his beard a tug. "Why not?"

"We could go down to the courthouse tomorrow."

"I want the store, though."

"Done."

He watches the progression of cars, of red and white taillights down the highway. She half expects him to turn, to pull her into his arms, to ask her not to leave, not this time. To tell her he still loves her. She's never before wanted a public display, would have abhorred the thought under any other circumstance, but to have Jared break down, just once, to have him profess his love—if he had done it, she doubts she could walk away.

But he doesn't do it. He looks defeated, his shoulders slumped. They stand there, side by side, and watch the snow coming down until it sticks to the grass. They let their hair get wet. They let their fingertips and noses go numb. And in the morning, they both show up at the courthouse at ten o'clock to sign the papers. Their assets will go to him. Their debt, what little is left, will be divided equally. There will be a two-month waiting period, and then they will be done with each other.

"One more thing," she says as they leave the courthouse. Jared turns to her, his face unreadable. He won't look her in the eyes. "Tell Deb to keep an eye on Steve. That man is not to be trusted."

Elizabeth DeWitt

20

After breaking up with Steve, I'm lost. What to do with myself without that relationship to maintain? Because I still want love, even if I don't deserve it. I want it to find me in spite of myself, to come barreling into my life and bowl me over.

I set up a dating profile. My name is now Loves2Laff.

The profile reveals just enough. My age, my hobbies, that I work as a line cook. A picture of me in makeup and a sunhat and a tight tee shirt. But these men see through the picture, the name, into the damage inside me. It draws them to me like flies to dead flesh.

They ask for my measurements. They ask for a full-body picture. They ask if I shave my pubic hair. They ask me to shave. They ask what I like to drink. They ask my dating history. They ask how many sexual partners. They ask me how tall. They ask my panty size. None of them ask my real name.

They tell me they want to take me to the hot tubs. They tell me they want to eat my cooking. They tell me they want to take me for drinks.

They tell me I remind them of someone. They tell me they want to eat my pussy. They tell me what trucks they drive. They tell me they love my lips, I have nice lips, my lips are big and soft and firm and snug. They tell me they want my number. They tell me they want to take me out. They tell me they want to lick my ass. They tell me I will love it. They tell me my picture looks sad, that they can make me smile for real. They tell me I look familiar. They ask my cup size; they tell me they've always wanted to date a D. They tell me they've never dated a black girl. They tell me about med school, about fire academy training, about working construction, about their grad programs. They tell me I look nice, I look fun, I look sexy, I look cute, I look shy, I look like a daddy's girl, I look light, and when I give them my number, they don't call, and when I ask them why, they don't message me, and when I ask again, they block me or they say I'm pushy, they say, Bitch, what's your damage? *They say they want a girl who is whiter or darker or taller or thinner or thicker, who wears more makeup, who wears less makeup, who knows how to have a good time, who has a better education, a better job, who drives a better car, who shares their interests, who has a daddy, who dresses better, who can hold a conversation, who can hold their gaze, who can hold herself together.*

THE LEAVING BEHIND

1998

You didn't have gas money, and I was working two jobs that summer, the deli and the bakery, saving what little I made for college. We walked around town on weekends, past the tool and die shop, through the warming grass of the cemetery, down the streets that crossed at irregular angles radiating from the river. I didn't have the guts to make the first move, because who would want me? Who would want this body and this hair? Deb had slender hips like a boy's. She had long red hair. Fair skin like a speckled egg. I'd seen you kiss her freckles, slowly, like you didn't want to miss one. You said you didn't love her, that you were waiting for the right time to leave, and I wanted to believe you. I didn't want to know you weren't mine.

At the park, we sat on the swings, our feet scuffing in the dirt, raising dust clouds that made me sneeze. When my hips were sore from sitting on a swing meant for a child, I ran to the merry-go-round. You took a wide stance, put your back into it and spun me, and the rusted merry-go-round whined and creaked. I watched you slip by, then the street, the swings, the slide. Sunlight through dark branches, bright green leaves, a kaleidoscope of foliage inter-lacing, orbiting a small pool of naked sky. You spun me around and around, the cars driving vertical on the street, the slide swinging sideways, the trees circling in the spring breeze, and when I couldn't stand it anymore, when my vision was looped, the park in retrograde, you stopped the merry-go-round. Steadied me from falling. And you kissed me.

Your mom came to stay with you a few days while your dad was drying out and cooling off. You asked me not to visit while she was there.

"I want to visit," I said. "I want to meet her."

"That's probably not the best idea."

She must have been bored, or wanted to make herself useful, because the next time I came over, your house was the cleanest I'd ever seen it. The windows had been opened, the cigarette smoke replaced with sunshine. Your counter, swept of crumbs. The hard-water stain, gone from your bathtub. The grout of your kitchen floor, bleached to the color of butter.

You were no good for me, my mother said. You would keep me from living my life. She had us sit outside on the balcony of her second-floor apartment, with the sliding-glass door shut, so I could break the news.

"Just like that?" you said. "You're going to let her wreck it, just like that?"

I tried to hold your hand, but you pulled away, rubbed your wrist as if I'd hurt you. Then you showed me the inch-long scar; you said that after you graduated high school, after you lost your job at the grocery store, you'd slit your wrists. How bad must the cut have been to still be such a vivid pink four years later? I wanted to hold you, to comfort you, but you said it wasn't my problem. So I watched you walk away, and made up my mind that this wasn't actually over.

We made a standing date, hanging out at the bluffs or in the abandoned River Bend Casket Company, or meeting at the movie theater. Once, when you arrived before me, you bought tickets and stood waiting outside. You'd brought me a bunch of gladioluses, and stood with them tucked in the crook of your arm. Your eyes were serious when you handed me the flowers, as if you were passing a fragile bundle. They seemed heavy in your hands. After the movie, we didn't want to leave, and so we sat in your car in the parking lot, the flowers wilting in my lap. We watched the rise and fall of the moon. I must have dozed off. In the darkness, you stirred. You wanted to get home, shower before heading to work at the creamery. I wanted you to stay just a little longer. In less than an hour, I knew, Deb would be waking up. Her mother had kicked her out again, and you told me you were letting her stay with you until she fixed things and made up.

I'm not sure you understood the idea of secret romance. After our date, I had to sneak the flowers into my room. My mother didn't have a vase large enough to keep them, and even if she'd had one, there wasn't a place I could put them without her seeing. I wrapped them in damp newspaper, laid them on the floor in the back of my closet, watched them wilting day after day, the smell of decay tainting my clothes. Their blooms started out red, yellow, purple, but soon they were brown and fluttered on the floor. And then I had to sneak the flowers out to the dumpster.

Maybe you understood the idea of secret romance perfectly.

Deb stopped at my deli counter to buy thick-sliced ham. She must have loved having me serve her, she in her pastel dress, me in my dirty apron, she with her pink knees showing, me with love handles blooming over the waist of my pants. I'd been working there all summer, had gained forty pounds from their Tuesday specials on fried chicken. That and the birth control. But then, she'd put on weight, too. Her legs were still skinny, but she was growing a belly. Her face had gotten plump.

I leaned over the counter to wipe a crumb away, and I saw that her cart held a can of Maxwell House, a pack of cigarettes, and a case of Old Milwaukee.

I could do this. I could serve her. It was the least I could do, considering her father had just died. She and I used to be friends. Now that we were adversaries, I couldn't let on how much I missed her.

The woman behind her said in a voice too loud for a grocery store, "Dear Lord, Deborah! I barely even recognized you."

I didn't know the woman. I'd lived in this town my whole life, and I didn't know this woman, and Deb did. I went to slice ham, trying not to look like I was listening to the women making small talk.

"Boy or girl?" the woman said, a hand on either side of Deb's stomach.

"Boy," Deb said. "Steve wants me to name him Layne after some football player."

I wondered whether anyone was really buying her story that she was pregnant again. She'd played that card before, had gone around faking morning sickness two years ago, but nothing had come of it. You had told me this was her go-to lie; she pretended she was pregnant for attention. It was one of the reasons you wanted to break up with her.

When I handed her her package, she kept her eyes on the other woman, on her cart, on the hands she'd rested on Deb's gut. She finally looked up at me, glaring, as if I were the enemy, as if I were the one making a fuss, showing her ass in the grocery store.

My mother, sitting in the kitchen. The light over the table warm, golden, a frizzy halo on her head. Why couldn't she straighten her hair like other women?

"I thought you ended it," she said.

The house was so tidy, the cereal boxes aligned on top of the fridge, the air holding only cooking scents.

She said, "Don't make that boy your everything."

And for a moment, I hated her. I hated her bright clothes and the way she twisted her hair in a scarf when she went out in public. She wore high heels, even though she was five-foot-nine, and she always walked with her back so straight. So proud on the surface, but I knew the whitening creams she kept in the bathroom. People watched my mother, everywhere we went. And I watched them watching her. You were always polite to her, your family had raised you with Southern manners, you called her ma'am. Even so, she never warmed to you. When my mother ran into you in town, she would hold her purse close to her belly, pucker her face, and turn away.

You helped me move into my dorm. I was nervous about college. You were so sweet, rubbing my back, trying to calm me. My roommate hadn't arrived yet, and we had the room to ourselves. We were gloriously alone. At your house, I always felt like the neighbors were watching me come and go. But here, nobody knew us. We hung a quilt from the top bunk, screening us from the world while we curled together in the bottom. I studied the squares of the quilt: red, purple, yellow, pink, red, purple. Finally, alone.

I told you I wasn't ready, and you told me you were, but that we could wait if I wanted. Which was stupid. I was stupid. It's not like I was a virgin anyway. Not for a long time. We lay together, fully clothed, draped in each other, and watched the maple leaves outside my window turning colors as bright as fire.

My mother called that night, and when I was short with her on the phone, she wanted to know what was wrong.

"Steve's here," I said.

I could hear her breathing into the phone.

"Someone had to help me move in," I said.

"This won't end well," she said.

I hung up on her. When she called back, I let the answering machine get it. I retreated into you, took shelter in your body, let you burrow inside me like a grub. Clothes off, all in. We were terrifyingly alone, feverishly alone, painfully alone, dizzyingly alone. In the morning, after you left, I could smell your aftershave all over me. You said you couldn't visit for a while. You'd lost your job at the creamery. And when you left, you left your scent in my quilt. At night, when I couldn't sleep, I would smell my way along the fabric, trying to find a path back to you.

You proposed two days before Christmas. In your living room, the snow climbing up to the bottom of the front door, you pulled me into your lap. Your eyes were trained on my face like I was a fast pitch, a finish line, a prize. You never actually spoke the words, but the way your fingers trembled said everything you didn't. You kissed me on the nose, you always said it was a perfect little doll's nose, then slipped the ring on my finger. And you said you had left her. You'd left Deb.

When I imagined getting engaged, I never thought it would be such a quiet moment, the deed hushed by the sifting snow outside, the world blanketed in bridal white.

My grandma came to visit around New Year's, said she wanted me to have my gifts. My mother wasn't speaking to me again, and I refused to go to Christmas with my family, where she would have made it obvious I wasn't welcome. I unwrapped presents out in your driveway. A Coach handbag, a pair of leather boots, a CD player for my car, a tiny gold watch. Snow gathering in my grandma's large wig. Her dark face smooth, placid from recent Botox.

"It sure is cold," she said.

"Yeah," I said.

"It's been years since we've had a December this cold."

"Yeah," I said.

"Won't you invite me in?" she said.

"Steve's sleeping," I said. "He works at the tool and die now. Long hours."

Really, I didn't want her to see your house, the cigarette haze, the walls stained yellow, the drafty rooms, the spoiled food in the fridge. Your house was heated only by the gas oven, because the electricity had been cut. I didn't want her to see the bed I shared with you, the thin wool blanket covered in gray feathers from the parrot you let fly around the house. I didn't want her to see the weight I'd put on while on birth control. The pickle jar I used instead of a bank and never thought to count at the end of each week. The grade report from my first semester in college detailing my 2.3 GPA, which I taped to the fridge like it was some fantastic joke, like it wasn't wrecking me that I was failing at my long-awaited exodus from River Bend. I was so lost at school, and ashamed of how lost I was. I could no longer look anyone in the eyes, and I didn't want my grandma to see that, either. Most of all, I didn't want to take my gloves off, because then she would see the ring.

You lost your job at the tool and die. You said you hated it there anyway; your boss didn't respect you, and your work was so mind-less, a monkey could do it. I had gotten you to apply for financial aid at the community college, but even that wasn't enough, so we took jobs at the roofing company working with your dad, shovel-ing snow. You worked with him all day, and I would join you both on weekends, driving the forty-five minutes from school.

At work, he treated you like an employee. You used to be a lot closer, you said. You used to go on fishing trips together. He tried to teach you how to hit a baseball. When you turned sixteen, he took you skydiving. Now we followed him up icy ladders, shov-eled until our backs were cursing, chiseled at icicles in cold silence as slush hit our faces and melted into our collars. My toes were always numb that semester. I felt as if I were made of winter, with

THE HOUSE OF DEEP WATER

a fog of hair and frigid limbs, skin rimmed in ice, snow pooled in my stomach, my eyes hard marbles.

It was maybe the worst job I'd ever had, but it paid ten bucks an hour, way more than my cafeteria job. Even with a decent paycheck, you asked to borrow money. You had to repay your financial aid, since you'd failed to enroll in classes. What did you do with your financial aid, then? You said you'd spent it on the ring.

You weren't at home, but your mother was there, bent over, scrubbing the kitchen tile. Without looking up, she told me you were visiting a friend. In your bedroom your African gray slept on top of its cage. I lay down on your bed.

"You're really just going to wait for him?" your mother said from the doorway.

"What's it to you?"

"Just wait for him? Like a good little puppy?"

I rolled over, showed her my back.

"Look," she said, "I know this is none of my business."

"You're damn right." I glared at her over my shoulder.

"I just don't think you two are right for each other. And it's not because you're . . ." Here she ducked her head to keep from looking at me.

"Because I'm what?" I said, rolling over to face her.

"Look," she said. "I have friends who are colored."

"Colored," your parrot said.

I stared her down, her gray hair, her gray clothes. Who was she? "Like you know what's good for him?" I said.

Her eyes, tired. A yellow bruise on her left jaw. "You think you're the only one in his life?" she said.

"He can't even stand you," I said. "He just feels sorry for you."

"I'm talking about Deb, stupid."

"Jay tame," your parrot said.

"You know she's pregnant again. And she's keeping it this time."

"That's just a story she's been spreading," I said. You'd told me all about it, how Deb was obsessed with you, how she was lying to try to get you back.

"Just keep telling yourself that." When she left, I went to your desk to check if you had emailed me. Before I had even logged in, a message came in on your ICQ: *Hey babe.* From a Sandra2000. I didn't even know a Sandra. I read through your conversations. I searched your email. I don't know what made me think to check if you had other email addresses.

You did.

You'd carried on dozens of conversations with Deb. You wrote to say that you and I had broken up. You said I'd cheated on you. You wrote to her in French, words I couldn't understand. *Je t'aime, je t'aime.* In the corner, your bird was plucking its feathers, its skin raw and weeping. I spent so long straining my mind, looking for cognates with the little bit of Spanish I knew, that soon even the English words seemed foreign. I could no longer grasp ideas like desire or need. Love.

You became quiet, sullen, moody. I started visiting daily, driving an hour from school, staying the night, every night, staking my claim. I felt like since I was failing at school, there was no way I'd make good there, but if I worked hard enough, maybe I could make things work with you.

You'd leave me at your house alone, to visit friends, to go to the bar, and I'd lie shivering in your bed while your parrot plucked itself bald in its cage. When I got bored enough, mad enough, I'd rifle through your room, search your desk. I sifted through the stacks of bills: car insurance, overdue cable bill, electricity bills, phone bills, receipts for oil changes and gas stations and fast food, and three receipts for Kmart diamond solitaires, each costing $219.

Your phone bill seemed unusually high. Most of the calls listed had been placed to me, but there was one number that appeared again and again, always around four in the morning. I dialed.

"Hey, hun." Her voice bright.

"Deb?"

"Jay tame," your parrot said, plucking the feathers from its wings, its pink skin scabby, pimpled like lizard hide.

"It's Eliza," I said. "Wait, don't hang up."

She was silent for so long, I wondered whether she'd heard me.

"Did he tell you we'd broken up?" I said.

"What's your game?" she said.

"Just tell me."

"The shit you put him through," she said.

"Please?"

"You ain't no good for him."

"I need to know."

"Yeah, he told me he'd dumped your skank ass. God, Eliza. How many men do you need? How many homes do you have to wreck?"

"I never cheated—"

"Bullshit," she said.

"But I should have," I said.

You wouldn't come to California for my cousin's wedding. We'd had such a fight after I confronted you about your phone bill that by the time the wedding came around a month later, you refused. I even offered to buy your ticket, which I couldn't really afford. I couldn't even afford mine. You said you were terrified of flying. You'd never been on a plane. Neither had I.

We all flew out of Kalamazoo: my grandma, who loved to travel; my mother, who still wasn't talking to me; my auntie, the groom's mother, whom my mother wasn't talking to, either. All for a cousin I hadn't seen in at least a decade, not since he moved to California. I didn't even want to go, but it was important to my grandma.

A gray day. Taxiing down the runway, the grass moving faster, slanting outside my window, followed by the lifting, the leaving behind. Misted windows and the jostling of ascent. And then, breaking through the clouds. Thin glorious sunlight. So much blue sky, it stirred something in me, something that, with age, I might have identified as hope. At the time I named it heartbreak.

Just before I left for this trip, I received a letter from my school letting me know I was on academic probation. I'd tried so hard to get here, and I was blowing it.

Then California's five-lane highways and taquerias and desert shrubs and dusty hills and palm trees. Michigan felt like something from my past. You should have been there with me, out in that orange grove, in the California sun. The altar adorned with a profusion of flowers, yellow, pink, pale purple. Yards and yards of red velvet aisle laid on the grass. The bride's gown, lace, with a train so long three bridesmaids had to pop under her skirt and bustle it after the ceremony, like something in a movie. You should have let me lean my head on your shoulder and cry as the bride walked down the aisle. You should have held my hand while they said their vows. You should have caught the garter. You would have looked nice in a button-down shirt, skin slick with sunscreen.

My mother sitting next to me at the reception, but still not talking to me. My auntie in her ridiculous gown, dripping in sequins, drunk dancing with the bride's brother. My grandma cutting tiny bites of chicken cordon bleu, chewing languorously. Sighing after each swallow. "Your cousin married money," she whispered. "And there's nothing wrong with that."

But first, the bachelorette party. A karaoke club. Red walls, black chairs, chrome bar. A woman thundering into a microphone, gripping it like a lover, beneath the spinning lights of a disco ball. She was dark-skinned and lovely, her hair in braids, her makeup unapologetic. She wore tasteful sequins. She was the kind of woman I never saw back home. I hadn't realized before how hungry I was for someone to look up to, someone who looked like me. Being around my auntie, whose life was every bit as messy as my mother's, and my cousin, who was light enough to pass, wasn't enough. But this? This is what I needed.

I ordered the first round, because I never seemed to get carded when buying rounds. A guy at the bar struck up a conversation. He wore a dress shirt, tight over his belly, and a loosened tie. His broad freckled face almost glowed in the dim lighting.

Why would he talk to me? I wore a baggy tank top and torn jeans because the only nice clothing I owned was my dress for the wedding. A line of sweat under my bra, down my spine, my blood too thick for California's heat. I was the only black woman in our group, and I was ashamed that I wasn't representing better. But he noticed *me*. He looked like money, like opportunity, like confidence, his face slackened by alcohol. He was talking to me, his mouth wide, the words lost beneath the karaoke. Then he palmed a wad of crumpled bills into my hand. Did he want to buy me a drink? I shook my head, but he insisted.

I took his money and retreated to my fellow bachelorettes. This was also new, this feeling of safety in a group of women. I hadn't had any girlfriends since Deb. Once he was out of sight, I counted up ninety-three dollars. I made a point of keeping a close eye on him, telling myself that it was only to keep my distance—but part of me wanted to see if he was watching.

I didn't even know what to order with the money. I didn't like the margaritas we'd ordered for our first round; they were way too strong. I let the maid of honor take the reins, gave her the entire wad of cash. We drank shots with his money, me fighting not to gag. Soon, the room was spinning along with the lights.

The bride on the bathroom floor, her head resting comfortably on a public toilet seat. The maid of honor combing damp hair from the bride's face. I held my liquor well; this made me feel powerful. I'd had so many drinks that they were beginning to taste better. I approached a barstool that was sometimes one barstool, sometimes two, sometimes one base with two seats. I crawled up onto the seats. Someone had left a pair of sunglasses on the bar, tea shades with lilac lenses. I put them on.

The bartender wouldn't serve me. Said it was for my own good. I'd never suffered such injustice. I let him know, about the injustice, about the unholy glare of lights on chrome, about the sickly lilac lighting, about the tricky barstools. He waved over a bouncer, which got me really amped up. I told him how the singing was off-key and the drinks were watery; I let him have it. An arm slid around my waist and guided me away from the bar, and I was telling them about the bartender, the injustice, the weak drinks, expecting them to commiserate, but instead they put their face in my face, their hands in my hair. They pressed me into a corner. *He* pressed me—this wasn't one of the women I came here with. His body on mine, his hands on me, that wide mouth on me, his broad freckled face had turned lilac. He was so close he looked like a cyclops; I couldn't focus on both his eyes.

"Boy," I said, pushing him away. "You don't touch a black girl's hair."

I got his zipper down, felt him tense, then relax into me. Playing like this was something I'd never been able to do before, not even with you. I couldn't do it sober; it brought back memories from my childhood. But with the flush of alcohol, the drone of music, the spinning lights, the space inside my head was somehow altered. For the better. I gripped him firmly in my fist, worked him until I felt him shudder, then wiped my hand on his shirt. This, too, made me feel powerful.

When I stumbled into my hotel room later that morning, my phone was already ringing. You'd been calling for hours. You wanted to know where I had been, who I was with. I'd been dancing.

You wanted to know how many drinks I'd had. I told you only two. By then, most of what we said to each other was lies. You always swore you never drank at all—not with your father as a model—though I'd seen cans of Old Milwaukee on the bottom shelf of your fridge, pushed to the back. I'd found bottles in your garbage. Sometimes your breath had the sour candy taste of liquors I couldn't name.

When I got back from California, you wouldn't see me for three days. Instead, we fought on the phone. You told me it was over, you were through with me, but I refused to let it end like this, so I stormed to your house.

Springtime. A cleansing. Baptism by sun. Driving in the country, windows down, wearing my lilac-tinted glasses. The weather unseasonably warm. Even though my air-conditioning never worked and the car seat riled a heat rash on the backs of my knees, in that moment, I didn't care. The glasses colored my world in Easter shades.

When I got to your house, Deb opened the door. She leaned against the frame, one arm stretched across, her hand resting on the other side. She wore an engagement ring with a lilac stone. The same ring I wore, as if she and I were the ones bound by love. Her face was lilac. I took my glasses off; I didn't like seeing her that way. I would never have admitted it, but Deb was lovely: gray feathers in her red hair, pale yellow sweater, thin white legs, a swollen waist stretching the fabric of her white dress. Behind her, the house was dark, smoky. The yellowed walls seemed likely to cave in on her any second.

"Steve's not here," she said.

"Where is he?" I said.

"I'm not his keeper," she said. "Neither are you."

Somewhere in the cave of a house behind her, I thought I heard your African gray squawking its bastard language, *jay tame, jay tame,* but as I listened, I realized the sound was more musical, more human. A wailing, squalling. An infant. Your infant.

All the fight went from me. I couldn't face Deb, my old friend, my enemy. I couldn't face her child. I put my glasses on again and drove to school, taking the back roads to get more out of the day. The suspension in my car was shot, and with each bump in the road, my car would bounce slowly, hypnotically, so that the ride was a continual bobbing, a gull on a lake. I passed spring fields, some of them planted, some of them tilled, some of them still overgrown with weeds and the remnants of last year's crops. All of them were lilac. The roads that rose and fell, passing between glacial hills, were lilac. The world, an eggshell-thin lilac globe.

You called and asked me to see you. I agreed, because, dammit, we were ending this on my terms. After I all but flunked out of school, I needed a win.

We met at your uncle's apartment. He lived two towns away, above a bait shop out on Robin Lake, kept a spare key duct-taped under the rain gutter. We used to meet here a lot. You thought he wouldn't mind, and maybe he wouldn't, but when we left you would make sure the toilet seat was up and the magazines on the kitchen table were arranged the way they'd been when we came.

Once inside, you led me to your uncle's bed. We shed our clothes as if we were molting. You threw the blankets on the floor, nested against me, your fingers in my hair, my face pressed into your chest. Very soon you heaved yourself off me and stilled, trapping me against the wall. The tiny window unit over the bed thrummed, working so hard there was frost on the pane above it, but the room was as warm and damp as a mouth. Past you, past the sliding-glass door, the porch, I watched a storm gathering over the lake. A line of ragged clouds, as dark as oil paint. A V of birds hung above the lake, gliding, their black bodies stark silhouettes. Lightning cracked, and the birds plunged one after another into the water. The sky like an open wound. Rain curtained the houses across the lake, and then the lake, and then the shore. There was only us, in that room, in that bed, your heavy body, the smell of you all over me.

I couldn't do this anymore. I couldn't breathe with you. I didn't know any better, didn't see any other options, but for the first time in years, I was at least looking. My vision was clearing.

You called the next day, and I unplugged my phone. You sent me emails I deleted. You wrote letters I didn't open. In my memory, your face blurred. I couldn't remember the shape of your nose or the curve of your mouth. I only remembered your eyes, the blue of the summer sky in the half hour before sunset, when the birds are roosting and the air wavers with dying sound. That is to say, looking at you always felt like a long day, ending.

Elizabeth DeWitt
21

I move in with my boyfriend after we've been dating for six months. I cook him butter burgers. I bake him hand pies. I clean his apartment. I wash his laundry. I want to keep this one.

He's invited to a friend's house, and I'm not invited to go with him. I don't want him to go. I don't know why, but it feels important that he not go. When he goes anyway, I am wrecked. On my way to the bathroom, to dry my face, I bang the wall with my fist. The drywall is damaged. He doesn't leave me alone again for a while, until he can't stand it anymore, until he leaves me alone for good.

THE GASLIGHT VILLAGE

Beth is in line at the grocery store, buying a turkey and potatoes and cranberries for Thanksgiving, and the woman in front of her keeps turning halfway around, squinting out of the corner of her eye, glaring, and then turning away again.

"Can I help you?" Beth asks with all the patience she can muster. It isn't much.

The woman wears a polyester pantsuit, her white hair sprayed into a dandelion puff. Pale powder cakes her cheeks. Her eyes are small, blue, and watery, and she blinks like she's fighting tears. "I'm sorry. It's just, you're Beth Hansen, right?"

Beth shakes her head. "DeWitt," she says.

"Jeanette's mother?"

"Is something the matter?"

"I'm Mrs. Schwartz." She stares at Beth like this should mean something.

"And?" Have they met? The woman doesn't look familiar. Beth

219

hates this about River Bend. Anyone who meets her can guess who she is simply by looking at her: That's the problem with being the only black family in town. She is always at a disadvantage, having been away long enough that people's faces have grown raggedly unfamiliar.

"I'm your daughter's history teacher?"

"Right." How is this woman still teaching? She looks like she has to be at least eighty.

"I really hoped the notes I sent home would have inspired some improvement." The woman's hands grip her cart a little too tightly.

"What notes?"

"The progress reports? Detailing Jeanette's poor performance in my class? You signed them." She slowly blinks those runny eyes.

Beth stares at her blankly, Jeanette's stare. She realizes now that it isn't a look of incomprehension, but one of barely concealed anger.

Oh, the strength required to hold your tongue, the queasy effort involved in swallowing, suppressing, the mental gymnastics needed to convince yourself it's better this way. Beth has stayed silent for so many years, about so many things, has spent so much time on hold that the slow work of unburdening, unclenching, feels almost like another kind of violation. Her very muscles ache as they loosen, and she quickly rebundles herself.

She isn't sure she has the strength to keep quiet today. She wants this damn checkout line to move, but the woman in front of Mrs. Schwartz has a stack of expired coupons and is trying to convince the cashier to accept them anyway.

"Your daughter's education is so very important."

No shit, Beth thinks, but what she says is, "How many notes?"

"There must have been four or five by now. Weekly. Really," she says, with that slow blink, "Jeanette is a bright child. If she only applied herself."

"And these signatures, were they right slanted, or left?"

"How should I know? My point is, Jeanette needs a solid foundation if she's going to attend college. And I do hope I can impress upon you the need for college, Mrs. Hansen."

"Ms."

Mrs. Schwartz pulls her neck in like a turtle. "Oh. I see."

"And I ask because my son is left-handed." She can't quite believe Dan would do this, but he is the likeliest suspect.

"Without college, your daughter's future is in jeopardy. You may not think much of college, but it really is important."

"I went to college," Beth says.

"Sorry. I just assumed—"

"And I will thank you to keep your assumptions to yourself." Beth has the pleasure of watching Mrs. Schwartz's cheeks flush.

"I just thought—"

"I can guess what you thought."

Mrs. Schwartz turns around and busies herself with rearranging her groceries on the conveyor belt, no doubt wanting to leave, but caught between Beth and the woman whose expired coupons have warranted a visit from the store manager. After a few minutes, Mrs. Schwartz turns around again.

"Tell you what. I would be willing to allow Jeanette to complete an extra-credit project. I don't normally do this, but, well, considering the miscommunication."

"What would she have to do?" Beth says, her eyes narrowing.

"Go to the Gaslight Village exhibit at the Muylder Museum in Kalamazoo. It's a nice little museum, not too expensive," she adds, eyeing Beth's groceries on the belt behind her own. "We've been studying River Bend's history, its roots in milling and agriculture, its pioneer work ethic. She can write a report on the exhibit. It really is quite lovely. I think you might even enjoy it."

When Beth was young, her favorite exhibit had been the Gaslight Village, a replica of how River Bend's Main Street would have looked in 1850. Her father took her to the museum often to see the village. It had the kind of gleam that comes only from a child's imagination; it sat off in its own corridor, the lighting dim, the hallway filled with the hushed echo of footsteps. While the village wasn't nearly as flashy as the museum's other exhibits—the dinosaurs, for instance, or the planetarium—its quietness was exactly why Beth loved it so much. It was easily overlooked, and so it felt personal, intimate. She always liked to pretend she'd stepped through a portal and found herself inside a frozen slice of history: a street paved in bricks, lined in storefronts and faux gas streetlamps flickering to simulate flame. In the middle of the road stood a stuffed horse yoked to a wooden carriage, a wax mannequin at the reigns. The village included the River Bend Casket Company, whose ruins still stand in River Bend today, and a replica of the Muylder Mansion, with wax versions of the tall, blond Governor and Mrs. Muylder and their butler standing on the porch, welcoming nobody. On the wall behind the mansion, a mural depicted the surrounding cornfields, the tall green rows of cornstalks growing smaller, bluer, as the fields drifted off into the distance. In and among the rows were workers, white men harvesting corn by hand. They looked so dignified as they worked, wearing trousers and jackets, wide swaths of fabric tied at their throats. As a child, Beth thought she would have loved to live in this time, to wear a bustled dress like Mrs. Muylder, to ride in a horse-drawn buggy, to shop at the haberdashery, to live in a fine big house surrounded by cornfields.

"It seems like such a hard life," Ernest had said once, gazing into the windows of the casket factory. Beth was twelve at the time; she lived with her mother and stepfather, and rarely saw Ernest those days.

"Those men must have worked so hard," he had said.

She'd moved on to the store windows, interesting for the myriad objects they displayed: leather-bound books on an old desk, a clothier sewing a bodice to a bustled skirt on a dressmaker's dummy. Standing in front of the window to the oculist, where inside a mannequin worked on a pair of round spectacles, Beth noticed other people entering the exhibit, two teenaged boys. They both had bowl cuts. One was wearing a football jersey, and the other a boldly colored sweater. The boys stood by the Muylder Mansion, whispering.

Beth thought the one in the jersey was kind of cute. He wore glasses and kept pushing his floppy hair back. She watched their reflection in the shopwindow, saw them coming closer. They were looking right at her. She was keenly aware that she hadn't done her hair that day, had just thrown it up in a puffy bun, the sides all dry and frizzy. She was wearing a pair of jeans that she hated, acid-washed hand-me-downs from one of her mother's coworkers. Even on a good day, she was always so awkward around boys, especially cute ones; she didn't know what to do, so she froze between wanting to talk to them and wanting to flee. At twelve, she was already lonely, yearning for a boyfriend, wanting to be touched, kissed, loved, but terrified of male attention. It was a problem, and one that left her angry.

When the boys came within earshot, she heard their whispers, heard the hissing syllables, the hard consonants. Something in their tone, in their energy, made them not cute anymore. Beth wanted them to leave; this was her exhibit, after all, and she didn't feel like sharing.

They didn't leave, and all she could do was ignore them, even as they continued to whisper. And then she heard one word, very clearly:

Nigger.

Out of the corner of her eye, she saw the boys staring at her. The one in the sweater was laughing.

"You have something you want to say?" Beth said, turning to them. The boy in the jersey looked down at his shoes, but the one in the sweater raised his chin, like he was thinking about it, until Ernest came up to put a hand on her shoulder. She watched the boys size him up, size up her white father, who was also tall and broad shouldered.

"Is there a problem?" Ernest asked.

"No, sir," the boy in the jersey said.

"We were just talking among ourselves," the sweater boy said. Both of them looked like they were fighting to keep a straight face, but their grins were breaking through. They wandered back over to the mansion, before the sweater boy said, "This is stupid," and they left.

"Why didn't you say anything?" Beth said when they had gone.

"About what?" Ernest asked.

"Didn't you hear what they called me?"

Ernest had gone back to the factory by then and stood staring through its window into the past. "I didn't hear anything," he said.

Beth felt her face heat up. Her hands were shaking.

"They called me the N-word," she said. How could he have missed it? Even now, it was all Beth could hear.

"Sticks and stones," Ernest said.

"That's bullshit," Beth said.

"Watch your language," Ernest said.

When Beth tells her kids they're going to the museum today, Jeanette goes into a silent huff. Dan begs to put it off until next weekend.

"I have plans today," he says.

"You should have thought of that before you forged my signature," Beth says. Still, part of her agrees. It's mid-November, and the sky is clear. Beth wishes they didn't have to waste the day indoors.

Much like River Bend itself, the village hasn't really changed since Beth was a kid. Also much like River Bend, the museum no longer feels benign to her, although she has a hard time pinning down why. Maybe it's the wax mannequins, once so lifelike, which now seem cheesy, the faces lumpy, the smiles like death rictuses. Beth supposes they have always looked this way, that her imagination has just grown weaker from years of watching CGI. The entire exhibit looks worse for wear, fingerprints smudging the shopwindows, bald patches on the stuffed horse's haunches and nose where children—Beth included—have petted it over the years, despite the sign asking patrons to refrain from touching the exhibit.

"This is it?" Jeanette asks. Her disappointment is so complete that she momentarily forgets to give her mother the silent treatment.

"This is it," Beth says, more harshly than she intends. "So you better find something to write about it."

Dan buries his face in the museum pamphlet.

Jeanette walks down the brick street, peering in the shop-windows. "The old-timey dresses are kind of cool, I guess."

Beth feels annoyed. She tells herself it's because of Jeanette's attitude, but really, she's disappointed, too: The village no longer holds the same magic.

"Come on, guys," Beth says. Even in her disappointment, Jeanette has to finish this assignment. "This is history. This is how River Bend actually looked."

"Real cool, Mom," Dan says, still studying the pamphlet. He pulls his phone out. "Next show at the planetarium starts at noon. We could still make it."

"How come he gets to use his phone?" Jeanette asks, going sulky again.

"He was just checking the time," Beth says. "Come over here. I want to show you something." She leads Jeanette to the factory window, where she peers in to see rows of men working. "This is how the factory looked when it was in operation. Maybe there's something here you can use for your report."

"Why are they dressed so fancy?" Jeanette says.

"People were a lot more formal in those days," Beth says. She always kind of liked the clothes the men wore. They seemed so romantic to her, maybe because she'd been a fan of historical romances when she was younger.

"They look hot," Jeanette says. "They would at least take off their jackets."

"They're dressed like they're upper class," Dan says. He finally puts his pamphlet away. "I doubt factory workers would have even owned cravats."

And isn't that just like kids today, to be so demanding? They can't appreciate the exhibit for what it is; they have to pick it apart.

THE HOUSE OF DEEP WATER

"They look ridiculous working in such nice jackets," Jeanette says.

"Okay, but focus," Beth says, trying to tamp down her annoyance. "This exhibit tells a story."

"I think it tells a lot more than it means to," Dan says.

"What's that mean?" Beth can feel herself getting flustered.

"Well," Dan says, "for starters, where are all the black people?"

Beth closes her eyes. Takes a breath. "Maybe there weren't a lot of people of color in River Bend in 1850."

"No, there were," Jeanette says. "We learned in class how a lot of free African American northerners came to work in the fields to escape racial tensions in Ohio."

Beth smiles at Jeanette's recitation. "And why are you failing history?"

Jeanette shrugs. "Homework is boring."

"Okay," Beth says. "So they worked agriculture, not in factories."

"I'm sure some of them had factory jobs," Dan says on his way past the museum's replica of the Muylder mansion. He studies the mural on the wall. "Also, there're no black people in the fields, either."

"That can't be right," Beth says, following him to the mural. She checks the fields, row by row. As hard as she tries, she can't find a single worker of color.

"Someone posted this thing the other day about the history of northern wage slaves," Dan is saying, but Beth isn't listening. Instead, she remembers that last visit with her father. They didn't stay at the museum long after the run-in with those boys.

On the car ride back to her mother's apartment, a news story had come on about the riots in L.A. that spring. Ernest quickly switched the radio off. He sighed twice and wiped his face.

"Here's the thing," he said, as if they'd been talking this whole time. "Those people, they think rioting is going to solve anything? They'll take any excuse for vandalism, and theft, and violence. And then they expect to be treated like everyone else. No, not even. They expect the country to bow down, to apologize for things that happened ages ago. You want to get ahead in this country? You work for it. You work hard, and you improve yourself, because we're Americans, and that's what we do. Enough of this garbage. We're not black, or white. We're Americans, all of us, and it's time we started acting like it."

Beth sat quietly while Ernest talked, and stared out the window. Even as a twelve-year-old, she thought his arguments were weak, because if there was one thing she'd learned living in River Bend, it was that some Americans seemed to be more American than others.

"If you ask me," Dan is saying, "they should call this the revisionist history museum." He looked quite pleased with himself.

Beth wants to unclench, to shout and rage. Inside, Eliza sinks deeper into the waters, only her nose and mouth above the surface. How has Beth never noticed this before? How had her father not noticed? He'd been so focused on the hard lives of the factory workers, he hadn't seen the interaction Beth had with those boys. But then, he'd always refused to see the truth if it was at all uncomfortable. And as Beth thinks about it, she feels her throat tightening, her hands shaking. She wants to hurt those boys, her father, Gilmer Thurber, Steve Brody, Mrs. Schwartz—every person who's ever wronged her. She wants to dismantle the system that demands she wait patiently, quietly, invisibly, that her children wait obediently; don't make a fuss, don't stir the waters, just be thankful to be alive, to be allowed to exist, and to be of use, to fill a role she never agreed to, to serve as a receptacle for their narrative, their opinions, their anger, their admonishments, their shame, their abuse, their damage.

But instead of shouting and raging, Beth takes a pen from her purse and ducks out of sight behind the Muylder mansion. There she draws a black family, a man and woman and child, their hair in braids and afros, their bodies clothed in rags, into the distant blue end of the cornfield. A family working to pull ears of corn they do not own, their bodies lashed with corn rash, but finally visible, and present, and together.

Watching from deep inside, Eliza shakes her head.

"You're acting the hooligan," she says. "Vandalizing."

"Fuck off," Beth says, and pushes Eliza's head under the water.

"Mom?" Jeanette says behind her, and Beth jumps, her pen trailing off of the body of the black woman. "What are you doing?"

"Fixing this," Beth says, capping her pen and stowing it in her purse.

Jeanette's face, for once, is not blank. It's full of as much color and life as that cornfield.

"The next show at the planetarium starts in four minutes," Dan says. "We could still make it." Beth doesn't have the energy to argue; all of her energy is focused on gathering herself back up. Instead, she lets her children lead her out of the Gaslight Village.

Elizabeth DeWitt
22

First date with the fireman. I want to date him because of his muscles, and because he wears nerd glasses, and because he tells me online that firemen work hard and play harder. I've never been a party girl, but I want to try.

I pay for dinner, to see if he'll let me, but also because I don't like to feel like I owe anyone anything. Even so, I find myself in a park with him in the dark. He sprawls out on the grass, pulls me on top of him. He's kissing me drunkenly. He's not a bad kisser. His hands go down my body, and I think he's feeling me up, but then I hear his zipper. I'm drunk, too, but not drunk enough. He stops kissing me, pushes my head down. I get to his belly before I come back up, but he pushes my head down again.

I can do this. I can know how to have a good time.

Second date with the fireman, and in his truck on the way home from the movie, he tells me his friend is also dating a black girl. His friend says black girls will let you do anal; you just got to throw it up there, ha-ha. Dummy that I am, I'm not sure why he's telling me this.

Back at my apartment, after he drinks all my wine coolers, he gets my clothes off quick. He flips me over and goes for it.

"That kind of hurts," I say, but he keeps fumbling, keeps trying. "I mean I don't like it."

"You're hella blunt," he says, but he stops, goes back to plain old vanilla. And I should tell him to get out, not to let the door hit him in the ass, but instead I let him finish because I never was good at thinking quickly.

WRECKED

On a Wednesday in early December, the doorbell rings. It's after noon. Beth tries to ignore it, but on the third ring, she gets out of bed, makes her way downstairs. She doesn't want to open the door, not when her hair's a mess and she hasn't showered, but then she reminds herself it's probably someone trying to sell her on Jesus. Who cares about making a good impression? What she finds instead is Steve Brody.

"What the hell?" she says, and he steps past her, into the house.

"Surprise," he says, quietly.

"I don't know where your niece is," she says.

"Down at the hardware store," Steve says. "Jared is showing her the ropes."

Beth's knee-jerk reaction is anger at Linda for leaving Ernest unattended, until she remembers that she's supposed to be watching him today. Linda told her at dinner last night that she had somewhere to be, only Beth assumed she was getting her hair cut or a prenatal massage.

"Shit," Beth says, and goes into the dining room to check on her father. There he is, his eyes open, though not exactly alert. She's not sure what she was expecting—that he'd run off on her? The thought almost makes her laugh.

Steve comes up behind her and wraps his arms around her, a hand covering each of her breasts. The nerve of him, thinking he can paw her right here.

"What time is it?" she asks.

"Quarter till one," he says. Her kids won't be home from school until three. She leads him upstairs. At the top, he hesitates when she turns toward the master bedroom.

"You sure?" he asks.

"We can't very well do this in the room I share with my daughter," she says.

He follows her inside. They don't even bother turning down the bed; they fuck on top of the flowered duvet that Linda, no doubt, had put on the bed. Even though it's been a month and a half since her father's stroke, the room still holds his green, fresh-mown smell. She imagines Linda coming home, entering the room where she now sleeps alone, and noticing something off. Maybe she would know right away, would recognize the smell of Beth's unwashed body, of Steve's cigarettes and drugstore after-shave. Maybe she would put it together, would realize what Beth was taking from Linda's family, the relatively small payment she collected in exchange for Linda's room and board.

As usual, Beth finds herself imagining some other couple, some other dynamic, like a boss and his employee, or a professor and his student. Always in these scenarios, she sees herself as the man.

And while Steve goes about his task—distractedly, it seems—while he keeps fucking her, slowly, rhythmically, Beth has the first orgasm she's had with him since they were twentysomething.

Afterward, in the stretch of infinity it takes for him to finish, it just now dawns on her that, no, he isn't fucking her. She's fucking him. She feels a surge of feverish energy at the thought, and when she realizes he is oblivious to this change in their dynamic, the energy only increases.

"Stop," she says.

He doesn't seem to have heard her.

"Stop," she says again, pushing him off her.

"What's wrong?" He looks genuinely confused.

"I'm done," she says simply.

"You're done?" His eyebrows lower. "Done with what? Done with us?"

"No, I mean I finished." She gets up from the bed, not bothering to cover herself with a sheet. She has always been a little unsure of her body, but today, she doesn't care if he looks.

"I didn't," he says, rolling toward her. He has a playful smile on now, and he reaches a hand out to grab a handful of whatever bit of her he can reach, but she steps away.

"That sounds like your problem," she says, and goes into the bathroom stark naked.

In the bathroom, she finds that she's shaking. She's never done that before—left a man before he completed his task—though Lord knows, plenty of men have left her unsatisfied. She has to fight the urge to go back in there, to let him finish.

"God, you're a bitch," Eliza tells her.

"Maybe I am," Beth says, her hands on either side of the sink. In truth, she knows she is. And she likes it.

. . .

At the end of the week, Dan and Jeanette want to go to Allison Dekker's Ugly Sweater Christmas Party. Beth knows the Dekker family. Allison Dekker comes to the house from time to time to invite all of the DeWitts to church. Beth doesn't really want her kids hanging around with the Dekker family, but she doesn't have a good reason to say no.

"Who's going to be there?" Beth asks them.

"Just some kids," Jeanette says.

"Will there be parents?"

"Of course. God, Mom," Dan says.

Dan comes downstairs later that evening wearing his normal clothes: tee shirt, blue cardigan hoodie, skinny jeans, tennis shoes.

"You too cool for ugly sweaters?" Beth asks.

"He wants to look good for his girlfriend," Jeanette says.

"You have a girlfriend?"

He shrugs. "Sort of."

"Well? Do you?"

"God, Mom. Leave it alone."

"Who is she?"

"Just a girl from school."

"Which girl?"

"Mandy Brody," Jeanette says.

"You're such a pain in my ass!" Dan stomps out of the house.

The news hits Beth like a tidal wave. Mandy Brody. She knew she should never have moved back here.

"How long have they been dating?"

"I don't know. A month?" Jeanette is eating Skittles for dinner, smacking her lips with every handful. She wears black pants and a fuzzy red sweater. Beth doesn't remember seeing either piece of clothing before, and she wonders where Jeanette got them. On Jeanette's neck, the scar from where Beth burned her is shiny and pink, bright against Jeanette's dark clothing.

"I suppose you're too old for an ugly sweater, too?" Beth struggles for normalcy amid the chaos in her brain.

"No."

"I think I have a reindeer one somewhere."

"I got it covered," she says, and tilts her head back, emptying the rest of her Skittles into her mouth. She goes to the fridge and pours herself a glass of Faygo before heading upstairs.

Why did Dan have to get involved with a Brody? Thinking of her son with that family, Beth can't ignore all the things she hates about Steve. His drunkard's drawl and old cigarette smell. His clothes, full of holes and stained with paint and roofing tar. His sense of humor, which he thinks is so wry, but is really just redneck. His gaze, shifty at all times except when he's lying; when he's lying, he looks you dead in the eye.

An hour later, Jeanette comes back downstairs with makeup on. Her eyes look professionally done, in heavy eyeliner and smoky shadow. Her sweater is pinned with felt candy canes and ornaments and snowmen. Worse yet, her little afro is pressed straight. Up close, Beth can see and smell that Linda at least used coconut oil this time.

"Nice sweater," Beth says, but she can't keep the bristles from her voice.

"Thanks," Jeannette says. "Linda helped make them."

"You need to scrub off some of that makeup, though."

"But it's a party," Jeanette says, her voice quiet, even. Jeanette, too, has a woman inside her, a woman who screams until the windows shatter. She's just better at containing her screaming woman, because she has to be.

"You're only twelve," Beth says, and for a moment, she finds herself counting back the years to make sure she's right. Is Jeanette only twelve? The look she gives Beth—calm, assured—seems so much older.

"Allison Dekker wears more makeup than this every day," she says.

"Allison Dekker isn't my daughter."

"This isn't the nineteen-hundreds," she says. And really, what's her mother's problem? It's not like she's wearing a short skirt or low-cut top. Some of the girls at school, they're always testing the dress code. Tonight, Jeanette figures it'll be a free-for-all.

"You can wear makeup when you get to high school." Beth's voice has gone higher, while Jeanette's is still even. "Now go wash your face."

"I really don't want to."

"Wash your face or you're not going," Beth says. She sounds shrill even to herself.

Jeanette doesn't move. Motionlessly, she stares her mother down. With so much eye makeup on, her eyes look huge, like those of a Disney princess. This makes Beth even more emotional. She doesn't want her daughter thinking she has to look like a princess, like a cartoon. The look Jeanette gives, though—her face placid, her eyes focused, squinted ever so slightly, as if she's studying Beth, measuring her—leaves Beth feeling proud of her daughter, but also scared at the same time.

When Beth was her age, she would have gone upstairs, washed her face, and then packed the makeup to reapply after she left the house.

"Never mind," Jeanette says. "It's going to be a stupid party anyway." And she goes upstairs. Quietly. She doesn't stomp, doesn't slam her bedroom door. Jeanette protests the only way she knows how: She plays country music in the sour bedroom she shares with her mother. Not loudly—she doesn't want to risk her mother having a full-blown meltdown. She figures it's just loud enough for her mother to hear downstairs, an assault calculated to grind her nerves.

Country is about as far from her mother's music as Jeanette can get. Her mother is ridiculous, though she dare not ridicule her. It's like her mother thinks there's danger lurking in this town, but how can there be? There aren't enough people here for real danger, and these farmers are too busy working and going to church and judging each other to pose any real threat. How Jeanette wishes she could move back to Charlotte, back to her old school. Her dad isn't nearly as strict, but then, her dad also doesn't want her there, she's sure of it. Or, no, maybe he does want her and Dan to live with him, but not as much as he wants to make things work with his new wife.

Beth hears Jeanette's music upstairs. She can only just hear it, though. She tries to convince herself it's not a personal attack. Her daughter is simply listening to music. She has more pressing issues anyway.

She finds Linda in the dining room, sitting next to Ernest's hospital bed. She's reading a book silently, holding his hand. Beth doesn't look at her father, at the face that she knows has gone sallow, at his boney arms. She looks at the wall above his bed, or at the floor, trying to fit him into her blind spot.

"I would appreciate it if you would stop smearing my twelve-year-old daughter in makeup."

"I'm sorry?"

"She's a middle schooler, for God's sake."

"Okay," Linda says, shutting her book.

"She can wear makeup when she gets to high school."

"I hear you. Loud and clear." Linda has her hands up in surrender. "I was just trying to cheer her up. She's having a rough time at school."

This deflates Beth. She'd hoped this would pass. "Bullies?" Beth asks.

"No, nothing like that," Linda says. "She's been having boy trouble."

"Boys her age are immature," Beth says, waving Linda away.

"The boy she likes? He likes her, but he's not allowed to date her."

"Fucking River Bend," Beth says.

"They are awful young," Linda says.

"And you thought pressing her hair would help?" She feels the urge to shake Linda, to wake her up. Instead, she folds her arms, keeps herself to herself.

"I just thought it might boost her confidence," Linda says.

"You can make her look whiter, but she still won't be white enough for this town," Beth says. Inside, Eliza cringes.

"What's her skin color have to do with it?" Linda says, and she looks genuinely perplexed. Of course she is. She's never before had a reason to question someone's racial motives. When Beth was not much older than Jeanette, she'd had a boyfriend who would date her only in secret. He said he was allowed to be friends with her, but his parents would never let him date her. What Beth hadn't understood—not at the time, although it falls into place now—was why he wouldn't even tell his friends.

"Her skin color has everything to do with it," Beth says.

Linda rolls her eyes. "Not everything is about race, Beth."

And how to make Linda understand? What she needs is definitive proof that this is about race, but Beth has been around long enough to know that trying to wake someone like Linda is an exercise in futility; there will never be proof enough.

"You're not her mother," Beth says, with more anger than is due her. Beth knows this isn't entirely Linda's fault, but she is fighting mad now, and Linda is the only person present.

"No. I'm not her mother," Linda says, sighing.

"What's that supposed to mean?"

"Nothing. I agree. I'm agreeing with you."

"No, you're sneering at me."

"No, I'm not, Beth," Linda says, her hands up. "I'm sorry. I should have checked with you before I let her use my makeup."

"And I'm perfectly capable of making an ugly sweater."

"I'm sure you are."

"There it is again. You don't believe me. But what do you know? You don't have kids. You don't know how much work and worry they are. You get to play stylist with my daughter, but you just wait. You wait until you have a twelve-year-old. You don't know, but you will."

"I don't know what you want from me," Linda says, hugging her arms to her chest.

"Just wait."

Linda gets up from her chair and moves toward Beth, who flinches, thinking Linda is going to hit her. Beth closes her eyes, waiting for the impact. Instead, Linda pulls Beth into a hug. "You're grieving," she says.

Beth shrugs out of her grip. "I don't need your pity." The side of her face is wet. "And don't you think it's time you moved out? You got a job now, right? At the hardware store?"

Linda's eyebrows lower, and her mouth scrunches to one side. "I'm not leaving Ernest," she says.

"I can take care of my father."

"Just think of me as the live-in nurse you can't afford."

"I can afford to care for my father."

"With what money? Your little cooking job?" The color slips from Linda's face.

"Then I'll sell this place and move somewhere smaller."

"Smaller," Linda says. Her voice sounds strained. She puts a hand on her forehead. "The four of you? In what, a two-bedroom house?"

"Don't tell me how to run my household."

"I'm not telling—"

"You're not even a part of this family. Nobody wants you here."

"I do," Jeanette says behind Beth. "Granddad does."

"Granddad's an invalid," Beth says.

"Don't say that," Jeanette says quietly, and Beth thinks she's finally crossed a line. She thinks Jeanette might be on the verge of wailing like she used to when she was a baby, of spilling over all the emotion she struggles to contain.

"He is," Beth says. "He's basically a high-maintenance house-plant."

Jeanette bursts forward, and again, Beth flinches. When she opens her eyes, she sees Jeanette catch Linda as she falls.

At the hospital, Derek Williams wheels Linda into an exam room. Beth sits alone in the empty lobby. Eliza uses the time to list all the ways in which Beth is failing.

"This is your fault," she insists. "You just kept pushing until this happened."

"Shove it," Beth mutters.

"You think Jeanette hated you before?" Eliza says. "Now you've landed her only companion in the hospital. Worse, you left her behind to care for her dying granddad."

"When did you become so honest?"

"I only say these things because your head is too far up your ass for you to notice on your own."

"Maybe you could tone it down a little." Even though Beth keeps her voice low, the intake nurse still eyes her like she belongs in the loony bin. Beth shakes her head, hoping Eliza will get the message.

"That's always been your biggest problem. You get so caught up in yourself, you fail to see how you're affecting those around you."

"Would you piss off already?"

"You did it during the divorce. And recently. You were so focused on you that you lost your job at the country club."

"I lost my job because the new owners didn't want a black woman in their kitchen."

"You lost your job because you stopped going to work."

"I didn't want to work somewhere I wasn't wanted."

"And then you got scared and came running back home."

The nurse at the front desk talks low into the phone, her eyes still on Beth.

"And another thing," Eliza says. "You know you're freaking that poor woman out, yet you keep talking to yourself."

"What am I supposed to do? Take your abuse silently?"

"You used to know how to keep your mouth shut."

"So did you."

A security guard shows up. He's not armed with any weapon aside from his sheer girth, his pale hard flesh straining against the fabric of his uniform.

"You can't keep this up," Eliza says. "You're ruining everything. And you brought your kids here, back to this town, dooming them to the same childhood you had. Gilmer may be gone, but what about the rest of these rednecks? What about Steve?"

"Steve would never," Beth whispers, and the security guard glares at her.

"You sure about that?"

Beth rubs her eyes like she can erase Eliza from her mind.

"You may be fucking him, but you don't know him any better than he knows you."

And even as she protests, part of her wonders what kind of man Steve really is, and whether she would even see the signs. Maybe Eliza is right, maybe Beth is so focused on herself, she wouldn't notice her own children in trouble.

Maybe she's no better than her father.

After an hour or so, Derek leads Linda back out front.

"I'm serious, though, Lin. You need to de-stress." He keeps a hand on Linda's back as they walk.

"Don't I know it," she says.

"Taking care of Ernest is too much."

"It's not that bad."

"I'd be more than happy to come help out again."

"Maybe," she says.

He hands her discharge papers. Then he hugs her, for a long time. Before he lets her go, he looks at Beth accusingly. No, not accusingly. She has to stop this. He looks at her. Just looks.

"Will you make sure she relaxes?" he says to Beth over Linda's shoulder.

"I'll do my best," Beth says.

At home, Beth finds Jeanette sitting in Linda's chair, next to Ernest's bed. She's texting on her phone. She still has on her sweater, her makeup. When she sees Linda, she hops up to let her sit down. Instead, Beth leads Linda into the living room, sets her in the recliner. She goes to make her a cup of hot chocolate.

"Is she okay?" Jeanette says, coming into the kitchen.

"She'll be fine. She just needs to relax."

Jeanette is silent.

"I'm sorry," Beth says. "You should go to your party."

"Nah," she says. "It doesn't sound like fun anymore." Beth turns to see Jeanette texting while she talks.

"You don't have to take off the makeup."

"I know," she says, her face still fixed on her phone.

"At least go and keep an eye on your brother," Beth says.

"You don't need to worry about him," she says. "He's not really that into his girlfriend."

Which is at least some comfort. Maybe it's just a phase, and they'll break up soon. And Beth can walk away from Steve, and the Brodys will be out of their lives.

Then Jeanette says, "Kelli's the one he's in love with."

In the dining room, alone with Ernest, Beth is at a loss. Does he really need the company? For all she knows, he has no idea she's even there.

She hates to see him like this. His body shrunken into the hospital bed. His hair so greasy it looks painted on his skull. The worst are his feet, sticking out of the bottom of the blankets. She can't recall ever seeing his bare feet; he always wore socks in the house, usually shoes, too. His feet are so pale, the toes long and skinny, the skin smooth, the nails gnarly. Beth pulls the blanket down.

"I suppose it shouldn't bother me," she tells him, for all the good it does. "This is your house, after all, and you should be comfortable here."

He doesn't move. His eyes are half open, pale blue irises peeking through purple-veined lids.

"Lord knows, I never was," she says, taking the chair next to him. Last she checked, Linda was napping. Jeanette is upstairs, in their shared bedroom, listening to her twanging music.

Beth never liked being alone with men, though she's a little surprised to find she's just as anxious with her own invalid father. She keeps trying not to look at him, but she can't help herself. She's staring.

"I always thought you were so strong," she blurts out. "Even as a girl."

Her mouth feels dry.

"Even when Gilmer was—" She swallows hard. "When he was—"

Ernest turns his head away. Beth doubts he is reacting to her, and yet she finds herself reaching out, taking his hand.

"You knew, didn't you? You knew and you did nothing." She squeezes his hand hard, even though he lacks the strength to pull it away. She stands up, leaning over him. "You know now. You're still in there. You see it. You see how broken I am. You know it's your fault. You were just as weak back then as you are now."

"What are you doing?" Jeanette says behind her. Beth hadn't heard her daughter on the stairs.

"I really need to put a bell on you," Beth says.

Jeanette takes her mother's hand away. "Granddad needs his rest," she says evenly.

"Yes," Beth says. "Granddad has certainly had it rough."

The way her mother talks. The venom in her voice. "What do you mean?" Jeanette asks.

Beth shakes her head. "I'm only joking."

"What did Granddad know?" She doesn't expect her mother to answer—her mother never answers personal questions—but her mother's response is even less than Jeanette hoped for. Beth sits down in the chair again, slumps really, her arms draped limply over the armrests. When she speaks, her voice has changed.

"Oh, you know," Eliza says. "Growing pains."

Elizabeth DeWitt

23

My boyfriend wants me to put my tongue in his mouth. His mouth tastes like bitter hops. He tells me to put my fingers in his mouth.

"Right hand, or left?"

"Doesn't matter," he says.

I put my left index finger in his mouth. His taste buds are rough, like he's burned his tongue.

"Push it deeper," he says.

When I twist my finger around, I can feel the ridges on the roof of his mouth, the smooth gums, the jagged surfaces of his molars, the oddly regular dips of his fillings.

"Deeper," he says, and I can feel where the back of his tongue curves down into the darkness of his throat. I'm an explorer, probing into him. I can feel his uvula. His tonsils. I wish I could probe deeper, to feel into the soft center of him, but this is as far as my stubby finger will go.

DRIVING LESSONS

1996

Ernest sat in the passenger's seat, waiting for traffic to clear enough for his daughter, Eliza, to pull out. It was probably a mistake taking her to drive in Kalamazoo so soon after getting her permit, but he thought it ridiculous that her driver's ed class never had them drive in the city. And Lord knew, Eliza's mother, Gretchen, wasn't going to take her. Eliza has been sneaking around with Steve Brody, that *no-good redneck tomcat*. Gretchen's words. And Gretchen would be damned if Eliza was going to get her license and a car to aid her in her poor decisions.

"There," Ernest said. "That was a perfect break." Traffic was heavy for a Sunday afternoon, but not that heavy. Eliza's problem was that she didn't seem to be able to gauge how fast cars were approaching. She sat there, all five feet five inches of her body rigid in her seat, her hands on the wheel at ten and two, her eyes so large that they pushed her eyebrows up into her furrowed forehead. She went long periods without blinking, and then her eyelids would flutter away the tears that were gathering in her drying eyes.

"There. Again," he said.

"I'm sorry," Eliza said, with enough edge in her voice to let him know she was less sorry and more angry. He didn't spend a lot of time with her these days, mostly just when she was fed up with her mother. She would get him to take her to the Soda Shoppe on Main Street, or the skating rink. Eliza didn't seem to want to be in his house with him. A few years ago, she had always wanted to go to the Muylder Museum in Kalamazoo, but she'd outgrown even that when she was twelve. What to do with a sixteen-year-old? He'd thought driving lessons were the perfect way to spend time together.

"Try this," he said. "Take a deep breath. Relax. Driving's not that hard."

In truth, Ernest couldn't even remember learning to drive. At ten, he'd already been driving tractors in the fields of his parents' farm, and he'd occasionally driven the truck on the dirt roads when he wanted to buy bait and go fishing. For him, the hardest part of driving had been unlearning the bad habits he'd picked up; he still had a hard time remembering to check his mirrors, and to use one foot for both the gas and the brake.

Eliza took a breath but still didn't pull the car out of the lot.

His daughter was always nervous, had been ever since she was a child.

"Ready?" Ernest asked.

Eliza nodded, but she still didn't step on the gas, couldn't bring herself to join the rest of the driving world. When did she learn that the world was so scary? He first noticed her nervousness when he and Gretchen decided to divorce. Eliza was four. He'd blamed it on the fact that her life was being upended. He'd figured she'd get better when the divorce was over and she'd settled in with her mother, but her problems only grew worse in the years after, and were especially bad whenever she came to visit him. She'd be irritable and jumpy, and always had her fingers in her mouth. He could imagine that being in his house again, the house where they'd all lived as a family, brought up painful memories. He couldn't help but think that the Section 8 apartments on the edge of town were a bad environment for her. If only he could get custody of Eliza, he could take her away from whatever it was that was bothering her. He'd tried, too. When that failed, he'd tried to get her to stay weekends with him, but she wouldn't.

When Eliza still didn't pull the car into traffic, Ernest tried a different tack. "Maybe we should start on something easier, work our way up to city driving." He'd meant it as a threat, a way to goad her into action. He wanted to prepare Eliza for the world, wanted her to reach this milestone. For as much as he hated to admit it, River Bend wasn't a place where Eliza would thrive. He knew that. She knew it. He'd heard her lament many times how much she hated this town, how she couldn't wait to leave. He wanted to soothe her, so she could head off to college in a couple of years.

Part of Ernest didn't want her to go—he didn't understand why everyone was always pushing kids to go to college. He himself never graduated, had dropped out after two years, and he turned out fine. Another part of him, though, wondered if getting out in the world would help Eliza see how good she had it in River Bend. Either way, the least he could do for her was make sure she was strong enough to go. Especially because he doubted he'd be able to pay her way. But instead of taking the bait, Eliza put the car in park, right there in the driveway to the bank parking lot. She unfastened her seat belt, got out, and asked her father to drive. In the passenger's seat, she kept her eyes fixed on her window, refusing to turn and look at him when he tried talking to her. In silence, she let him drive them both home.

Elizabeth DeWitt Hansen
24

I meet a good man. I tell him nothing for fear I will tell him everything. Steve cured me of that impulse; I will never again be that intimate. It seems to work. Greg thinks I'm normal, whole. He finds me attractive. He says he wants to know me, because knowing is loving. He tries so hard to make me feel good, his head buried between my legs. We lay in bed in the morning, our bodies so close. I'm not attracted to him. I remind myself that he's a good man, and tell my body to shut up its cravings. He's the kind of man I would want my son to be. I manage to seem whole long enough that he marries me. I take his name.

I give nothing, have nothing to give. Most of my insides have been scooped out and buried, rotten, in someone else's yard. What little is left I've shoved down deep, hoping to hold on to it, terrified of it being discovered.

But my husband is smart. He intuits the pieces of me I've shoved down deepest. He asks me about myself, and when I'm evasive, he asks me, "Why so secret?" He only wants to know me.

"You're inscrutable," he says. "Unknowable."

I hate him for making me remember that I'm insufficient. I hate him for not knowing me, for not guessing.

JESUS COW

Christmas morning, and Paula is up to her elbow in a cow's vagina, feeling around for a head or a hoof, something to grab hold of. The calf is breech. Jared called this morning because the vet is out of town, and with Dinah beside herself, he could think of nobody else who'd have the stomach for this.

She doesn't flinch, doesn't pull a face. The woman has nerves of iron. Her whole body is made of iron. The heifer is lying on her side, she won't stand, and Grandma Dinah fears she's injured herself while thrashing. Jared and Steve squat to hold on to her legs, trying to still her kicking, to keep her from further harm. Derek sits with his legs folded, the cow's head in his lap. Paula crouches behind her, her free hand braced on the ground. Jared watches that hand, focuses on it as if it will anchor him to this world. The back of her hand is very tan, the veins protruding. Even in the cold of the barn, Jared has worked up a sweat. It streams from his hairline into his eyes, but he doesn't dare mop his brow.

"I'm going to have to turn the calf," Paula says.

"All right," Jared says.

"And mamma's going to kick."

"All right."

"Hard," she says, and both Jared and Steve brace themselves.

"Oh," Linda says from behind them, turning her face away. She has her arms wrapped around her belly, not because she's cold—she's been hot ever since she got pregnant—but because she's wondering whether her own baby is positioned right. At twenty-three weeks, she's just beginning to feel the baby kick. Derek wishes he could cross the barn and hold her.

Most of the family has gathered in the barn, because that's where Grandma Dinah is. Even the dogs are here, pacing back and forth outside the door. Dinah is in the barn because it's where Maribel is, her prized cow, the one whose milk used to win ribbons at the county fair. She knows she should get in there and get her own hands dirty, but she's too emotional. Inside this stall, Dinah feels the space press in on her. It isn't an entirely unpleasant feeling. It comforts her, in fact, this closeness, her family gathered together.

In the kitchen, Christmas dinner prep has fallen to Deborah, the only one not outside. She thinks there must be a joke in there somewhere: How many idiots does it take to birth a calf?

Paula, she understands. The woman isn't much of a homemaker. Hell, she's really more man than woman. But where's Linda? She isn't needed out there. When Deborah was pregnant with each of her children, she never once slacked off like Linda does now. Worse yet is Paige, who hasn't even shown up yet. No doubt she'll arrive when supper is ready, and she'll disappear soon after. Those girls are nothing but leeches, just like their mother. The longer Deborah thinks, the madder she gets. How pathetic that Jared is still hung up on Paula, that he's put his life on hold for twenty years to raise another man's kids, even after his wife up and left. The family could say whatever it wanted about Steve, but at least he's still here.

Deborah visits her mother's house maybe four times a year: Mother's Day, Dinah's birthday, Thanksgiving, Christmas. But for years now, she's been kept from handling the turkey, the beef roast. Ever since she married Steve, a man her mother disapproved of—loudly and often—Deborah has been cut out of holiday preparations.

Now, suddenly left to cook dinner for all these people, she feels another kind of exclusion. Deborah works slowly, peeling and chopping potatoes, in her head hearing her mother suggest—not tell, for she would never say it outright, but suggest—that Deborah is doing it wrong, and how could she, a grown woman, not know how to make a simple Christmas dinner?

When Deborah was seventeen, when her father took ill, Deborah found any excuse she could not to be home. She couldn't handle her father's diminishment. She didn't know it, not then, but when her father started chemo she was already pregnant for the first time. Her mother fell to pieces—tiny shards that were lost in the corners of the kitchen, swept under the refrigerator, ground into the carpet in the living room. Dinah had never been much of a housekeeper—preferred plowing fields and baling hay to cooking and cleaning—so as her husband got sicker, she retreated deeper into the fields, the barns, leaving the household maintenance to her children. Jared did what he could, but he didn't have an eye for housework. He didn't see dust on a shelf or crumbs on a counter. He'd wash dishes only when the sink was full. And

Deborah would clean grudgingly: She wanted her own house to take care of, her own kitchen to cook in. She would make dinner for her family, meatloaf with too much oatmeal and not enough meat, and dream of the day when she moved out.

"You're going to have to do better than dry meatloaf, you want him to marry you," Dinah would say. Even at eighteen, Deborah understood she hadn't caused Dinah's bitterness. She knew she should be patient with her mother, she should go to her and hug her, let her have a good cry, but she was also at an age when her mother's grief, her raw need, was too much. She couldn't take it all for her mother, and so she took none of it.

Deborah's cooking never improved, but Steve married her anyway. Eventually. After she ended her first pregnancy and he got her pregnant with Layne. Once they were married, Deb found Steve was just as happy with frozen pizza from the gas station as he was with a home-cooked meal.

Now, in her mother's kitchen, she feels overwhelmed. The spice rack has herbs Deborah has never heard of. And this damn potato peeler. Not the good one with the rubber grip; she could only find the peeler with the slick metal handle, its blade perpendicular. Deborah keeps scraping her knuckles as she pries tiny scraps of skin from the potatoes. It occurs to her, halfway through peeling the bag, that the goose should be in the oven already. She's never cooked a goose. She goes into the living room and logs on to the computer. A Google search suggests she should start by removing the feathers. Her stomach turns watery at the thought. She's never had to de-feather a bird.

Back in the kitchen, she's relieved to find the goose on a plate in the fridge, feather-free. Its organs have been removed and placed in a separate dish. This she can do. She can rub butter on the skin; she can salt and roast it.

The back door opens, and Paige blusters in with that woman and their little boy. They stomp their boots in the doorway, knocking off the snow, and bring in shopping bags full of wrapped presents. Not a word passes between the two women. The little boy, Sage, lifts his arms to Diane and says, "Up," and Diane hands Paige her shopping bag without looking at her, then stoops to lift him. Paige lugs the gifts into the living room. As unnatural as their relationship seems to Deborah, she has to admit, Diane's child is a handsome little boy, with piles of black curly hair and cheeks as pink as a sunset.

Neither woman bothers to acknowledge Deborah. Not a "Hello" or a "Merry Christmas." Deborah returns to peeling potatoes, making short strokes with the dumb metal peeler. It occurs to Deborah that they're not simply being rude; their silence is a lovers' quarrel. (The word *lover* makes her a little uneasy here, but what else do you call it? A wives' quarrel? A domestic dispute? Is it still a domestic dispute if it carries outside the home?) Paige and Diane have been together a long time, long enough for the initial shock of them to have worn off. Still, at times like these, Deborah can't help but wonder, how do they decide which one of them should help here and which should be in the barn? She wonders, but doesn't ask, who does the laundry, who mows the lawn. She guesses Paige is the one who should help cook. She stays home with the child while Diane goes to work. Although Diane works as a nurse. But then, so does Derek. It all seems unnecessarily confusing.

Still, sometimes Deborah envies Paige. She wants her niece's freedom. When Paige is restless, it's not unusual for her to upend her life: quit her job, go back to school, take off on a road trip. There's a wildness to Paige that a man like Steve would have stomped out. Deborah worked for a time ringing up groceries at the gas station, until Steve stopped in one day and saw her talking to a male coworker. They had an argument that night. Nothing that wouldn't have blown over, except the next day, the coworker called Deborah at home. He'd only wanted to see if Deborah could cover his shift, but Steve wouldn't hear it. That had been the end of Deborah working.

Now Skyla wafts into the kitchen, bringing the cold in with her. She's in one of her rare feminine moods, and her body shows it. She somehow manages to glide as she walks, her limbs long and lean even under so many clothes: jeans, tee shirt, sweater, winter coat, wool socks, mittens, hat, scarf. She pulls off her outerwear in the doorway, and when she removes her hat, Deborah sees that she's cut her hair boy-short. Her first thought is that Jared must not know—no way any decent father would let his daughter out like that—and that Deborah is the first person in the family to see it. But, no, there's no way she can be the first, no way Dinah hasn't already seen it. This is a professional haircut, not something Skyla did to herself in the middle of the night, standing in front of the bathroom mirror with a pair of kitchen shears. She spent money on this haircut, which somehow makes it seem worse.

"Your hair," Deborah says. "It's different."

"Thanks," Skyla says, sidling up to her aunt and giving her a sideways hug. "And Merry Christmas." She rummages in kitchen drawers until she finds the potato peeler with the rubber handle. She takes over peeling where Deborah has left off, humming "We Three Kings" as she works.

The goose, Deborah sees, is still sitting on the counter. "You're in a good mood," she says, rubbing butter on its skin.

"'Tis the season," Skyla says. She's working slowly, dreamily, peeling potatoes at about half of Deborah's speed, even though she's got the good peeler. Soon, Linda shows up, rubbing the cold from her forearms and cheeks, and takes over as if the kitchen were hers, as if she'd never left this place. She's not even blood, Deborah thinks. Linda is another problem. That baby she's growing outside of wedlock. With Ernest bedridden, there's no way Linda can get him to marry her now. It isn't that Deborah's own family is spotless—yes, she knows about Steve, but he's been bewitched by a woman you'd expect to act the hussy. And Deborah knew about Beth before she married him. It's just what you did, though. You married the father of your child.

Linda's whole generation seems to make themselves at home wherever they are. These millennials, they have no qualms about taking, feel none of Deborah's debilitating self-doubt. Their efforts scream, "Look at me! Look what I've done! See how clever?" And they get by with it, too. Deborah can't recall Dinah ever scolding Linda or Paige for failing to live up to her standards.

When Paige finally returns to help, Deborah takes it as a sign she's no longer needed. The sisters work with their own rhythm, perfectly in sync with each other. Deborah feels suddenly old, an outsider. She finishes the goose and slides it into the oven before she leaves. On her way into the living room, she sees Linda turn the oven on. Stupid, stupid.

Hannah plays up in the hayloft, jumping around like it's a playground, and Mandy and Kelli join in to distract their sister from the situation below. Steve feels grateful to his oldest daughters for keeping Hannah occupied. He'd tried to get the girls to stay in the house, to help their mother, but not ten minutes after he got to the barn, the girls showed up, peeking their heads into the stall. Hannah immediately started asking questions he wasn't ready to answer. Let her stay ignorant, innocent, a little longer.

He'd started drinking early today. He'd needed it after turning on the news this morning and seeing Gilmer Thurber again, with his pansy-ass mustache. Thurber has been sentenced to life in prison. When Steve was younger, when he and Beth were first dating and she told him about a man who hurt her, it had all seemed so distant. Steve never even thought about who had done it and whether the man still lived in town. Without even asking Beth, though, he'd put it together in the wake of the arrest: It was Gilmer.

Who else in this town had Gilmer hurt? Steve watches his girls up in the hayloft, and for a moment he's filled with so much rage he's shaking. He feels dizzy with fury.

Paula is up to her shoulder in Maribel now, her whole body rigid, every muscle tense as she tries to turn the calf. Even with two men steadying her legs, the cow kicks, and Steve loses his balance. With her front legs free, Maribel tries to scramble to her feet, her right leg buckling under her weight. Paula's arm is twisted around inside the cow.

"God dammit, Steve." Paula should have guessed he was already drunk. "Derek, you want to step in?"

"I got this," Steve says.

"Move," Dinah says.

Steve stumbles to his feet and slaps the cold from his arms, as if to blame his lack of balance on the weather.

"You hold her head," Dinah tells Steve. "Just lay it in your lap, make sure she doesn't knock herself out."

Sitting, Steve is much more stable. Derek takes hold of the forelegs, averting his eyes from his stepmom's business. He's a nurse, so he shouldn't be squeamish, but the whole thing—Paula with her arm up a cow's backside, her face way too close, as if she wanted to crawl inside—makes Derek nauseous. There's something that clicks in his brain when he's at work that keeps him from feeling this way, but watching someone else, he wants to throw up. Maribel twitches, grunting, trying to pull herself up or push the calf out, Derek can't tell which. He half wonders whether he might break the cow's legs if she kicks—he's holding on so tight—or whether the cow's legs might break him. Uncle Steve is holding Maribel's head in his lap with both hands, and when the cow is still, he strokes the sides of her face, damp with saliva. Steve is humming softly, and Derek thinks this can't be the same man who gave him shit last week as he changed the valve on Derek's water heater.

"Almost there," Paula says. The straining muscles in her back are visible through her shirt, and her free arm is bulging, tense. She has her eyes closed, and Derek realizes his dad is staring at his stepmother.

"There," Paula says, and withdraws her arm. God, the gore that coats her. Jared tries not to look, but he can't help seeing the thick mucousy fluid, wet enough to plaster down the hairs on Paula's arm. Once Paula has fully extracted herself, she searches around for a towel. The best she can do is a saddle blanket, and she cleans her arm as well as she can before rolling her sleeve back down.

As soon as Paula moves away from Maribel, Dinah is on her knees, her palms flat on the cow's side. She leans down to kiss her fur, a rare tender moment. Maribel is still working, still trying to give birth, her flanks pulsing irregularly, her breath making short puffs in the cold air. There's steam rising off her body, and Paula wonders whether she should fetch a blanket, make the poor thing more comfortable. Sickness and blood don't bother Paula, not when it seems likely to pass, but Maribel's labored breathing, her quivering haunches, all scream Death at Paula. The rest of the family has been in and out of the barn all morning—Deborah brought them hot coffee—and while they were concerned for the cow, none of them seem alarmed. None of them seem to hear Death, to recognize the stench of it. Only Paula hears it, Paula and the dogs, who whimper from the doorway but won't enter.

"Christ," Paula says. "The feet should be out by now." She rolls her sleeve back up, kneels by the cow. She feels around inside for the legs again. "Do you have obstetrical chains?"

"We don't normally calf them anymore," Dinah says, "but that Hudson bull got in our field—"

"Any thin chain will do," Paula says. "Or a leash? A choke chain?"

Dinah sends Derek off, tells him where to find a leash. He's a good boy, Dinah thinks. He would have made a good veterinarian. When he returns, Paula slips the leash into the cow and uses it to hold on to the calf's legs. She pulls, gently, trying to time her tugs with Maribel's pulsing flanks. A stream of fluid shoots out of Maribel, and for a moment, Derek is certain he will throw up. He's always thought, but now he's sure, that he would make a terrible OB-GYN. He looks around to compare how his dad and uncle are doing, and finds they both have their eyes averted. Behind the cow, the straw is damp. The calf's legs are now poking out, the fur matted and wet, the leash darkened. Paula tugs like it's nothing. When the legs are far enough out, Paula removes the leash, the cow still working at the calf, until the dark wet mound of fur—Derek can't yet think of it as a living thing, since it doesn't move, doesn't breathe—is spat out onto the straw.

"Jesus," Derek says.

Paula pokes a piece of straw up the calf's nose, again and

again, until the calf coughs, and breathes. Dinah watches, morbidly anxious. Steve's head nods; he's falling asleep with the cow's head in his lap. Even the kids have stopped playing, peeking down from the hayloft to bear witness.

"It's a Jesus Cow," Derek says.

Nobody but Steve laughs.

After the birth, after the calf has been cleaned and dried—Derek does this, for cleaning and drying are all normal parts of his job—Derek returns to the house. He wants to take up residence here, in this kitchen, with Linda. He hasn't seen the sisters all together in years, and he watches for a moment. How comfy, how in-her-element Linda seems. She and Paige cooking together almost looks like choreography. Linda stretches for the spice rack, and Paige hands her the rosemary. Paige carries chopped onions to the stove, and, without looking up, Linda leans aside so her sister can dump them in the frying pan. They're talking, but not about the task at hand. It isn't until Skyla speaks up that they start arguing, amiably, as only grown women can do. Skyla loves this, thrives on the chaos.

Linda stirs a pan of gravy while the potatoes boil over. The Brodys' dogs, in and hungry from the cold, wrestle on the floor over raw goose organs. They're all snarls and wagging tails. The dogs each claim a bit of offal and carry it off to separate corners.

Paula arrives, strips down to her bra, and scrubs her arm in the sink. She leaves her flannel shirt on the floor. Jared brings out a clean tee.

"Thank you for coming," Jared says, his hand going to his beard.

"No worries."

"I would have said it before, but you seemed preoccupied."

Paula laughs. Her laugh is the only distinctly feminine thing about her. It's always reminded Jared of wind chimes.

"What's the word?" Paige says. She keeps sneaking glances at her mother while rummaging in the fridge. She and Paula had coffee a couple of weeks back, and something about sitting at a table across from her mother made it feel like Paige couldn't really study her. It was too close, too intimate. Here, though, she feels free to look. Paige finds that Linda's assessment is accurate: Paula hasn't aged. She's still as hard and pretty as ever.

"We had a cow," Derek says. "A Jesus Cow."

Steve cracks open a beer.

"Shit's never going to come off," Paula says, still scrubbing her arm in the sink.

As hard and pretty and potty-mouthed as ever.

Paige edges around her mother to fill a pot with water. She keeps staring at her. Up close, her mother's face has a few sun spots and more lines, mostly around her eyes and on her fore-head, not so much around her mouth. Her eyes are brown. Paige couldn't remember, but they are, they're brown, like her own.

"I'm not an alien, you know," Paula says.

"I'm not convinced," Paige says.

"Out with it."

"Out with what?" Paige asks, her eyes narrowing.

"Whatever it is you want to say."

But Paige has nothing. Her confidence is shaken.

Diane comes to the doorway now, watching both Paula and Paige. Paige looks to Diane for help, and for the first time in months, Diane's face softens. Paige wants to go to Diane, wants to bury her face in her wife's neck, her skin so different from Paula's, as smooth and pale as the moonlight. Paige wants to cry into her, wants to weep like an exhausted child. Instead, she opens the oven, checks the goose. "You're letting the damn potatoes boil over," she calls over her shoulder good-naturedly. Diane slips back into the living room.

"Hell, they're barely hissing," Linda says. Even though they're swearing, they're both smiling. Skyla stands on the opposite side of the kitchen island, away from the heat. "I can only take so many hours of these women bickering," she says to Derek, but she's smiling, too.

Paige nudges Linda aside with her hip and takes up stirring the gravy.

"You let it clump," Paige says. "You must have learned to cook from Ma."

"I can hear you," Paula says.

"Why isn't Skyla helping?" Linda says.

"I'm waiting to carve," Skyla says.

"You're going to be waiting a long time," Paige says.

Skyla gives Derek a wink.

"You want to grab these potatoes?" Linda says. She's taken the gravy back from Paige, stirs it furiously as if she could beat the lumps out of it.

"I would, but I don't want to leave these knives unattended," Skyla says.

"Diane's watching the kids," Paige says.

When Skyla still doesn't move, Derek goes over, grabs the hot pads, and pulls the potatoes from the stove. He drains them and leaves them in the sink. Linda barely looks at him as she mumbles a "thanks."

This is too much for him. Linda's awkwardness. She's been like this for months.

He escapes to the living room, seats himself near the Christmas tree, pretends he's ventured into the forest to watch these strange creatures in their natural habitat. What he finds is confusing. Steve is in the middle of the living room letting Hannah climb him like a jungle gym. Sage sits on the floor nearby, clapping his hands and squealing. He crawls over to Steve, raises his arms, and says, "Up," and Steve lifts the child, standing with Sage in his arms and Hannah clinging to his back like a monkey. He tosses Sage in the air. Diane is clearly uncomfortable, watching closely for any falter in Steve's balance.

On his way back to the kitchen, Derek stumbles upon Paula and his dad, standing in a doorway, kissing. She doesn't belong here, never did. Their kiss looks halfhearted, obligatory, as they stand in the hallway underneath the pointy leaves and red berries of the mistletoe. There's a sadness to it, a chasteness. It makes Derek turn away even faster than if it had been passionate. These are the men he holds himself up to, the men he compares himself to, always finding himself lacking. They are his *How to Be a Man* template. He wonders now whether he has ever really seen them clearly. He's always blamed his stepmother for leaving, for breaking his dad's heart. But now, after seeing his dad with Paula, his arms draped loosely around her body, with enough space between them to see daylight from the window, kissing under the mistletoe—which isn't even mistletoe, he realizes; those pointy leaves and berries are holly—Derek wonders whether he shouldn't make a new template.

After goose and fixings, after pie and coffee, Hannah begs them to finally, *finally* open presents. The family crowds into the living room, the children on the floor.

"I'm not a kid anymore," Mandy mutters, but she seats herself next to her sisters on the hardwood. She motions for Skyla to join them, but Skyla shakes her head, lingering near the doorway like she wants to make a fast break.

Steve also hovers in the doorway between the living room and the kitchen, where the drinks are.

Diane is shivering in her seat by the drafty window. Paige goes to the fireplace to light a fire, as if her attentiveness, the anticipation of her wife's needs, could erase the fight they're having. *See how sweet I am? See how caring?*

When the presents are all doled out, after the children have littered the floor with torn wrapping paper from their gifts, Paige makes sure Linda sees the package from her and Diane first. "For baby," Paige says, handing over the gift, and when Linda opens it, Paige watches her sister's face go soft with tears.

"Cute, right?" She'd gotten a doll with springy curls in her hair, a stiffly starched dress.

"Oh, Paige," Linda says.

"It was nothing," Paige says.

"You know I'm having a boy."

"Ah, shit," Paige says.

"It's fine," Linda says, holding the box with white knuckles. "Did you get a receipt?"

"Shit, shit, shit," Paige says.

"That's my daughter," Paula mutters. Jared laughs and pats her knee.

"Maybe your son will be gender nonconforming," Paige says.

"Let's hope," Diane says.

"I hate Christmas," Paige admits.

"Everyone hates Christmas," Derek says.

"At its essence it's good, right? I mean the bastard child, the idea of extending hospitality to those in need, no matter how mangy or Arab they might look." Paige bounces on the balls of her feet. "But what does that have to do with gift giving in the name of a morbidly obese old guy? Like, what the fuck, America?"

Paige looks to her wife, hoping her little rant has at least amused her. It has not. When Paige went on like this, Diane used to kiss her forehead and call her her Little Radical. Now Diane gets up, picks her way through the family, and goes to the bathroom. Paige listens for the toilet flush, but even after the door opens again, Diane does not come back.

"I was reading about Finland, I think," Paige says, "where they just give each other a new book and a chocolate bar on Christmas Eve, and maybe a new pair of pajamas. You go to bed early in your new fleece and eat chocolate and read. Doesn't that sound nice?"

Those two are doomed, Derek thinks.

Steve gulps from a coffee mug.

Give it a rest already, Paula thinks. Part of her is still in the barn with the calf, its skinny, slick legs, its nostrils twitching when she tickled them with the straw. The newborn was much smaller than a calf should be. When they left, it had yet to stand, hadn't even tried stretching its legs. How certain she had been that it was dead, that it would never breathe. But it had breathed, Paula reminds herself. She had done all she could.

Her daughters are bickering now, still opening presents. Linda and Paige—those two were never close in the way Paula thought sisters would be. Yet in a lot of ways, they were much closer, and Paula wonders whether there is something about age proximity that drives sisters apart, each one struggling to outgrow the other, to shoot above them like a sapling trying to break through the canopy. Maybe they are close, just in their own way.

For a moment, just a moment, Paula thinks she could stay here and pick up her old life. She had felt something earlier when she kissed Jared, and even though it wasn't exactly sexual, it was familiar. Familial.

Nobody notices Skyla sneaking into the kitchen to answer her phone. When Steve goes in for a refill, he finds Skyla waiting by the window.

"You know Santa already came," he says, and Skyla rolls her eyes so hard, he worries she might detach a retina. He looks a little sheepish as he pours whiskey into a coffee mug. "Our little secret," he says, as if anyone in the living room were fooled. Her uncle makes her sad, and she doesn't like to feel sad. She doesn't really like to feel in general, so she usually lets him know, nonverbally, how incredibly lame he is. When the eye roll doesn't work, she realizes she's going to have to say something before he'll leave her alone.

"I invited someone. He should be here any minute."

"Attagirl," Steve says, raising his newly refreshed mug. She's not his daughter, so he can condone such acts.

He doesn't get it, but then he never does. Rumor has it he's sleeping with Dan Hansen's mom—and how can Aunt Deb stand it? At sixteen, Skyla's already done with romance. She'd chased after Dan along with her cousins, but he didn't even notice her. It seemed like such a pointless pursuit.

No, her guest isn't for her, but for her mother.

When the rental car pulls up in the driveway, Skyla goes outside to greet Jorge. This is her gift: She's spent the last month talking to Jorge, convincing him to come here. She knows her mother will be angry, and that her father will be heartbroken. But she also knows her parents are becoming too chummy again; all throughout dinner, she watched them sneak glances at each other. In a sense, bringing Jorge here is really a gift for her father.

. . .

Jorge pulls into the driveway and turns off his GPS. The farm, built up on a hill and covered in snow, looks to him like a Christmas card. *Season's Greetings, Warm Wishes,* and all that. For a moment, he wonders if he's made a mistake. He didn't expect a full-on farm, with barns and a silo, and he realizes how seldom Paula talks of her old life, how few details she's provided.

From the driveway, he can see into the picture window in the kitchen, straight through to the living room, where Paula sits in a chair next to a man with a full beard and glasses, a heap of wrapping paper at their feet. Jorge has no doubt the man is Jared. Watching her framed in the doorway like this, it's almost like watching her on a movie screen, and Jorge finds himself wondering how the scene will play out, waiting for Paula's body language to tell him what's really going on. She holds a mug in her lap and smiles, presumably watching the rest of the family unwrap presents.

Part of him wants to head back to the airport, but then the back door opens and out steps a teenaged girl who's the spitting image of Paula, wearing an oversized sweater, leggings, and unlaced men's boots. She clomps toward him with a smile, her arms wrapped around herself to stave off the cold.

"You coming in or what?"

She doesn't bother introducing herself or asking who he is. He can still see through the window behind her; Paula is leaning toward Jared, who says something in her ear and then laughs, his fingers buried in his beard.

When Paula left, Jorge spent the first month trying not to call her, trying to give her space. He'd imagined going with her to

Michigan, meeting her daughters, her old friends, convincing her husband it was time to let her go. When Paula said no, this was something she had to do herself, it sounded sensible because it was a line so often used on TV. Of course he understood.

But then, despair set in. She wasn't coming back. And even though he felt certain of this, he found himself unable to let go. He called daily, they argued daily, they made up—as well as a couple can make up while fifteen hundred miles apart.

When he was beginning to come to terms with the loss—about the same time Lola had stopped whimpering in the evenings, stopped staring at the spot in the drive where Paula usually parked her truck—when he was beginning to find other things to occupy his mind (nights out with friends, remodeling the bathroom, finishing the porch, having the neighbors over for brisket), when he was starting to feel like he might be okay, he got a call from Skyla. She sounded eerily like her mother, the tone and timbre of her voice. The cadence, though, was distinctly teenaged.

"She misses you, you know," she told him after minimal small talk.

"She sure doesn't act like it," Jorge said. He was outside when she called, up on a ladder, painting the eaves, and he hadn't bothered to climb down when his phone rang. He clung to the ladder awkwardly, his phone held with his shoulder while his paintbrush bristles stiffened with paint.

"You should come for Christmas." Skyla said it so casually he found himself agreeing without really thinking it through.

Standing in the snowy driveway, though, watching Paula through the window—Jorge decides he's not leaving here without a fight.

. . .

Derek's gift for Linda is cheap, he realizes now. Questions of gender aside, Paige's gift is thoughtful, tuned in to Linda's future in a way that Derek's gift is not. He got her a pound of coffee, ordered online. He imagines Paige spending hours looking for a doll, the perfect doll, a doll that reminds her of her sister. All he did was click some buttons on the computer, the whole time remembering a trip they took in high school. They drove with some friends to Seattle, where the family of one of the friends lived. Derek remembers being crowded into the backseat with Linda and arguing over what to listen to on the radio, taking shifts driving through the night, eating at fast food restaurants because they'd all pooled their money for gas. And after days in the car, when they finally arrived in Seattle, the first thing they did was find a coffee shop. He remembers the look on Linda's face when she took her first sip, the contentment. He was hoping to see that on her face again when she opened his present.

But she's pregnant. As much as he doesn't want to think about that, doesn't want to acknowledge that she's having another man's baby, it's undeniable. She can't even drink coffee right now. God, he's so stupid.

He won't give it to her, he decides, and steals his own gift from her stack when nobody's looking. But before he can make it out of the living room, he finds the doorway blocked by a man he's never met before.

Jorge enters to find Paula with her hand on Jared's knee, her eyes trained on his face, her laugh quiet, meant only for her husband. He barely has time to compose himself before Paula sees him.

"Surprise," Skyla says from behind Jorge.

"Baby," Paula says. "What are you doing here?" She presses her hands to her mouth, not quite obscuring her awkward smile.

His appearance has the desired effect: She leaves Jared sitting alone and goes to hug Jorge.

"Merry Christmas," Jorge says.

"Who're you?" Dinah says from her seat by the tree. It isn't that she means to be rude, but she's had a very long day, and his arrival surprises her. She'd been so focused on Christmas, and Maribel, that she'd failed to hear the car pull into her driveway. She scolds herself. You can't be too careful, especially in this day and age. Why, just this week, that Thurber man was in the news again. It's getting to the point where you can't even trust the people you've known your whole life.

"Everyone, this is Jorge. Mom's fiancé," Skyla says. The look on her father's face breaks her heart. She can tell that seeing Jorge in his home has made the man real for the first time. He takes off his glasses, rubs his eyes, his beard. He looks so old to Skyla. She had thought that bringing Jorge here—that getting her mother to leave—was the best thing she could do for her father, but now she's not so sure.

Dinah is sure, though. She looks from Jared to Skyla, and when she realizes Skyla's plan, she whispers a silent thank-you to her granddaughter. "Goodness, you've come a long way," she says, putting an arm around Jorge. "You must be exhausted. Can I get you a plate? Cup of coffee? I'm Dinah. The kitchen's this way." And she steers him away from her son.

"I'm not really hungry," Jorge says.

"Nonsense. It's Christmas, and you're family." She pulls leftovers from the refrigerator, fixes him a plate.

"I can't believe you're here," Paula says, retrieving coffee mugs from the cupboard. She's more shocked than surprised, and it occurs to her how long she's been here, how easily she's lost track of time. What was it about River Bend that bred such complacency?

"I should have come sooner," Jorge says as Dinah pushes a plate into his hands.

"You're here now," Dinah says. "We'll give you two some time to catch up." She stares pointedly at her grandchildren. Skyla hovers behind her mother and Derek, who's trying to hide a gift in his coat. She lets him finish, then shoos him back into the living room.

Jorge sets to work on his food, while Paula pours them each a cup of coffee.

"You've had a nice little reunion, I see," he says when she sits down with him at the table. It's out of his mouth before he can stop himself.

"Is that what this is? You came to take back what's yours?"

"I didn't mean it like that," he says.

"Then what did you mean?" She blows on her coffee, even though it's old, almost room temperature.

"It just seems like you and your family have gotten close."

She can hear the jealousy in his voice, not only jealousy over Jared, but over the roast goose and the farmhouse, the wood-burning fireplace, the children and grandchildren and great-grandchildren, the snow-covered hills and gray sky, the harsh Michigan winter that has forced the family to huddle together for warmth. She knows this scene would appeal to Jorge, and there's no way she can tell him everything else that goes along with it: the lack of privacy; the judgments made about how you run your business, how you raise your children, how you feed your family, how you love your spouse. Taking his hand, she decides she's ready to be done with all of it. She nods, smiles, and says, "Let's go home tomorrow."

. . .

The Jesus Cow dies two days later. Of course Grandma Dinah is sad, but she's mostly concerned for Maribel, who Linda found in the barn, licking the ice from the stiff calf's coat. Linda shows up at Derek's house to share the news.

"I can't stand any more death," Linda says. She wants to say more, but her voice has gone too thick to speak. When she has recovered, all she says is, "That coffee smells amazing."

"Want some? I just brewed it."

"No. I mean, yes, but no. It's bad for the baby."

Stupid, stupid, stupid, Derek thinks.

"Well," she says, "maybe half a cup." Her stepbrother has been awful sweet these days, and when she thinks about it, she realizes he's always been sweet. They've been best friends since before their parents even married. She's closer to him than she is even to Paige. Wouldn't it be great if she could make herself feel even a tiny bit of the love he feels for her?

Derek goes to pour her a cup of coffee, adding just cream. *And what now?* he thinks when he hands it to her. She's here, in his house, and how can he get her to stay? He wonders whether this is a family trait, the inability to get women to stick around. He heard from his dad yesterday that Paula is gone. No goodbyes, she just skipped town three days before the divorce became final. Linda drove up this morning in Paula's truck. Not that his dad had expected Paula to stay forever—they knew she was getting remarried—but something about the kiss Derek had seen made him wonder. Because his dad was a different man, a more present man, with Paula around.

"I see you got her truck," Derek says, nodding to the window where it sits in his driveway.

She shrugs. "Whoopie. The damn thing's running on borrowed time."

Linda takes a sip of coffee, and her face brightens. This is how Derek gets Linda to take off her shoes. This is how he gets Linda to stay awhile in the house he bought three years ago, the house that just now, today, starts to feel like home.

Elizabeth DeWitt Hansen
25

About a year after our son's birth, a change takes Greg like a cold front. It's subtle: He leaves piles of folded clothes on the floor, he cooks all the meat from the freezer, then lets it spoil in the fridge, he makes a full pot of coffee and drinks only a cup, he turns the air conditioner down to sixty-five without telling me. To compensate, he buys me sweaters, three sizes too big. He stores gallons of orange juice and leaves them to ferment in the fridge. He moves us to a bigger house, a bigger yard, a bigger city, more space to lose each other in. He plants a garden that takes up the entire yard, then lets it go to seed and weeds, green and glossy and so thick the grass underneath dies.

I tell him all this: He doesn't take care of himself, he doesn't take care of me, he doesn't take care of the house, the yard's a mess. He won't pick up after himself, he doesn't appreciate all I do around here, he puts too much into work and not enough into this marriage, he doesn't know how hard I work. He paws at me constantly, wants my body, demands my body, as if he could dig into me, as if he could unearth me.

He waves me off. Tells me, "This Angry Black Woman act is getting old."

PIG PLOP

On a damp sunny day in early March, the Muylder Mansion holds its annual fund-raiser in the park. Beth has fond memories of the park from when she was a teenager; of lying in the sun on the picnic table, of winter snowball fights with friends. It was where she and Steve had their first kiss, on a green spring day.

Spring has technically sprung—Punxsutawney Phil was pulled from his hole a month ago and failed to see his shadow—but the trees are still bare, showing only the earliest yellow buds. The first robins have been spotted, and sparrows hop around in the tree branches. The sun shines so weakly it may as well be cloudy. After hunkering from the cold for all of January and February, the people of River Bend are coming out of hibernation. They wander down to the park, which is a mess of muck, the last of the dirtied snow heaps still crushing in on themselves. Even so, children run around with no coats. Some of the adults have on short sleeves.

Beth can see the temperature on the bank sign downtown. It's fifty-two degrees.

In the driest patch of dead grass, the Hudson boys—men, really; Slick and Mikey—have fenced off a section with chicken wire, a grid spray-painted on the ground inside, bingo-style. Beth has never attended the annual Pig Plop. She can't stand the smell of pigs, has always hated those damp days in the summer when the wind comes up just so, carrying the stench from the farms south of town.

When Beth left the house, Jeanette was hiding in her room. She would stay until her granddad's nurse came at ten. Beth wishes she could have stayed behind instead. She didn't want to get out of bed this morning, certainly not to watch her boss herd a pig. She's here only for Dan, who stands at parade rest in his marching uniform, stonily rigid beneath the weight of his bass drum. He's had a growth spurt when Beth wasn't looking; just last fall, it seemed he would topple under the weight of his instrument. Today, he bears the drum's weight easily.

If Beth has missed his growth spurt, the girls in school certainly haven't. Kelli and Mandy Brody both eye Dan with the awkward, guilty lust of small-town teenaged girls. Deborah Brody notices, too. It's concerning. That boy spends entirely too much time with her daughters.

Next to Deb, Steve stands far enough away to keep from touching her. In a way, they look like they fit together perfectly. Both wear worn men's jeans and flannel shirts with the sleeves rolled up. Steve's hair is thin, with so much gray creeping in that it looks pale. Deb's hair is limp and stringy, dyed too red, with three inches of gray roots showing. The longer Beth watches, the more she decides that Deb is every bit as distant as Steve said. Deb keeps her head angled away from her husband. There's nobody talking to her, nothing to occupy her attention, but she very studiously keeps from looking at Steve.

As the Hudson boys arrive with the pig, Mandy Brody steps forward and cues up the band. They play a processional march befitting a king. Mikey drives up in his pickup truck, the pig trying hard to stay standing in the back. Over the heads in front of her, Beth can just see him. Beth remembers Mikey standing in Gilmer's bedroom, his bare feet on the carpet mere inches from hers.

Seeing him again, she feels her stomach drop out of her. The crowd goes silent, and she feels the sky darken. She takes a deep breath, closes her eyes. When she opens them again, Mikey is still there, getting out of his truck. He still has the same dark eyes, the same thick eyebrows. And yet he's smiling, laughing. For all she can see, he looks like a normal guy who has lived a normal life.

When Slick lets down the tailgate, he leans a wide board against it as the pig skitters toward the cab of the truck bed. Mikey hops in and chases the pig toward the makeshift ramp. The band plays on, equal amounts pep and missed key signatures. Beth tries to focus on Dan, that steady *bom, bom, bom*. The pig squeals and scrambles, wary of the ramp, but eventually Mikey drives it down and Slick shepherds it toward the grid. Mud flecks Slick's tee shirt, his jeans, his bare forearms, but not his pale face, not his sail of strawberry-blond hair worked free of its copious gelling. Beth stays at the back of the crowd, where she can barely see the grid, but at least can't smell that wretched animal.

Now that the pig has arrived, the betting begins. The idea of a Pig Plop is to wait and see which square the pig does its business on. When Mrs. Schwartz comes by with a bucket and tickets, Beth looks in her purse, but all she can find is a twenty-dollar bill. She needs it for groceries; the Muylder Museum will just have to do without.

"Mrs. Hansen," Mrs. Schwartz says. "So good to see you."

"Ms.," Beth says. "DeWitt."

"I'm sorry to say, your daughter is still behind in my class."

"Perhaps the problem is not my daughter," Beth says. "Perhaps you might reconsider your rubric."

Mrs. Schwartz seems not to have heard Beth. "How are you? How is your father? We're all praying he makes a full recovery."

"Save your prayers. My father's as good as gone." She hopes this will get the woman to leave, but Mrs. Schwartz continues to hold her bucket out until Beth relents and opens her purse again.

"The Lord hears all prayers. It's not for us to decide what's important and what's not."

Across the grid, Beth watches Mikey approach Steve, who pulls out his wallet. When he opens it, Deb puts a hand on his arm, stands on tiptoe to whisper to him. Steve leans his ear toward his wife. He smiles, the briefest smile. Was this how Beth's own husband was when they were married? Beth imagines he had another woman, too, one he would lie in bed with long before the divorce, telling her how miserable he was in his marriage.

"It seems the two of you have become close since your return," Mrs. Schwartz says, her eyes following Beth's. "I wonder what your mother would say, were she to find out."

"Probably, she'd tell you to mind your own goddamn business," Beth says. "But then, my mother always did have a mouth on her." Beth has the pleasure of seeing a flush settle into Mrs. Schwartz's cheeks.

"Your mother's not the only one," Mrs. Schwartz says.

"I read somewhere that Governor Muylder was a gambling man, that he racked up some serious debt in his day. The scandal broke about the time he was seeking reelection," Beth says. "Ironic, don't you think?" As she tries to set the twenty in the bucket, a breeze catches it, threatening to carry it away. She crumples it in and picks which squares she wants to bet on.

"Yes. Well. I look forward to teaching Jeanette again next year," Mrs. Schwartz says, handing Beth four tickets for her bet. "Thank you for your donation." And she continues on.

As Steve fusses with Deborah over how much money they can spare, Deborah catches sight of Beth. Even as she talks with Mrs. Schwartz, Beth watches Steve. Beth has no right to even be here; she left River Bend, bragged on social media about how she became a successful chef, how she worked at a fancy country club, how she married a man with money. She always looked down on this town.

Now she's back, with her hands on Deborah's husband. And that boy of hers has his eye on Deborah's girls. The DeWitts need to leave, need to go back to their fancy life. Beth wears equestrian boots and skinny jeans, a wool peacoat. She has her hair pressed straight, except that the spring humidity makes it frizz at the temples. What a mess. The scarf she wears is silk or satin, something shiny and cold looking.

Slick and Mike Hudson wrangle the pig onto the grid, and the pig begins rooting around for acorns. Across the grid, Beth hugs her purse to her body and wrinkles her face. Little Miss Priss. When Mrs. Schwartz had come around with a bucket, taking money, Deborah had watched Beth pull a twenty from her purse, flashing the bill around for all to see before she set it in the collection.

Really, the woman is too much. Worse yet is that daughter of hers, her hair cut short, puffed out in an afro. At least try to fit in. That nappy-headed child looks like she, too, thinks she's too good for this town. Just like her mother.

Deborah tries to clear her head. Her daughters. She's here for them. Kelli plays tuba, and Deborah is surprised to hear how good she is, how confidently she plays. Even better, this is the band's first performance since Mandy made drum major. Deborah is proud, and she tries to focus on that.

What'd you bet on?" Jeanette says, and Beth jumps. She hadn't seen her daughter walk up. She'd thought herself alone at the back of the crowd. Beth shows her the tickets.

Before long, the crowd has dispersed around the park. Children run in the mud, playing tag. The chains on the swings clank and squeak as kids pump themselves higher and higher. The merry-go-round, having sat motionless and rusting all winter, creaks loud enough to be heard over the music. Boys make snowballs and throw them at the band members, trying to see if they can make them break formation; the band, for the most part, remains still, but when Skyla Williams takes a dirty slush ball on the side of her face, she pockets her piccolo and chases the boys down.

Jeanette soon wanders off to talk to one of her classmates. Her hair has grown out some, and she has picked it out into an afro. She wears a scarf that hides the curling iron scar on her neck, and earrings and eye shadow. Since December, Beth has given up the makeup argument. Now she wonders when her daughter became a young lady. It won't be long before she's an adult, before she goes off to college, where Beth won't be able to protect her. Already, Jeanette is out of the house more and more, hanging out with kids Beth doesn't know. When Jeanette is gone, Beth can't help but imagine things happening to her. Horrible things. Car accidents, tornadoes, kidnappings, school bombings, mass shootings. And when Jeanette wants to go out in the evenings, Beth always imagines her getting separated from her friends. She imagines Jeanette in a damp mall parking lot, checking her phone and finding it drained. Jeanette turning to go back into the mall, only to realize it's closed. A strange car pulling up, the car door opening, a thin strip of interior light showing around the door. Stale cigarette smoke wafts out. A man grabs Jeanette by the arm, hauling her in.

"We're right back in the Thurbers' coat closet," Eliza says from deep in the well.

Beth shakes her head. She goes over to her daughter, intent on taking her back home. This Pig Plop is a waste of time and energy; who knows how long it will be until that smelly animal relieves itself. But as soon as Beth sidles up next to her daughter, a friend takes Jeanette by the arm and pulls her over to a group of boys. Beth has never felt more alone, more desperate. She feels sick, and she realizes she's now close enough to the pig to smell it.

And who are these kids? They look like any other River Bend teens: most of them blond, although only one—the girl who'd grabbed Jeanette's arm—looks like the color might be natural. The girl is shorter than Jeanette, but that won't last. She'll no doubt have a growth spurt in a few years and leave Jeanette in her shadow. By high school, the nice boys won't notice Jeanette standing next to this girl; only the trashy ones will. And Jeanette will feel like it's her fault, like she's not good enough. Beth hates these blond kids. She wants so desperately to save Jeanette from the heartache they will cause her.

"Beth, how are you?" Linda says, approaching hand in hand with her stepbrother. *Poor dumb boy,* Beth thinks, noting the glee in Derek's eyes. For a moment, Beth can't remember what it feels like to hold a man's hand in public. She doesn't want to talk to

Linda, doesn't have anything to say, but Linda is still in the process of moving out, and Beth tries to keep things friendly. She doesn't want Linda to up and change her mind, decide to stay. Really, Derek Williams is a godsend.

"How's Ernest?" Linda asks. Now that she has a substantial baby belly, she keeps her hands braced on her back.

Beth shrugs. "About the same."

"Mind if I stop by and see him this afternoon?"

Derek visibly bristles, but says nothing.

"That would be nice," Beth says, still watching her daughter.

Linda leans in and hugs Beth goodbye before taking Derek's hand again and moving off to talk to someone else.

Without Linda to distract her, Beth can feel Steve's presence in the crowd, like a quiet surrender. She feels herself leaning into it. Her hands grow warmer with him near, as if in anticipation of a touch. All winter they've been meeting at least once a week, but it's not enough. She wants more than she can get from him.

Jeanette and her friends are near the band now, a stone's throw from where Mandy stands, cueing the next song. Mandy is skinny, so like her mother at that age. In fact, if Mandy had red hair, if she were a few inches shorter, she could be Deb's clone. And yet there's a confidence to Mandy that Deb always lacked.

The girl is trouble.

The whole family is trouble.

Beth searches the crowd and spots Deb still across the way, talking to Mikey. She watches for a moment, hoping to see some hint of flirtation—Deb's hand on his bicep, maybe—something that would ease her conscience, but Deb stands an arm's length away.

Beth knows she needs to end it with Steve. She can't let her children get mixed up with that family. She can't let them get trapped in this town like she was. But, oh God, she wants to curl up inside the man, to incubate there until she can burst back out of him, strong and healthy. He's behind her now, so close he blocks the wind. So close she can smell him, the cigarettes and Aqua Velva. She stretches a hand back slowly, and finds his hand similarly stretched. She just touches him, just grazes him with her fingertips.

Deborah sees the touch. The brazenness of it all. She's had enough. She's been quiet long enough. She's put up with enough. As she makes her way over to her husband, she feels her face heat up, her whole body shaking. She wants to bark commands and make him obey. She wants to bring him to heel.

She's on them all too soon. Instead of wielding words, she finds herself mute, her voice having left her. She grabs her husband and yanks him away from that woman, that whore. Beth looks startled, as if she'd thought they were alone. As if she'd forgotten Deborah was even there. This is almost worse than her publicly flaunting the affair. Beth has completely forgotten about Deborah.

Deborah lunges at Beth, grabbing handfuls of hair, clawing at her face. Beth offers no resistance. Even though she's been waiting for this, waiting for an attack, now that it's here, she's in shock. She realizes she doesn't actually know how to fight—has never had to—and at first, she shrinks away. This makes Deborah even madder. She launches herself at Beth, and the two crash through the chicken wire fence, stumbling onto the pig grid. The pig squeals and skitters into the far corner. Something in Beth awakens and she kicks Deb, her boots slipping in the mud. Her jeans are so tight that she can't move well, her thighs straining at the fabric. The best she can do is kick at Deb's shins, spattering Deb's shoes with mud.

Deborah knocks Beth down. A swipe of Beth's legs, and Deb is also down, the two women slapping and clawing inexpertly. The band stops playing and breaks formation in confusion as the town crowds around the grid. The pig scampers around the two women and escapes where the chicken wire has been knocked down, Slick giving chase. Deborah grabs handfuls of mud and rubs them into Beth's hair, and Beth pushes Deb's face down onto the grid.

Steve watches from a distance, a dumb smile on his face—what man wouldn't want his women fighting over him?—but when it occurs to him that both women mean business, his smile evaporates. What if Beth actually hurts Deb? What if she hurts the mother of his children? He knocks his way through the crowd, trying to come to Deb's rescue, and brushes past Tabitha Schwartz, who nearly topples over. *Trash,* she thinks. *This town has only changed for the worse.*

Linda wants to intercede, but can't squeeze through the crowd with her belly. Derek would intercede, but there are women mud wrestling, so . . . Kelli Brody buries her face in Dan's shoulder, wanting to pretend the whole thing isn't happening, and Dan pulls her to him, her tuba knocking into his bass drum. The sounds makes her jump away from him, to glare at him like *he* had attacked her. Just as Steve is about to jump in, Mandy lunges, breaking Beth and Deb apart, getting one quick kick at Beth's shins before pulling her mother away. Her uniform is muddied in the process, but it's worth it to get to kick someone.

"You leave my family alone," Deborah yells, while Mandy pins her arms behind her back. Beth lies breathless on the grass, her peacoat caked in mud.

The silence that follows is brief, broken by the distant squeals of the pig as Slick finally catches it. In the aftermath, Beth feels deflated, tired. Even Eliza is breathless as she berates Beth.

"Was it worth it?"

Beth looks up and sees Jeanette, her hands over her mouth. Are those tears in her eyes? What has she done? How will she live this down? She looks around until she finds her son. He isn't looking at her but at Kelli, who glares at him.

"You ruin everything," Eliza says.

It isn't until both women are escorted away that the band director notes that the pig, while cowering in the corner, has done its business on square A1.

Derek Williams is the big winner.

Elizabeth DeWitt Hansen
26

Our house is a combat zone; neither my husband nor I risk spending much time there. I take a job working nights, and Greg keeps irregular hours. I can't bring myself to leave our son with a babysitter. We fight, and I mean really fight, over who will give a little: We yell, we cry, we cuss, we break dishes, we blame each other's upbringing, we question each other's moral character. We resolve nothing.

Our two-year-old latches onto the chaos. He upends a box of Cheerios onto the kitchen floor. He pulls the pots and pans from the cupboard, moves around the house clanking them against each other. He fills the cat's bowl until it's spilling over. He empties the silverware drawer, a cymbal crash on the floor. He does this all quickly, with more speed than I would have thought possible. When I catch him, he's reaching for the drawer that houses the kitchen knives.

BREAKING DOWN

After the Pig Plop, a singular energy charges through Beth. She doesn't know what to do with it, so she goes on a weeklong cleaning binge, scouring the house in the evenings after work, staying up long after her kids have gone to bed. She shampoos rugs, clears cobwebs, scrubs mildew from grout, bags up most of her father's clothes for charity, repaints the kitchen cupboards from an old can she finds in the basement. The entire time she works, she imagines violence inflicted on the Thurber house: tornadoes hitting it, the siding peeling off one slat at a time, the roof torn away. She imagines fires blazing through, leaving nothing but a charred skeleton.

She's ashamed of her public display in the park last week. In the aftermath, she has even less desire to show her face in public, so instead she will see to it that her house is in order; she's claiming the space for herself, ensuring that she has room to exist outside her own head. She knows the house needs repairs that are outside of her budget or her DIY skills, but she will do what she can. When the house is as clean as she's ever seen it, she falls into the recliner in the living room.

Her kids come home, and she follows them into the kitchen, where they're already rummaging through the newly painted cupboards.

"Want me to make you a snack?" she says, and Jeanette looks at her like she's lost her mind.

"We got it," Dan says.

She wants them to notice how clean the house is, to comment on it, but they don't. They pull together cheese and crackers, Faygo RedPop, and head upstairs to do homework in Dan's room. From the bottom of the stairs, she can hear them talking. About her.

"She's acting so weird," Dan says.

"She's lost it," Jeanette says.

Her kids are wary of her. Even Steve has cooled. They didn't meet this week; instead, he said he had a big job a few towns over and wouldn't have time to see her. Which is probably good.

With the house clean, there's only one thing left to do. Beth gives her father a bath. Around seven-thirty, as she is tucking him into bed again, she hears Jeanette making dinner.

"Go," Eliza says, and for once, Beth obeys. When the sun goes down, she takes a walk. Before she realizes it, she finds herself walking south, past the Thurbers'. Until today, she has worked very hard not to see the house; whenever she drives by, she looks away. Now she stares. Studies. It's still as derelict as ever, the front porch heaped with junk—broken appliances and boxes and clothes and tools—piles stacked so high they're pushing against the screen, poking holes.

She's disappointed to find it in one piece. Outside, the house looks much the same as it did in her memory: the same blue paint with green trim, the same pink gingerbread near the roof. The roof itself has visible holes. Several of the windows have been smashed. When she enters, she finds the walls molded, draped in cobwebs so thick they look like Spanish moss. It smells like mushrooms, but then it always smelled like mushrooms. Mushrooms and cigarettes. But the cigarettes have faded, replaced with the scent of old leaves.

She knows coming here isn't healthy.

The interior of the house has been demolished. Someone took a crowbar or something to the walls, and smeared God knows what—mud? feces?—on them, acts of violence that suggest the Thurber family had no hand in it. This is a different kind of anger, and it enters Beth like a virus. It invades, multiplies. Her body blooms with rage.

She returns to the porch, finds a pipe wrench. With a good swing, she lodges it into the living room wall. It takes a while to work the wrench back out, but then she slams it again and again into the wall. She'll finish the work someone else started. She feels connected to this house's demolitionist in a way she hasn't felt connected to anyone in a very long time.

She whacks the slats of the staircase railing, takes out the banister, smashes through the closet door—the same closet where she hid all those years ago. She wrecks the bedroom door, the bathroom door. In the basement, she dents the pipes until they drip stagnant, rusty water. She breaks windows from the inside. She'll dismantle the house, inch by inch, breaking down its darkness. She rips up carpet like an animal digging in the earth. She shatters mirrors, light fixtures, bathroom tile; she tears up linoleum. Her fingers bleed, but she has work left to do.

"Hands where I can see them. Drop your weapon."

The wrench clunks on the floor.

"Are you alone?"

"Yes."

"Turn around. Slowly."

When she turns, a flashlight hits her face. She's dazed out of the darkness. It takes a moment for her eyes to adjust, and then she sees his outline, his arms stretched out before him, wrists crossed, one hand holding the flashlight, the other holding the gun, both pointed at her. Her heart stops for a moment, then kicks into overdrive. She tries to tell herself she's okay, but he's a police officer. He has a gun on her. She moves her hands up in increments. Her eyes adjust slowly to the light; she squints, and is just able to see him, his dark hair and darker eyebrows. Mikey.

She knows him, but she also doesn't.

"Now you've done it," Eliza sneers at her.

"I'm okay," Beth whispers. "I know him." She's trying to convince herself as much as Eliza. She takes a deep breath. It's okay. She's okay. She can hear cars on the next street over. She smells the mushroom and leaf scent of the house. The night air coming in through the smashed window is cold on her face. She's okay.

"Eliza?"

"Yes," Eliza says. Beth lets her surface. This is what Eliza is good for: being calm, complacent. Compliant.

He lowers the light, and after a moment's hesitation, he lowers his gun. Eliza blinks the water from her eyes, trying to adjust to the light once more.

"Well, I'll be," he says, and holsters his gun. "I heard you three houses down. Come on outside."

She can't make her legs work, though. She stays rooted in place, staring through the busted window. A streetlamp outside makes the yard shadowy, but it lets in enough light that she can see him now, his face and dark eyes. Mikey Hudson and Eliza DeWitt, in the same house where they first met as children. Glancing out a side window, she can see her house next door, her own bedroom, and she catches movement at the darkened window. She knows Jeanette is there; she must have heard the ruckus. She must have gone looking when she called Beth for dinner.

"Can you tell me where you are?" Mikey stands at a distance, moves slowly, as if Eliza were armed and dangerous. He's wearing a coat, and his hands hover by his belt.

"Where are you, Eliza?"

"The Thurber house."

She wishes he'd move his hands away from his gun.

"That's good," he says. "And do you know what you were doing here?"

"I was wrecking up the place," she says simply.

He laughs. "Yes. Yes, you were. You really were." His hands relax.

"Are you going to arrest me?"

"No. I'm not going to arrest you. But you have to promise me you'll stay out of this house. I can't have people trespassing, even if it is to destroy this place. It's condemned for a reason. It isn't safe." He looks around, at the damage that's months old.

In the pale glow of the streetlight, she can see his face. Drained of detail by the dark, he's the spitting image of the boy she remembers.

"You know he's gone, right? In prison? He's doing life in Chicago." His hands are hovering again, shaking a little, but away from his gun. He's reaching for her.

"Yeah, I'd heard," she says, taking a step away.

"So you can go home, okay?"

His face, still pudgy after all these years. How did he do it? How did he stay in this town and not let it break him? He's a cop, and a good one from the looks of it. At least he didn't shoot. Elizabeth DeWitt didn't become one more statistic, one more news report.

Beth wants to finish her work here, to raze the house until there's nothing left but glowing cinders. She wants to wreck it all night and into the morning; she wants to burn it down. Anything rather than going home and explaining to her daughter what she was doing. Even more, she wants to understand how Mikey is still whole. She begs Eliza to ask him.

"What about you?" Eliza says.

He seems caught off guard by the question. His hands are still shaking, down by his sides. They stand in silence, in darkness, long enough to feel truly awkward. Then Mikey leans down, picks up the wrench Beth had dropped, and walks to the front door, where he pauses, then drives the wrench, just once, into the wood. It splinters, a chunk landing at his feet. Then he nods, drops the wrench, and walks out the door, leaving Beth alone.

After a time, Beth goes home, dragging her feet. She's so tired. When she walks in, Jeanette doesn't comment on what she must have seen, doesn't even look at her mom; she just says, "Dinner is ready."

"It smells great," Beth says, and watches her daughter, until Jeanette turns to meet her eyes.

Elizabeth DeWitt

27

I'm seven months pregnant with our daughter, and my belly is so big it looks like I'm lugging a garbage bag in front of me. My husband cowers from the excess. I hate him for making me feel like I'm too much. He comes home later and later, sullen, a presence that feels like an absence. Our daughter is born in one of those absences, and she fills the void with her howls. She screams my heart out; all the words I've kept inside for decades come pouring from her in that eerie music that predates language.

As I suspected, my husband can't take her raw emotions. He won't wake in the middle of the night to comfort her, he barely wants to hold her. He comes home even later from work. Then, one night, he doesn't come home at all.

The next time I see Greg in person, we sign divorce papers. I slip back into my old name, and with it, every moment assigned it in the past: the violence, the anger, the humiliation, the damage. My name is a garbage bag, tied around my head. If I am to ever breathe again, I must begin the slow work of ripping it wide open.

FLOOD

It's the first Thursday in April, and the sky has been dumping rain on River Bend since Monday morning. The St. Gerard River has swollen and stretches out past its banks. Around midday, the rain lets up, though low, dark clouds still crowd the sky. Birds hunker in trees, wishing they had stayed south a little while longer.

Dan Hansen and Kelli Brody are playing hooky. Figuring the rain is finally done, they ride their bikes to the abandoned River Bend Casket Company down by the river. The stone houses near the old factory are listing and falling; moss grows on their sides, their roofs sag, their yards are full of puddles. Inside the factory, the building echoes, cold and dark; the floor is dirty with rodent and pigeon droppings. The windows are small, meant to keep workers from getting distracted by the world outside. The glass has been smashed out of them.

Kelli and Dan sit with their backs against a wall, its surface cold through their tee shirts. Kelli has an arm around Dan, who pulls a book from his back pocket. He reads while Kelli watches dark clouds lowering the sky.

She won't date him. First of all, her mom would kill her. And if not her mom, then Mandy would; Dan broke up with Kelli's sister only a few months ago. Worse still, Kelli couldn't face her friends, the way they would make fun of her if she was dating an underclassman. They already tease her for how much time she spends with him. But what they don't understand is that Dan is comfortable to her in a way that nobody else is. She doesn't feel as if her energy is drained by him, doesn't have to recover after spending time with him. She doesn't have to try to be someone she isn't when she's with him. She can just sit in an old building and listen to the water dripping from the trees outside, watch the spiders creep across the ceiling. The thrill of skipping school is augmented by the weather—the rich earthen smell of almost a week of rain, the danger hanging in the air.

Dan reads with his face close to the page. He seems oblivious to the risk. His eyes are so dark, so serious, he looks like he's scowling. She likes to watch him read, likes it when he leans against her, likes scrubbing her fingers over the lamb's wool of his short-cropped hair. Just last month, their mothers had fought each other in the park with the entire town crowded around, bearing witness. Kelli avoided Dan for a week afterward. Something about their mothers' fight had seemed personal to Kelli, almost like she and Dan had had the fight. Now Kelli wants to talk to him, wants to see if they are okay, but she isn't even sure how she feels—she doesn't understand what the fight was about. All she knows is her mother told Beth to leave her family alone.

Dan reads on languidly, tucking his finger behind the page long before he has to turn it.

Kelli breathes deep. The winds out of the south carry the smell of the pig farms outside town. She doesn't mind. It smells like country air, like home. When the rain starts back up, at first it's only a spritzing; Dan doesn't even notice. Kelli watches the windowsills go damp, the water beading on old wood. The factory roof is leaky, and a small drip splashes on Dan's head. He still doesn't notice. What she wouldn't give for his focus. She has a terrible time paying attention in class. Her mom wants her to go to college, but her grades aren't good enough for the kinds of scholarships she would need.

Dan notices only when the leak gets going for real, when his book is wet. The rain has gone from spritzing to spilling, like from an upturned bottle, or an open spigot. Soon, water runs into the building from the sidewalk outside, and as Kelli and Dan race to their bikes, the rain comes harder, lashing against their faces, turning their fingers numb. On their bikes, they pray no cars come every time they approach a stop sign; their brakes have given up. They fight through the slashing rain, and when their skin is stinging, when they pass over the bridge into town and see the St. Gerard River rising, they make the unspoken decision to go to Kelli's house because it's closest. There are no cars in the driveway, but Kelli peeks inside to make sure nobody is home before she lets Dan in.

School gets out early because of flood warnings, and Jeanette arrives home soaked through, looking as though someone tried to drown her. She stands at the kitchen sink and upends her book bag to pour out the water.

"Guess I can't do my homework," she says when her mom comes in the kitchen. Jeanette lays the sodden papers on the counter.

Beth still hasn't showered, has her hair up in a scarf like her mother always wore. She hopes Jeanette won't comment. "Where's your brother?"

Jeanette shrugs without looking at her mom. It's the shrug that means *I'm not telling* instead of *I don't know*.

In the dining room, Ernest lives a life of stasis, of waiting for what comes next, unaware of his surroundings, of the torrential rain, unaware even of Linda sitting beside his hospital bed, dozing in a recliner. Ernest is dreaming of powerful steam-driven engines, of machinery, of industry, of progress. Linda has a book open in her lap, and when Beth shakes her awake, she, too, looks completely unconcerned about the rising water.

"Have you heard from Dan?"

Linda has not.

"I've called him twice now."

"Don't worry," Linda says. "It floods like this every few years. The water's not going any higher." She stands and smooths Ernest's hair along his forehead. His hair is oily; it will need another dry shampooing soon. When she rolls him over to check his diaper, Beth turns away.

Maybe this is why you find someone to love, someone to love you, someone to live with: so your own daughter won't have to change your diapers.

Beth calls her son again. This time, he picks up.

"Where are you? Are you okay?"

"I'll be home soon," he says. He sounds breathless.

"It's raining too hard. I'll come get you."

"It's okay," he says. "I've got my bike. I'll be right home."

He hangs up before she can argue. A few minutes later, her phone rings.

"My gears are locked up," he says.

"Where are you?"

He takes a deep breath. "Kelli's."

Beth is soaked before she gets into the car, her shoes sloshing on the accelerator. Jeanette shivers beside her in the passenger's seat. Beth has a hard time keeping control of her car, the water is so high in the street. At the river, the dam is holding, but the St. Gerard is marching over its banks and rising up to lay siege to River Bend. By the time Beth knocks on the Brodys' door, she's freezing. Her clothing sticks to her skin; her hair has gone curly under her scarf, even though she pressed it just yesterday, using plenty of oil. There are no cars in the Brody driveway.

"Where are your parents?" Beth asks Kelli at the door.

The girl winces at the question.

How like Steve. Nowhere to be found during a crisis.

"I'm sorry, Mom," Dan says. He would have tried to explain, would have launched into the excuses he has at the ready—that he only stopped here in hopes that the rain would let up, that Kelli's parents just stepped out—but the look on his mom's face makes him shut up.

Beth finds herself transported, feels a stirring until she pushes Eliza back down.

The house smells exactly the way it used to. Too many animals, not enough care cleaning up after them all. Two big dogs jump on Beth. The walls are still bare, primed but not painted, a white that has yellowed with age. Looking past the kitchen, she can see a bare concrete slab where the living room carpet has been removed.

"Get in the car," she says. "You, too," she nods to Kelli.

In the living room, she can hear a parrot squawking. She

swears it sounds just like the bird Steve had all those years ago, but that can't be right. That bird has to be long dead.

"What about the dogs?" Kelli says.

Each dog is about eighty pounds. Beth really doesn't want her car to smell like those dogs, like this house. Still, it isn't their fault their owners have abandoned them. It's Steve's fault, and Steve's mess, which she will once again clean up.

"And the cat."

Beth sighs, pinches the bridge of her nose. "Where's the carrier?"

"She doesn't have one."

They rummage the house looking for a box to carry the cat. As soon as Beth steps into the living room, she sees it, that horrible bird, its feathers ripped out.

"Colored," it says.

The little fucker remembers her.

They find a box, wrestle the cat in. When they open the back door, the dogs burst out, snapping at the rain. *This is great! The rain! New people! A new car to ride in!*

"What about the bird?" Kelli says.

"It's up off the floor," Beth says. "It won't drown."

In the car, the dogs jump around in the backseat. Kelli tries to restrain them, to at least keep them off her lap so they don't crush the box the cat is in. Beth can tell that she already smells like that house, a stink that will travel with her all day.

"Do you have somewhere I should take you?"

Kelli directs Beth to her grandma's farm.

The dirt road has turned into a river of mud, but Beth's car somehow manages to pick its way up the hill. Grandma Dinah's house sits at the top, protected from the river, from the town. When Beth pulls into the long gravel driveway, she sees a figure hunched in a raincoat, waving down the truck in front of her. It seems the whole family has turned up at Dinah's. Beth sees the driver of the truck—Steve's truck—in front of her get out, hand her keys over to Steve, and make a dash for the house. Steve is about to get into his truck when he realizes he's blocked in the driveway.

He comes back to Beth's car.

"Pull around back," he shouts, winding his arm in circles over his head. When he gets close enough to see who the driver is, he stops for a moment, looks between Beth's car and the house. Then he comes to her window. She rolls it down, and the rain pours in. His face, wet and shaded by the hood of his raincoat, looks old, his forehead lined, his mouth sagging.

"I don't have time," he says. "I need to find my daughter."

At the sound of Steve's voice, his dogs go crazy in the backseat. *We're in the car! Back here! We're in a new car with new people and it's raining!* The smaller dog, the brown one, tries to climb into the front seat with Beth, tries to poke its face through the open window. Jeanette does her best to muscle the dog down. Steve looks into the back then, and Beth watches the tension wash off his face. He leans toward Beth, intent on kissing her, but he catches himself. Instead, he goes around to the back of her car, opens the door, and pulls Kelli into a wet hug. He kisses the top of her head. The dogs shoot out of the car, jump up with muddy paws onto Kelli and Steve. Deb comes running out of the house, shoes unlaced, no coat. Steve holds Kelli at arm's length, as if to make sure she's real, that she's unharmed, then hands her over to her mother. Deb hugs her, too, and over Kelli's shoulder, she and Beth lock eyes through the windshield. They look at each other only for the briefest moment. It's enough.

When the Brody women go off inside the farmhouse, Steve comes back to Beth's window.

"Come inside. Dry off."

But she will not. Even if it is the safest place right now, Beth will not go inside that house. She hopes Deb felt how sorry Beth is when she looked at her. She tried to convey that she regretted everything, that things will be different starting now, starting with her leaving this place. She backs her car out of the drive quickly and makes her way back down the hill, only to find a lake forming in the road. She sits in her car, positioned on the brink of submersion.

"What do you think?" She turns around in her seat to look at Dan. Instead of a response, she hears a meow. The box with the cat is still in her backseat.

Ernest DeWitt is dreaming of water. In his dream, he is aboard a large fishing ship on the open ocean, hauling a net laden with slick, shimmering bodies up from the water, the pull of long limbs, of trapezius and deltoids, the salt spray and gray skies blurring the horizon. He's had this dream since his boyhood, a child's vision of an adulthood he would never know. He watches himself work from a small remove, across the deck—that battered wood expanse flaked with fish scales—and he becomes aware that he is quite comfortably alone on this ship. There were other people, he is sure, but now they're gone, and how easily he could let go of the net, the fish, and slip overboard. His body would melt the moment he touches the water, his boundaries dissolve—yes, how naturally he integrates with sea, horizon, sky.

In her car out on a flooding dirt road, Beth feels him go, feels him slip beneath the surface.

In his last seconds, Ernest DeWitt is unaware of the hospital bed with its gray blanket, the woman in the chair beside him, dozing with a book in her lap. She will waken, stretch, take his hand, still warm, feel for a pulse, and know that he is gone.

W here've you been?" Mandy says when her sister walks in. All afternoon, all anyone could talk about was where Kelli was. You'd think the world were coming to an end.

"Go on upstairs and find some dry clothes in Grandma's room," Deborah says. Mandy follows her sister.

Upstairs, while they rummage through Grandma Dinah's dresser, Kelli shakes silently.

"It's really that bad out there?" Mandy says.

"No," Kelli says. "I don't know. Maybe." She pulls off her wet clothes and shimmies into a flannel shirt and jeans, still wearing her wet underwear.

"What's your problem?"

"Don't worry about it," Kelli says, throwing herself down on Grandma's bed, burying her face in a pillow.

"Hey," Mandy says, shaking Kelli by the foot. "What's your deal?" It isn't like Kelli to be such a drama queen.

"Leave me alone," she mutters. At least that's what it sounds like. It's hard to hear Kelli with her face stuffed in a pillow.

"Is it Dan?"

Kelli only hiccups.

"What'd he do?"

After a time, Kelli pulls her face out of the pillow. She gulps down air like she'd been suffocating.

"Beth DeWitt's sleeping with Dad."

"Don't be ridiculous," Mandy says.

"She drove me here. I saw them together."

"So?"

"The way they were with each other. You could just tell."

There have been rumors around town, rumors that Mandy had dismissed. But now Mandy is on her mom's side. Beth was bad news, just like Dan. "I'm telling Mom," she says on her way out of the room.

"Mom already knows," Kelli calls out behind her.

Kelli stays in Grandma's room all afternoon. Her dogs scratch at the bedroom door, whimpering to get in, but she ignores them. Her phone dings with texts, but she ignores those, too. She doesn't want to talk to anyone.

Eventually, Mandy comes back in the room. "Dan and Beth are here," she says. "His sister, too."

Kelli sits up. Looks at her phone. Dan has sent her several messages.

We need to talk.

I'm here.

Please come down.

"What are they doing here?"

"I guess they're flooded in," Mandy says.

Kelli shoves her phone in her pocket. "How's Mom seem?"

"Strangely normal," Mandy says.

They hear footsteps on the stairs, a knock on the bedroom door.

Mandy opens the door to find Dan and Skyla on the landing. "What do you want?" She stands in the doorway, blocking their entrance.

"Can I come in?" Dan says.

She hesitates, but Skyla walks in without invitation. After a second, Dan follows.

"They've already closed school tomorrow," Skyla says.

"Go away," Kelli says from under her pillow.

"Hey," Dan says, sitting down on the bed next to her.

"I don't want you here."

He looks to Mandy, who busies herself with her grandma's jewelry box on the dresser, sneaking glances at them out of the corner of her eye. Skyla just shrugs.

"We could use your help rounding up the cattle," Skyla says to Mandy. Her cousins aren't strong riders, but she figures Kelli and Dan need some time.

When they've left, Dan puts a hand on Kelli's back. He knows what this is. He saw it, too: the closeness between his mom and her dad. "Can we talk?" he says.

Kelli sits up in bed, holding the pillow in her lap like a shield. "What's your mom thinking, sleeping with a married man?"

"What's your dad thinking, stepping out on your mom?"

They stare each other down. Finally, Kelli says, "Go away," and buries her head again. Dan grabs the pillow off her.

"My parents are probably going to split because of your mom," Kelli says.

"Yeah?" Dan says. "It takes two to screw."

"Fuck off," Kelli says, and shoves him off the bed. How could he even take Beth's side? Kelli knows her dad has a history with Beth—and her mom must know it, too, must have already known that Beth and her dad were sneaking around again. Kelli heard from kids at school that her mom had started the fight, that it was your typical redneck brawl. But now she understands that her mom must have been fighting for her husband, for her family. Maybe her mom is right. Maybe the Hansens are no good.

Kelli hears the door and peeks out from beneath her pillow to see that she is alone. *Good,* she thinks. He could just go home and drown for all she cares. Mandy comes in a while later to tell Kelli that Beth is leaving for the hospital because Ernest DeWitt has died; Dinah has directed Beth out to a back road.

"Good riddance," Kelli mutters from under her pillow.

"Damn, bitch," Mandy says. "That's cold."

"Get out," Kelli says, and to her surprise, her sister doesn't argue. Mandy can go drown, too, Kelli thinks as she hears her sister leave the room. Anyone who takes the Hansens' side is dead to Kelli. Linda is a sucker for getting involved with that family, for being roped into taking care of a dying old man. At least Mandy has saved Kelli the humiliation of dating Dan.

When the sky outside grows fully dark, Kelli hears the bedroom door again. She lies very still, hoping whoever it is will think she's asleep and go away, but then she feels the weight, the heat of someone sitting down on the edge of the bed.

"Supper's ready," her grandma says, rubbing Kelli's back.

"I'm not hungry," Kelli says.

"That may be, but you have company waiting for you."

"I don't want to see him."

"Look," Grandma says. "I know what you think you saw, but it's very complicated."

"It seems pretty simple to me," Kelli says, pulling the pillow off her head. "Dad's sleeping with Beth DeWitt." She waits for her grandma to deny it, but Dinah does not.

"And don't think he's not going to hear from me," she says instead. "But right now your friend is downstairs, and he needs you."

Kelli doesn't answer, doesn't move. Eventually, Dinah gives Kelli one more pat on the back and leaves the room. When her grandma is gone, the silence in the bedroom is somehow emptier, more complete. It lets the sounds of the rest of the house intrude: Kelli can hear people moving through the rooms downstairs, plates being filled with food, silverware pulled from drawers. Her mother and father, her sister and cousin and grandma, sit down to dinner together. Jeanette Hansen is there, too. She sits down with a full plate, and, apart from them, Dan sits in the living room, alone with his grief.

Kelli finds Dan in a chair by the cold fireplace, with her cat curled up in his lap. He has his book open in front of him, but his eyes aren't moving across the page. For a second, Kelli thinks she can hear his mind, too full now to even read: She can feel his loss, his grief, not only over his grandfather, but over his mother as well, the same loss she feels for her dad, the loss that comes with realizing that parents are profoundly human and helpless, pitiful even. Dan's pain is so palpable to her that she can't help herself. She goes over and hugs him.

Elizabeth DeWitt
28

After Greg moves out, the house seems impossibly large. It was too big when we bought it, with four bedrooms and high ceilings, but now those sunny rooms seem swollen with space, grossly obese with excess. The ceilings are too high for me to dust the cobwebs. When I sweep the floors, the corners always recede from my broom, and I can never catch all the crumbs. With an infant and a three-year-old, the light carpets are a nightmare, stains so big and dark they seem like they might rear up and swallow my children.

I take them to visit my father, up in Michigan. He hasn't even met Jeanette yet. We stay in a mid-tier hotel, one with two king beds, a cramped bathroom, a microwave hidden in the television cabinet. People come clean the room while we're out visiting my father, a chore made even more awkward by the latest tramp he's dating—a woman in her forties with frizzy blond hair, too much eyeliner, sun-damaged cleavage, and jeans so tight her tiny belly hangs over the top of them. I swear, his women keep getting younger.

Cooped up in his house, drinking his coffee, trying to keep Dan enter-tained. I laugh when he gets ahold of one of my father's Civil War books, tearing it to shreds, and cringe when Miss Thing wants to hold Jeanette—can she even hold a child with those fake-ass nails? In these moments the divide between my father and me feels insurmountable. I count the days until we fly back to our sunny house in Charlotte.

FOR FEAR AND LOVE

Linda watches other families, at the store, in the park, for clues about how to behave. When to hold a child, when to scold. How to talk, how to coax. If she had stuck around, she could have spent some time with her nephew. As it is, she knows only what she sees on TV and in movies, what she reads in books and gleans from people watching.

It's been three weeks since Ernest's death, and she can finally admit that she'd had her doubts about what kind of father he would be. Beth seemed so broken, and Linda can't help but wonder what part Ernest played. Derek, though, has a nurturing side that, she realizes now, she's never really experienced before. Not from her mother, not from Nathan. Derek will make a good father. But what kind of mother will she make?

And so she watches people, everywhere she goes. At a basketball game, as her cousins and sister play in the pep band, she sees parents scold their young children for not sitting still. In line at the bank, a young mother blows raspberries on her baby's cheek, and the baby in its kangaroo pouch squeals and squirms. At the hardware store, a father comes in to buy his ten-year-old a hunting rifle to shoot mourning doves, and grabs the boy's wrist when he reaches for candy at the register. At the grocery store, where a mother shoulders her cellphone to give her whining toddler a swat on its diapered butt. At the hospital, where she brings Derek a cappuccino in the middle of a double shift, and sees a father rocking his daughter in his lap, gently guarding the leg she broke riding her horse. Linda watches these moments, judging them as only a person who is not yet a parent can, with the certainty that comes only from safe distance.

And because she is watching a mother (scolding her daughter for not using the restroom before they left the house), Linda doesn't see the little shoe, a baby shoe kicked off and lost, on the stair in front of her as she's leaving the salon; she steps sideways on it, and her ankle, already strained from her pregnancy, gives out, and then she's clawing at the railing, trying to slow her fall. She twists severely at the waist, and thuds on her side down the stairs.

Back at home, Linda finds blood, a bright red spot on her maternity pad—not a lot, but enough to visit the hospital, where they admit her and place her on bed rest. Linda suspects it's nothing, that they are being overly cautious because Derek has insisted, and yet later that night, she wakes in her hospital bed with a slick hot wetness between her legs.

Derek Ernest Williams is born by emergency cesarean on April 22, weighing seven pounds four ounces. Afterward, the first person to visit (besides Derek, who had been with her throughout) is her sister Paige.

"There she is," Paige says with feigned cheerfulness.

"You made the drive by yourself?" Linda says.

"About that," Paige says. "How would you like some help settling in at home with the new baby?"

So Diane has left her, Linda thinks. The Williams girls are incapable of maintaining a relationship, just like their mother. As pale as her sister is and given the gifts her sister has brought—flowers and balloons and a plush dog, not even from the hospital gift shop—Linda understands that Paige is scared; like their mother, fear seems to be the overriding force directing Paige: fear of rejection, fear of falling behind, fear of being left alone, fear of commitment, fear of death, and perhaps most especially, fear of life.

After the fall, after her son decides he's through waiting, that he will be born now, Linda lies in the hospital bed, feeling the wound of her belly, her body sliced open to retrieve the child and stitched up like a football. It's been two days, and she doesn't want to hold her baby, will only concede when the nurses and lactation specialists insist. Not that his cries leave her unaffected, but she isn't sure her incision is as sturdy as the doctor says.

Deep down, Linda worries that she doesn't have a chance of being a good mother, having no model herself. She worries she holds a deep deficit inside; isn't her failed marriage proof that she's tainted?

In the time since Ernest DeWitt's final, fatal stroke, Linda has been reconsidering what love is. Having loved Ernest so briefly, she figures that, logically, it should be easier to let him go. Yet she wants to suffer—suffer deeply—and the fact that she suffers so little weighs on her conscience, as if it belittles Ernest, the importance of him. She begins to wonder if it was love, or if love comes only after much more time.

She's known many women whose lives left them bereft of love, and she doesn't intend to become like them: gray, sullen, with a kind of maniacal energy simmering lewdly beneath the surface. So in the interim—for that was how she'd thought of it; she never harbored delusions that Ernest would recover—she began moving her heart toward Derek. It didn't occur to her to move her heart toward her son. She always took for granted that after the birth she would just—snap!—love him.

Before Ernest, when she was still in Texas with Nathan, she lived in fear for his life. Whenever he worked late, when the news reported a fatal car crash on U.S. 290—which seemed to be every day—Linda tried to steel herself for a phone call. When she was a preteen, when her grandfather battled cancer, Linda had watched Grandma Dinah try to cope. Linda saw her grandmother's denial, her anger, watched her heart break day after day, as Linda's grandfather let go a little at a time.

Linda was thirteen, Paige eleven, the first time their mother left. Paula and Jared had fought all afternoon, and around dinnertime, Paula said she needed some time to herself, and she got in her truck and drove off. She did this from time to time. Not to be the one waiting, Jared left in his truck, too. Derek had retreated to his bedroom. It felt like the sisters were alone in the house.

The night air that pressed in through the window screens turned cool and damp. Linda and Paige fell asleep in front of the television and were jolted awake when an infomercial started up, some middle-aged man shouting about his miracle cleaning product. It was a Wednesday night in mid-April. The sisters didn't talk as they slipped on their nightgowns, brushed their teeth side by side in the cramped upstairs bathroom. But neither wanted to go to sleep. They left the doors unlocked and the windows open, as if afraid that a secured lock would deter their parents from returning. Yet, with the house unsecured, anyone might walk in. Linda was starting high school next fall, so very grown up, but this situation made them both feel like children. She was keenly aware of how small they all were, she and Paige, and also Derek, who was twelve and hadn't yet hit puberty.

To distract themselves, the girls popped popcorn, the smell of which brought Derek down from his room. They threw more of it at one another than they ate, jumped on the couch, then raided the pantry and drank a warm two-liter of Faygo cream soda while a tape played in the VCR. They slept that night on the couch, piled together, the snow on the TV a welcomed glow after the movie finished. This is how her stepdad found them when he sloshed in the next morning.

At least he had the good sense to realize he was in no fit state to parent. He moved his stepdaughters and his son to his mother's farm. Didn't the fact that Dinah had allowed them in constitute a kind of love? They may not have been blood, but they were still family.

Was love simply a willingness to put someone else's needs before your own? Beth had done that, moving her children back to River Bend to give them a more stable life even though she was obviously miserable here. Her sacrifice had to take a lot of strength, more than Linda has given her credit for.

During Linda's hospital stay, Derek visits regularly, both during and after his shifts. On the third day, he picks up the baby, nuzzles his face into the newborn's soft neck, and removes his shirt for a kangaroo session, skin to skin. Then he places the baby in Linda's arms. She's too tired to protest.

"I'm worried about you," he says, and she manages a smile. For him.

And as Linda holds her child, holds him just for the sake of holding him, as she feels him against her bare chest, the flutter-beat of his heart and the fuzz on his head, she decides that love can come instantly. She feels certain that it will deepen with time—she can feel it already deepening now—and understands that that won't cheapen the love she feels in this moment.

Elizabeth DeWitt
29

Coming home from a long day of work, I no more than step into the house when the babysitter takes me quietly by the sleeve and shows me into Dan's bedroom. I just want to make dinner and relax, but she insists, a serene smile on her face, and when we get to the bedroom, I find both of my kids in there together, a sprawl of toys and stuffed animals around them, Dan sitting in the middle of the mess, a book in his lap, his sister snuggled up against him. He's reading to her. My five-year-old is reading to my two-year-old, and it instantly breaks and remakes my heart.

BITS AND PIECES

The McFadden Funeral Home is the only house left in River Bend older than the DeWitt home. It sits across the street from the park, as if to bookend the journey: from childhood to the grave. At present, the north-facing wall of the funeral home is torn away and tarped for renovations. All the windows are open, a box fan droning in each. The day is hot for mid-May, and the fans manage only to blow the hot air around. The marquee in front announces today's service in memory of Ernest De-Witt. Beth had a terrible time scheduling the funeral because her mother, Gretchen, insisted she come, but couldn't make it to River Bend any sooner than today.

Beth holds herself perfectly still in the front row, head bowed so that her neck seems to melt into her bosom. Her eyes are heavy, with dark circles exaggerated by her makeup, which has smeared from the heat. She looks tired enough to sleep for a week. Her hair, normally pressed sleek, has gone nappy and gray at the roots. It's so hot and humid, the summer just starting up, that Beth figures what's the point anymore? Why torture her hair straight, when it'll just go frizzy the second she leaves the house? If the weather would just break. It hasn't rained since last month's flood.

Linda has lost so much weight since Ernest's death that if you didn't know her, you might not even realize she'd just given birth. She wears a drab dress that sags off of her, revealing the top of her bra's satin cups. She holds hands with Derek Williams. Next to Derek, Skyla sits wearing a black skirt that's far too short for a funeral. She keeps leaning forward, her knees not quite together, and making a show of not looking across the aisle at Dan Hansen. At the end of the row, Paige bounces Linda's baby, making the most ridiculous faces at him, even though his eyes are too new to really focus. Paige has been staying with Linda and Derek—to help with the baby, she says, though, really, she needs some time to get back on her feet after splitting with Diane.

Up front, the pastor rambles on. It's hard to hear him over the drone of the box fans. There's a laziness to this day, a kind of comfortable tranquility that isn't wholly unpleasant. Beth feels as if she could stay in this folding chair forever, as if her rear, which went numb ages ago, is now a part of it. Her family surrounds her, Dan restless, shifting in his seat regularly, Jeanette still and quiet in her eerie way. Between Beth and Jeanette, Beth's mother, Gretchen, sits with her head on Beth's shoulder. She's crying loud enough to be heard over the fans. Divorced over three decades and weeping like a new widow. Meanwhile, her teal pantsuit and the matching satin headscarf look celebratory. Still, Beth's whole family is here—what's left of them at any rate—and for the moment, she almost feels okay.

When the service is over, Beth and Linda both stay seated.

Beth studies the enlarged picture of her father at the front of the room, printed on poster board and leaning against an easel. In the picture, Ernest is not smiling. They'd been unable to find an in-focus picture where he was, as if his happiness were a covert thing.

After hesitating, Linda rises from her seat and takes her baby back from Paige. Linda jiggles the baby a little as she makes her way over to Beth. "Want to meet your brother?"

Beth looks surprised, then alarmed. And then her face relaxes. She even smiles, sort of.

"What's his name again?" She reaches for the baby and runs a finger along his soft baby toes, which curl and kick at her touch.

"Derek Ernest Williams."

Derek steps up next to Linda, resting one hand on the small of her back. He kisses the top of Derek Jr.'s head. Jeanette slides in next to Beth, wrapping her sweaty arm around her mother and letting it hang there limply. Dan soon joins them, if for no other reason than to avoid Skyla.

This is what Ernest DeWitt has left behind: bits and pieces that almost resemble a family.

After the funeral, the town shows up at the DeWitt house bearing casserole dishes, flowers, ice cream, ham sandwiches on white bread. Beth has not invited anyone for refreshments, but they've come anyway. Someone, Linda maybe, opens all the windows in the house. Paige sets out paper plates, napkins, utensils. Beth finds herself in her own backyard—for it is hers now—under the shade of her own mulberry tree, eating Frito pie with people she always thought hated her.

"Your father was a good man," Derek Williams says, setting

out lawn chairs. He takes a seat next to her. "Don't give me that look. I mean it. He was a truly decent person. I can't tell you how many times he came out to fix our tractor when Dad couldn't get it running. He was more than happy to let us pay him in corn, too, come fall."

"He kept my car going," Linda says. "At least until the engine crapped out."

"He helped with the fall harvest, too," Skyla says. "The year Grandma was sick."

Beth feels her face pinching up. She can't help it. What's their game here?

"Point is, you can listen to the gossip from people who didn't know Ernest," Linda says, "but they only saw his faults."

Beth takes a bite of Frito pie. In the shade like this, with a breeze blowing, if she sits perfectly still, she's almost comfortable. She figures it won't last, this closeness, this kinship. As soon as the day is over and they go their separate ways, she'll likely never speak to these people again. Her mother drove back home as soon as the funeral was over. A three-hour drive, she said—even though it was only an hour, tops—and she might as well get going. She'd made her appearance, her show of grief. She was done. Beth has no doubt Linda and Derek will leave soon, too, and will be done with her. But then again, they might surprise her. Sometimes people do.

Beth wanders into her house in the afternoon to put away leftovers. Gatherings like this, people tend to leave food out in the sun—sandwiches and salads laden with mayonnaise—ripening and covered in flies. Nobody will be getting salmonella on Beth's watch.

As she's rearranging items in the fridge, she hears the toilet flush. Someone clomps down the hall in work boots. She'd thought herself alone in the house, and now her instinct is to freeze, to slip into the space between the fridge and the wall, but she fights the urge. Instead, she peeks her head out of the kitchen to see Mikey making his way back to the door.

"Hey there," he says, and in the daylight it occurs to Beth that his voice is too deep for a man his size: He's scarcely taller than Beth. He sounds like a man who has put years of practice into speaking. He stops in the kitchen doorway.

"I wanted to tell you how sorry I am at Ernest's passing." His thick eyebrows knit together. He looks truly sorry, his hand raised slightly as if he's considering taking her hand.

Beth hesitates. She isn't sure whether she wants to ruin Mikey's opinion of her father, on the day of his funeral of all days, but on the other hand, Ernest is gone, and there's no need to protect him anymore. And her needs matter.

"You know my father was friends with him?"

Mikey's eyebrows knit even closer, almost joining each other.

"Gilmer Thurber," she adds.

"I didn't know that. I didn't know Gilmer Thurber had any friends."

"Yes, well. My father believed in giving all men a chance."

"That was right decent of your father," Mikey says, "but it must have been very hard for you."

"He invited him into this house. He was here, many times."

"Beth—"

"One time, my father saw Gilmer coming out of the bathroom with me. My father had knocked on the door, and Gilmer zipped up so fast he pinched himself. He pulled my pants up—didn't even bother pulling up my underwear—and walked out of the bathroom with me. We were both walking funny, Gilmer because he'd zipped himself, me because my underwear was all bunched in my pants. He told my father I'd needed help in the bathroom, and my father didn't even question it, didn't question this grown man 'helping' his six-year-old daughter go to the bathroom."

"Beth, your father must have—"

"All day, everyone has been reminiscing about how great my father was, but Ernest DeWitt was a child, incapable of facing anything the slightest bit uncomfortable."

"I'm sure he did the best he could," Mikey mutters.

"You know that's shit," Beth says. "You of all people know how that should have gone down. There should have been police cars screaming to a halt in their driveway the first time it happened. Or the day the school talked to my parents. Or any number of times he should have seen the warning signs. How many more children were hurt because my father did nothing?"

Mikey backs away from her now, retreating to the door. Beth thought he would be on her side, but he's just like her father. With his hand on the doorknob, he turns back to her. "You know he wanted to testify, right?"

"Bullshit," Beth says.

"No, he did. He was on the list, but by the time it went to trial, he was already—" Mikey waves his hand here, looking for a way to say it delicately.

"An invalid?" Beth offers.

"He meant well, Beth."

"Why didn't he go to the police when it was happening?"

Mikey shakes his head. "We'll never know why. But he wanted to."

"Yes, well." She doesn't even know what to say. Ernest wanting to help her isn't the same as him actually helping her, but maybe it's a start. Maybe. She feels the fight draining from her.

"My point is, he was sorry he hadn't been able to protect you. And he held on to that guilt his whole life."

Beth hears footsteps behind her. She crosses her arms over her chest. She won't cry in front of these people.

Mikey shakes his head. "Take care, Beth. If you need anything, I'm here." He lets himself out into her shady backyard. Through the screen door, she watches him retreat down the alley.

"It was that guy on TV, right?" Jeanette says behind her. This time, Beth thinks she might really buy her a bell.

"The guy who did it? He was the one on the news last fall."

Beth turns slowly to find Jeanette standing just behind her, close enough to be her own shadow. She puts a hand over her eyes to keep from seeing Jeanette, so strong and lovely in the pink sundress she put on after the funeral. Beth can't find the words to explain what happened here, in this house, decades ago. But then, she doesn't have to, because Jeanette's eyes grow round, and she says, "Oh."

Elizabeth DeWitt
33

I took the kids to the park today. At nine, Dan decided he was too old to play on the equipment, but he entertained himself by collecting fall leaves for a while, then sat down in the shade of a live oak to read. Jeanette, though, wanted me to swing with her, then wanted me to go down the slide after her, not because she was scared, but because, as she said, she wanted me to have fun, too.

We had a little picnic of bologna sandwiches, oranges, and juice boxes, and afterward, when we trekked over to the dumpster to throw our trash away, Jeanette pointed out a sunflower growing from a crack in the concrete. The cement around it was stained aquamarine; some groundskeeper had poured copper sulfate on it, as if it were a weed. Even so, the sunflower was at least four feet tall, taller than Jeanette, its head nodding down to her, heavy with seeds. My daughter grinned up at this perfect sunflower.

This is all I want for her: I want Jeanette to grow with the same strength, the same resilience, as that sunflower.

ALONE

As soon as school lets out for the summer, Dan and Jeanette board a plane to their father's house. I have three months to myself, and nothing to occupy my time besides job searching and home improvements. That first night, alone in my father's house, my house, the muggy hot day unravels into a breathless night. There's the blink of fireflies in the yard and the rhythmic chirp of crickets.

I go around and in each room I turn on lights, place fans in the windows. In the master bedroom—Jeanette's room now, since I figured she'd earned the extra space in this past year—I find her bed made, her teddy bear leaned against the pillows. She's grown so much, she left her favorite stuffed animal at home for the summer.

Maybe I haven't wrecked her after all.

I am constantly surprised by my kids' ability to adapt. I worried this town would destroy them, like I'd completely failed when I had to move them back here. But they're okay.

Jeanette didn't run away to her room that day after the funeral, or get angry that I'd never told her. She didn't pull away as if I were contagious. Instead, she shook her head and said, "I can't even imagine." And then she hugged me. My trauma is so far out of her experience that she can't imagine it. For that, I am truly grateful.

I also take some pleasure in knowing my kids didn't want to go to Greg's this summer. Dan didn't want to be apart from his girlfriend. An entire summer seems like a lifetime to him. He has no idea how short it really is—a lifetime, I mean. Three months is just a blip. When Linda moved into this place, I bet my father thought he had years, decades to go, that he was just starting another phase of his life.

Dan would go to his father's only after Greg agreed to fly Kelli down to Charlotte to visit. Not that I think Deb will allow that. Still, it seems like something of a win that Dan and Jeanette both feel at home in this town, that they have connections here, unlike I did at their age.

In my bedroom, I take stock of River Bend, the roofs I grew so familiar with over the winter. They are transformed, stripped of snow, and their chimneys stand out dark and bare. There is a gap where Gilmer's house used to be. They finally tore it down last week, the house, the crabapple tree. They've ripped the yard out, which makes me think someone has bought the property, is starting over from scratch.

In addition to his house, my father left me a small sum of money he had squirreled away. He was, above all, a thrifty man. Tomorrow I will begin searching for contractors: new pipes and, if there's money left over, a new back porch. The rains in April flooded the basement, mostly, but there was some damage to the carpet, too. I hoped insurance would pay, but I'm still arguing with them. I'll probably have to foot that bill myself. Then, too, the kitchen could use remodeling. For now, it's enough just to air the place out.

I go to the kitchen, pour a glass of white wine, and sit on the back porch with my laptop. Before my father's last stroke, he spent most mornings out here with a cup of coffee. I never joined him; I stayed in bed until I could hear him puttering around in the garage, because I didn't want to be that close, that quiet, with him. Now it's like he's still kind of here. I visit a few Web pages, request some quotes on pipes. There are holes in the porch screens, and pretty soon the mosquitoes chase me back inside. After some preliminary pricing, I realize that the job will cost way more than I can afford, that the money my father left isn't even close to what I would need. Unless I knew a handyman who could do it on the cheap. Which, of course, I do.

I need a better job, and so I carpet-bomb my résumé over every decent restaurant, country club, resort, and bed-and-breakfast within fifty miles. After an hour of filling out job applications, I feel really helpless, and go to the fridge for another glass of wine.

When I enter the kitchen, a mouse scurries across the floor, and it startles me so badly I drop my wineglass. Add *hire an exterminator* to the list of things I need to do with my inheritance. And maybe *adopt a cat*. After cleaning up the broken pieces, I go for another wineglass. Pushed toward the back of the cupboard is an old pink teacup, printed on the inside with flowers. It seems terribly out of place among my father's dishes. I wonder whether this was Linda's, if she forgot it here when she moved out. It's so small, it seems like it could belong to a child. All of this stuff should be replaced with decent tableware. Still, this teacup is kind of sweet, pretty. So I pour my wine into it.

I'm about to leave the kitchen when there's a knock at the back door. It's eleven o'clock at night, and there's a knock at the back door.

I know who's there. I can picture him in the dark, swatting mosquitoes from his neck. Who knows how long he's been knocking? I could have easily missed it with all these fans running. He knocks again and I'm frozen, standing in the kitchen with a teacup full of wine. A chill starts where my fingertips make contact with the cup and spreads up my arm, and I hear, or think I hear, him whisper my name, so quiet, like he must know I'm here, even though he can't see me from the stoop.

And, for once, I can imagine a day when I won't even want to open the door.

ACKNOWLEDGMENTS

It takes a village to raise a book baby, and this book is no exception. I'd like to thank my thesis adviser, Alex Parsons, for his insight and artistry, and David Haynes, whose feedback proved invaluable. Also, Robert Boswell, whose prompts got me started on this whole thing. Big thanks to Dino Piacentini for his feedback, as well as his camaraderie during the long and grueling agent search, to Laura Jok for her keen eye and many reads as I filled in the vowels of this n(o)v(e)l, and to Talia Kollouri, David Messmer, Liz Davies, and Ashley Wurzbacher for their reads and feedback. Shout-out to my entire Kimbilio family for great conversations and insights, but especially my 2016 workshop group: Asali Solomon, Nana Nkweti, Donald Quist, Lakeisha Carr, and Ty Coleman. Of course, I got to thank my bae, J. P. Brandenburg, for putting up with me while I was moodily processing. Thank you, too, to Nancy Emmerich, for encouraging me at a time in my life when not a lot of people did. Much love and gratitude to Janet

ACKNOWLEDGMENTS

McFarland-Idema for her unending support, and Aliah Lavonne Jahan-Tigh for our many conversations on grief and trauma, and for all the ways she helps me make sense of other people. Thanks to Darlene Campos for her advice on querying, and Jason McFarland for all those hours on the phone talking about all the things that needed to be said. And to Lee Romer Kaplan for our bespoke writer's retreat on the fly! And thank you to Andrea Morrison for her feedback, support, and an amazingly painless submission process. And, finally, a huge thank-you to Helen O'Hare for her fantastic editing, and to the rest of the team at Putnam.